DATE

UNDER A WAR-TORN SKY

L. M. Elliott

Hyperion Books for Children
New York

Printed in the United States of America.
First Edition
3 5 7 9 10 8 6 4
The text for this book is set in 11-point Deepdene.

Visit www.hyperionchildrensbooks.com

Library of Congress Cataloging-in-Publication Data
Elliott, Laura.
Under a war-torn sky / L.M. Elliott.— 1st ed.
p. cm.
Summary: After his plane is shot down by Hitler's Luftwaffe, nineteen-year-old Henry
Forester of Richmond, Virginia, strives to walk across occupied France, with the help of
the French Resistance, in hopes of rejoining his unit.
ISBN 0-7868-0755-5 (trade) — ISBN 0-7868-2485-9 (library)
1. World War, 1939–1945—Underground movements—France—Juvenile fiction. 2.
France—History—German occupation, 1939–1945—Juvenile fiction. [1. World War,
1939–1945—Underground movement—France—Fiction. 2. France—History—German
occupation, 1940–1945—Fiction. 3. Air pilots—Fiction. 4. World War, 1939–1945—
Aerial operations—Fiction. 5. Guerilla warfare—Fiction.] I. Title.
PZ7.E453 Un 2001
[Fic]—dc21   2001016633

For John, who has steadfastly believed in me;
For Megan, whose astute questions helped build the story;
And for Peter, whose unspoiled joie de vivre
I would wish for all boys growing into men.

Chapter One

March 1944.

"Pull her up, Hank! Pull her up!"

Henry's arms were locked through the steering wheel of his B-24. He was yanking with all he had, but the wheel was stuck solid. "I can't! She won't budge!"

The bomber was in a death dive. Henry's pilot had hurled them into the dive to put out a fire in the plane's engines. The fire had erupted after a Nazi fighter shot up their wing. The force of the winds against the bomber as it hurtled toward the ground was the only thing strong enough to snuff out the flames. Still, Henry knew the pilot's strategy was a real gamble. There was no guarantee that once the plane was rocketing to earth her two pilots would be able to wrestle her level again. Right now the plane was bucking and rattling enough to shake a guy's teeth loose.

Over the intercom Henry listened to the panic of the crew: "We're going down!"

"Do something, Hank! Please! I don't wanna die!"

In his mind, Henry heard the distant growl of his father: *Do* something, *you idiot.* The surly voice slapped him into action.

Henry had learned to cheat death at the very last second during flight training. Hadn't he repeatedly yanked his plane up just before smashing into something, forcing out a big-man guffaw to hide the fact he'd almost wet his pants, he'd been so afraid? He could do this. Just yank the wheel, Henry, yank it hard, to level the plane off.

BANG-BANG-BANG-BANG.

A German Messerschmitt zoomed past to strafe the bomber's cockpit one last time. Henry couldn't believe the pilot would take the trouble to target a plane already in flames. Ha, you missed me, he thought.

"Do something, Hank! Pull her up."

Henry looked down at the wheel. He stared at the metal half-circle. *Put your hands on it, fool.*

But he couldn't. The Messerschmitt's bullets must have ripped his arms clear off. He stared. He couldn't find them anywhere in the cockpit.

Henry looked up through the shattered window and saw the green, leafy domes of treetops racing toward him. Closer, closer. There wasn't anything left to do but die. He tried to scream.

With a choking gasp, Henry lurched up. He clenched his hands. They were there. He felt every finger. Henry recognized the stink of burning coal, wet woolen socks hung up to dry, lingering cigarette smoke. He was in his Nissen hut on base in England. It had just been another nightmare. He was awake. He was alive.

Quietly, Henry eased himself back down on his cot. He was grateful not to have woken up the other fliers who slept in the cold hut. They could be tough on a fellow if they smelled his fear. It was hard enough being the youngest copilot there. Henry was just barely nineteen.

He rolled over, still trembling. He wanted to get up and walk off the nightmare, but he couldn't without waking everyone. So he flipped onto his back, whacking his ankles against the cot's iron rails. It creaked loudly. With embarrassed irritation, he wiped leftover dream sweat from his face and stared up at the bottom of the shelf over his head. On it, where no one else would see it, he'd taped a poem called "High Flight." A nineteen-year-old American pilot, flying with the Royal Air Force, had written it just before he'd been killed. Henry knew every word.

He closed his eyes and tried reciting it silently to ease himself back to sleep:

Oh, I have slipped the surly bonds of earth,
And danced the skies on laughter-silvered wings;
Sunward I've climbed and joined the tumbling mirth
Of sun-split clouds—and done a hundred things
You have not dreamed of—wheeled and soared and swung
High in the sunlit silence. Hov'ring there,
I've chased the shouting wind along and flung

3

My eager craft through footless halls of air.
Up, up the long, delirious, burning blue
I've topped the wind-swept heights with easy grace
Where never lark, or even eagle, flew;
And, while with silent, lifting mind I've trod
The high untrespassed sanctity of space,
Put out my hand, and touched the face of God.

That's how Henry had thought flying would be—
dancing the skies, skating the winds, playing tag with
angels. But flying bombing missions hadn't been anything
like that. The missions had been teeth-gritting beelines to
targets, dogged all the way by men shooting at them. He
didn't know how many planes he'd seen explode, scattering debris and bodies through the clouds, how many
screams of pain he'd tried to ignore during the past few
months.

With a groan of frustration, Henry put his hands over
his eyes and rubbed his forehead to clear his mind. That's
no way to go back to sleep, he told himself. He listened
to the deep, steady snores of his bunkmates. See, they're
not afraid.

Suck it up, boy. A whiner won't last long in this world.

Henry pushed his father's voice out of his head. He
was sick of that voice and its harsh assessments. It had
been a real struggle for Henry not to see himself the way
his father seemed to. He'd thought he'd be free of his
father here, overseas, in a war, a chaotic world away from
their isolated farm. But the voice haunted him still.

Henry made himself think about blueberry pie. To

4

smell his Ma's blueberry pie—that would calm him down. It always did. He drifted home to Virginia and dreamed of his mother, Lilly, standing by the kitchen sink. She was awash in Tidewater sunshine:

"Get your fingers out of my pie, you sneak," Lilly chided. "It'll be cool soon enough. Then you can have a proper slice and sit down to the table like civilized folk." Her dimples showed as she said it, though, so Henry knew he could push it. He pulled out another small wedge even though it scalded his fingers. He popped it into his mouth.

Grinning, Lilly picked up a wooden spoon and shook it at him. "You're a hambone," she said and caught him for a hug.

"Lieutenant Forester?" A voice cut through the bleary warmth of Lilly's kitchen. "Get up, Lieutenant. You're flying today."

Henry forced his eyes open. Sergeant Bromsky stood by his bunk, shining a flashlight. The blueberry pie evaporated.

"I'm up, I'm up," Henry said and stretched himself awake. He was used to arising at 4 A.M. on his family's chicken farm. But most of the other fliers weren't. Sleepy groans filled the Nissen hut as the sergeant and his flashlight beam moved from bed to bed to rouse fifteen other pilots, navigators, and bombardiers—the officers of four bomber crews.

"Where we heading, Sarge?" Henry asked. "Any idea?"
Sergeant Bromsky came back to Henry's cot. It was

next to the small black stove that heated the thirty-foot-long hut. Built like a tin can cut in half and turned onto the ground, the hut had only one door and two windows at each end. It was dark and damp. Winds from the nearby North Sea found every crack. Even right beside the stove, the airmen shivered.

Sergeant Bromsky faced his backside to the stove. "The word is Germany, pretty far in. But keep it to yourself. You know the rules, Hank."

Henry ground his teeth. That meant about a thousand miles round-trip under attack by enemy fighter planes and antiaircraft guns on the ground. They'd just hit Berlin and lost almost half the base's crews.

"What number is this, Hank?" the sergeant asked.

The sergeant always asked Henry what number the day's mission was, as if he were rooting for him to get home. His support helped Henry. In return, he gave Sergeant Bromsky his cigarette rations, even though the other guys in the hut made fun of him for not smoking them himself. Henry had been born and raised in tobacco country, and he just hated the stuff.

Today, though, superstition slowed Henry's answer. To finish his tour of duty and go home, Henry had to survive twenty-five missions. But every airman had figured out that the average life span of an Eighth Air Force bomber crew was only fifteen. Everyone was afraid of the fifteenth mission. It was a make-or-break flight.

"It's my fifteenth," Henry said quietly. He watched the sergeant's face tighten.

"Yeah?" Bromsky looked away. His eyes fell on a photograph pinned to the wall beside Henry's cot. A pretty teenage girl smiled back at him.

"I hadn't noticed her before," Bromsky changed the subject. "Who's the dame?"

"Oh, she isn't a dame, Sarge. That's Patsy. We grew up together. Her family has the farm next to ours. She's almost like my kid sister."

Sergeant Bromsky leaned forward to get a better look at Patsy's thick, wavy hair, heart-shaped face, and serene smile. "Wow. She's a real looker, Hank."

Henry was mortified to feel himself blush. He tried to seem nonchalant. "To tell the truth, Sarge, that picture kills me, because she looks so ladylike. What I love about Patsy is that she's no sissy. She's a real spitfire. We could use her fighting the Germans."

Henry could tell from the Sarge's smile that his attempts to seem indifferent to Patsy's beauty were failing. He was just so confused about Patsy these days. Until right before he'd joined the Air Corps, they'd been buddies, best friends. But somehow their relationship had changed when he'd received his orders. And her letters, well, her letters brought out a longing in him he'd never felt before. Henry couldn't sort out if the longing was for her or home or just peacetime. But it was a strong feeling. She wrote him and he answered every week. He started to ask Sarge what he thought about the wisdom of romancing a girl through letters, but changed his mind.

"When I was about ten I was in a fight in the school yard," Henry continued. "This dopey boy, Jackson, was giving me trouble because my family raises chickens and the farm smells of them. He thought he was better than all us farmers. His dad hauled cargo at the Norfolk docks and didn't have to work the dirt the way we did. He was yelling: 'Henny Penny, what a chicken.' Well, I'd given him a sharp punch like my dad showed me. But he'd knocked me down and was kicking me good. Patsy came tearing up out of nowhere. Her face was red as a tomato. She kicked Jackson's shins so hard he cried!"

Henry paused to look at Patsy's face and felt his own flush again. "Anyway, she's . . . special, you know, Sarge?"

Before Bromsky could reply, Henry rushed to wrap her up with a safe comment. "I mostly appreciate how Patsy checks up on Ma for me. Dad doesn't talk much except when he's mad. Living on a hundred and fifty acres all alone with him and two thousand chickens could drive anyone crazy."

"Two thousand chickens! I'm not sure I've ever even seen one live chicken," said Bromsky, who was a native of New York City. He gave Henry a quick clap on the back. "Good luck today, Hank. I gotta roust the rest of the crews."

Henry dressed hurriedly to prevent the concrete floor's icy cold from seeping up through his entire body. He kept his blond head low as he pulled on his mission gear. The ceiling was eight feet high in the center of the Nissen hut but it curved downward to the ground from there. Henry was a lanky six feet tall and still stretching, as his ma always said.

Over his long johns, he pulled blue flannel underwear

that was wired to connect to the airplane's electrical system and protect him from severe frostbite. If thick clouds and enemy flak forced them to fly at 24,000 feet—four and a half miles up—the temperature inside the bomber's open bays could be thirty below zero.

Next came wool pants and shirt, plus a black wool tie. Over that, Henry pulled flying overhauls and fleeced-lined boots. Finally, he picked up his fleeced-lined bomber jacket and strapped on a .45 pistol. He'd need the gun if he had to bail out somewhere over Nazi-controlled Europe.

Across the aisle, Billy White, another copilot, was inspecting his beard. Dark haired Billy was just six months older than Henry, but his beard grew thick. Henry had to look close to find anything to shave. Still, he did it. During a flight even the slightest stubble caught condensation that could freeze and leave a string of icy beads right where the oxygen mask gripped his face.

Billy rubbed his smooth face and grinned. "Gotta be close, boys," he said to a bunkmate who cat-whistled at him.

Billy was peering into a tiny mirror hung next to a sultry photograph of movie star Rita Hayworth. He caught Henry's dimpled, babyfaced reflection in the mirror. He tapped Hayworth's photo and said, "Hey, Hanky, this is a real woman, no prudish kid sister. But would you know what to do with a real woman if you ever caught one?"

Henry straightened up. He'd gotten used to the raunchy humor around the barracks. He'd also flown a lot more missions than Lieutenant White. "You know what,

Billy," he said. "I've learned a thing or two flying *all* my missions. When guys are scared, they talk big."

"Whooaaa," laughed a few of the men as they scrambled to get ready.

Billy White shrugged. "We'll see who flies the most missions, farm boy."

"All right. Save the spit for the Germans," interrupted Henry's pilot, Dan MacNamara. Dan was twenty-five years old, married, and the father of a baby girl named Colleen. He'd been the oldest brother in a rowdy clan of seven Irish siblings in Chicago. He could control the barracks and crew with just a few words.

"Billy," Dan said. "We'll let it stand that you've danced with every girl this side of London. Of course, whether you've gotten anywhere with them, we don't know."

He turned to Henry. "Hank, you're one hotshot pilot. Nobody flies a tighter formation than you do. Let's just get over there, drop our bombs, get home, and I'll buy you both a beer. That's root beer for you, right, Hank?" Dan winked at Henry as he said it.

"Yeah, yeah," Henry said and smiled.

Today would be Dan's twenty-first mission. He had even survived the legendary raid on the Ploesti Oil fields in Romania the previous August. Dan had told Henry how the bombers had gone in at treetop level to avoid detection as long as possible. They didn't know about the antiaircraft guns hidden behind haystacks. A third of the planes went down in flames, too low in altitude for any of their crews to bail out.

After hearing that, Henry was certain Dan could

survive anything. Henry's first four raids had been under a different pilot, last name Cobb, a real wildcat flier. He'd bled to death on their fourth mission, as Henry fought on alone to get their plane up and over the Dover cliffs and crash-land on English soil. Only then had he realized he was covered with Cobb's splattered blood. Henry had crawled out of the cockpit and vomited for fifteen minutes solid.

With Dan in command, no matter how bad the flak or fighters were, Henry knew he at least had a chance.

Dan threw open the door to a wet wind and a sea of slippery, icy English mud. "Let's get to Group Ops," he said. "Briefing's in ten minutes."

"Jeez," said Billy, pushing his way out past Henry. "It musta poured last night."

"Isn't it always raining in England?" muttered Dan. "Let's hope the weather officer knows what he's doing."

They all looked up at the black sky, trying to assess the clouds. No stars visible and no sunrise yet. The only lights were on the distant airfield. Out there, the ground crews were loading bombs and fueling the aircraft. If it wasn't mechanically perfect, a B-24 loaded with 2,000 pounds of bombs and glutted with gasoline was a flying deathtrap. "God bless the ground crew," murmured Henry aloud, without thinking.

Then he wanted to kick himself for opening the door to a put-down. He'd been dismissed as "a Boy Scout" before and knew some of the older fliers were merciless with a devout Baptist gunner who got down on his knees to pray before getting into his plane. Henry could see a jeer forming on Billy's face and braced himself.

But instead Billy agreed: "Amen to that." The ground crew and their work were sacrosanct for everyone.

"Hey, didya hear Lord Ha Ha last night?" asked Henry's navigator, Fred Bennett, as they slogged across the mud-washed base.

"Naw, I never listen to that guy," said Henry, even though he did. "He's full of baloney." Broadcasting in English almost every night, Lord Ha Ha was a Nazi trying to unnerve the British and American fliers.

"I don't know, Hank," said Fred. "He seemed to know we'd be flying today. He said the Luftwaffe would be waiting for us."

Fred was a small guy, a washout from flight school, a real worrier. He'd finished two years of an English literature major at Harvard before volunteering. He was always quoting some writer named Thomas Hardy—very depressing stuff. But he was a great navigator. He seemed to have a sixth sense for direction, even in heavy cloud cover. And Henry just liked him. "You know what we can do tonight when we get back, Fred?" said Henry.

The navigator shook his head.

"I'd love it if you'd read aloud some more of that Dickens, that _Tale of Two Cities_. I've got to keep up my studies, you know. Virginia said they'd keep my scholarship active for me for two years as long as I don't go stupid on them."

"I didn't know you were going to be a college boy, Hank," said Dan.

Chapter One

"When I get home. I promised Ma. It about killed her when I joined up two weeks after graduating high school. Schooling is real important to her. She's the one who taught me there's more to the world than chicken coops. She used to read to me even when I shelled peas and beans, so my mind was working too. The Bible, Sherlock Holmes, a poet named Emily Dickinson she loved. My personal favorite is Jules Verne, *Around the World in Eighty Days.*"

"Good for you, Hank," said Dan. "I dropped out of high school when the Depression hit. I needed to work to help Da. Seven kids need lots of shoes. Read to us, Fred. Gotta get me some book education to impress my baby girl when I get home. Rose wrote that she said her first word."

"What was it, Dad? *Goo-goo blah-blah?*" It was Henry's turn to tease.

"No," said Dan goodnaturedly. "It was *wa-wa.*"

"*Wa-wa?*" Henry laughed. "I don't seem to have *wa-wa* in my vocabulary, Captain. What's it mean?"

"She was asking for water," Dan said, laughing at himself. "A budding genius, she is." Then he grew quiet. "I tell you what, though. The first word I'm going to work on her saying when I get home is *Daddy.*"

"You guys are making me sick," Billy interrupted. "You know what I did last night? Some important scientific research. I figured out that these flight getups have thirty-six feet of zippers. I'm getting mighty good at unzipping fast. That'll come in real handy with the girls someday soon, boys, if you know what I mean. Do you have any idea what I mean, Hank?"

13

Patsy's pretty face came to Henry. He knew how much Billy's off-color jokes would insult her. And he was startled and mad with himself that for a few fleeting seconds Billy's crude comment had sent Henry imagining Patsy in a vivid, not particularly respectful way.

"Stow it, White," Henry snapped. "I feel sorry for any girl who gets stuck with you."

The group had reached the operations building. Billy turned to ridicule Henry in a forced Southern twang: "And whom do you all date, farm boy? Some bucktoothed swamp queen?"

Henry's nightmare had left him feeling thin-skinned and homesick. He stepped in front of Billy to block his path. Leaning toward him, Henry whispered in a menacing manner, "Y'all want to see some swamp-boy boxing?"

"Hey! Cut it out," yelled Dan. He pushed them apart with a big, practiced shove. "Remember what you're here for. Shake hands."

"No way," muttered Billy. "The guy's a lunatic."

"Shake hands. That's an order."

Reluctantly, Henry extended his.

Reluctantly, Billy took it.

As their hands touched, Henry regretted his outburst. That was the kind of threat his Dad would have made. Henry had always promised himself that he'd never be like his volatile father. He took a deep breath and tried looking at things from Billy's side, the way his ma forever told him to. Heck, Billy was probably just as nervous as he was. And what could you expect from such a jerk on a morning like this, anyway?

Chapter One

"Tell you what," Henry said as he let go of Billy's hand. "When the war's over, I'll come to Philadelphia to meet those country-club lady friends of yours. Then you come to Richmond. My ma will fix a meal that'll melt in your mouth and teach you some manners without your ever realizing she's doing it."

Billy seemed to relax. "Done." He opened the door and whistled as he walked through. "Off we go, into the wild blue yonder. . . ."

Dan followed behind Henry. "What's the matter with you, Hank?"

"Sorry, Captain." Henry's green eyes hit the ground. "I don't know what's wrong with me this morning. Got the jitters, I guess."

"Don't get flak-happy on me, boy," Dan said, putting his hand on Henry's shoulder. "I mean it. You're the steadiest copilot I've ever seen."

Henry nodded, bolstered.

"I want to get home, too, Hank. I've only got four more to go. Let's make sure we both get back today."

The pilots' eyes held each other's for a moment. Dan's belief in him made Henry feel years older, stronger. He wasn't just a scared farm boy away from home for the first time. He was someone Dan could trust. "I'm with you, Captain," Henry answered.

Dan smiled. Then he resumed his flyboy swagger. He called after the group, "Okay, boys, let's see what part of hell we're visiting today."

Chapter Two

Henry followed Dan and Fred to the front of the briefing room. Their bombardier, Paul Sabatino, trotted up the aisle to squeeze in with them on the wooden bench. Paul was always late.

"Nice of you to make it, Sabatino," said Dan.

"Aw, I was here before you guys." Paul pointed his thumb toward the back of the room. "I wanted to get a doughnut from Abby."

Abby was one of the Red Cross girls at the door handing out doughnuts and coffee as the fliers filed in. Even at 4:30 in the morning she was fresh, her lips perfect with red lipstick, a ready smile, and a kind word. Half the base was sweet on her, especially Paul. But she had a beau in the 303rd, flying B-17s.

Henry stared nervously at the wall ahead, covered with a white curtain. Behind the curtain hung a map of Europe. Henry knew that a red piece of yarn traced their flight to the day's target. But the curtain still hid the map. Henry checked the position of the yarn pulley to the left of the curtain. If the pulley were near the top of the curtain, that would mean all the yarn was used up to point their way. It'd be a long mission deep into Germany. If the pulley were hanging pretty far down, they'd have a short flight, a "milk run," into France or Belgium. Today the pulley was rammed up to the ceiling.

Henry exhaled a low whistle and began fumbling in the flap pocket of his shirt. He jostled Dan.

"What's worrying you now, flyboy?" the captain asked.

"Just looking for my good luck," Henry said. He pulled out a beautiful marble. Swirls of red and gold floated just under its surface.

Dan smiled. "I had one of those when I was a kid."

Henry dropped it into the captain's palm.

"It's a cloud, isn't it?" Dan asked as he rolled it around his hand.

"That's right," Henry nodded. A cloud was an "end-of-day" marble: a large, one-of-a-kind marble that glass-blowers made from leftover glass. "It's my shooter. I won it off my old man. He *always* played by the rules. Even before I was in grade school, I had to shoot knuckles down or I'd lose my turn. And he played for keeps. Whatever he knocked out of the circle, he kept. Even if it was my favorite marble. He'd say," —Henry adopted a low, gruff drawl—"'That'll teach you to shoot better, boy.'"

"Nice guy," said Dan.

Henry paused. "That's Clayton Forester for you. Dad

17

can be . . . well . . . kinda harsh. He has his own set of rules for right and wrong. You gotta be a man. When I was eleven years old, my dog, Skippy, got hit by a truck. Skip had been out on the road looking for me to come home from school. I'd told him and told him to stay by the house. He was the best dog, so loyal—a beautiful English setter—but he didn't mind worth a dime.

"That truck hit him hard enough to break both his back legs. Skip was in terrible pain, dragging himself along the ground. Dad said he was my dog, so it was my responsibility to stop his misery." Henry's voice cracked. "So I got my rifle. And I shot him. Skip died looking at me with those big, trusting brown eyes of his. I don't think I'll ever forgive that old bastard for making me do that."

Henry took the marble back and looked down at it. "Ma would try to sneak back the marbles Dad won off me when he was asleep. But what I really wanted more than anything was to beat him fair and square. When I was fourteen, I shot this out of the circle and claimed it. It had been Dad's since he was a kid. I used it as my shooter for the rest of that game. And you know what?"

"What?" Dan asked.

"I knocked out every single one of my old man's marbles on one turn. Even his steelies. He about had a fit." Henry laughed. "So this is my good luck, my cloud. It'll keep me up there in the blue."

Carefully, Henry put the marble back into his pocket and buttoned it in. He tried to wait patiently for the C.O., the commanding officer, to arrive. The exact location of the target wouldn't be revealed until then.

"Tenn-hut!" The fliers stood up, straight and still, as the C.O. passed to the front podium.

"Be seated, gentlemen," the C.O. called out. "Before we show you today's mission I want to congratulate you on the past month. You've done a hard job well. One that had to be done if we ever want to liberate 'Fortress Europe.'" As he uttered the last two words, the C.O. stuck his finger under his nose and adopted a thick German accent to make fun of Hitler's term for his empire. The fliers laughed appreciatively.

"Here's what you have accomplished: Air Intelligence tells us that during January, when weather kept us grounded, the Nazis increased their aircraft production to one plane every fifteen minutes. That's four Luftwaffe killers an hour." He paused to let that number sink in. "We had to break that production before it broke us. That's what all those back-to-back missions in February were about.

"I'd like to give all of you a week's pass to London," the C.O. concluded—he held up his hand to stop the men's cheers—"God knows you deserve it. But it's crucial that we weaken the Luftwaffe before General Eisenhower tries a land invasion. Otherwise, thousands and thousands of American boys will die for nothing. We have to push forward to keep the Luftwaffe from regathering its strength." He sat down and nodded to his S-2, the intelligence officer. The S-2 pulled back the curtain with a flourish.

The red yarn ran across the English Channel to the

Belgian coast, took a sharp turn down to France, and ran a long diagonal across it. From there, the yarn skipped along the northern edge of Switzerland to a point in southern Germany. It would be a long, long flight.

Henry and the other airmen shifted in their seats. "Is this trip really necessary?" shouted a smart-mouthed pilot, quoting a gas-conservation slogan well known back in the States.

"Yes, it is, men," said the S-2. "And let's do it right. Drop the bombs right in the pickle barrel." He slapped the map with his pointer. "Your target is a ball-bearing plant. Without ball bearings, Messerschmitts can't fly, Rommel's tanks can't roll."

The S-2 put up a photograph of the factory. The Nazis had tried to hide it among homes, schools, and churches. Accuracy was critical or many civilians would die. The S-2 talked about the number of fighters and flak guns the crews could expect to come up against. It wasn't pretty.

Then the weather officer explained how to deal with the weather. The clouds would be low and broken up as they left England. Once they hit the European mainland, however, cumulus clouds billowed up solid to 20,000 feet. They'd have to fly over them. The target was overcast but predicted to clear by the time the bombers arrived at 11 A.M. Everything was strategically timed: the moment they'd rally with other bomb groups taking off from bases all over England; the time they were to hit the target.

"Gentlemen," the C.O. stood up again to synchronize the men's watches. "Here's our time-tick. It is now five-oh-five minus twenty seconds." The fliers looked down at their watches and set them to 5:05, keeping the stem that started the watch pulled out, waiting for the C.O. to say, *hack*.

"Five seconds . . . four . . . three . . . two . . . one, *hack*." Henry and a hundred other men clicked in their watch stems. Whatever their various fates on this mission, they were tied together in time.

"Let's get some chow," said Dan after the briefing. They headed to the flying officers' mess hall. There were "combat eggs" this morning, real eggs, not the powdered, green-tinted ones. Henry took mounds of scrambled eggs, bacon, and pancakes. It would be night before he ate again.

Billy crowded up behind Henry in the food line and banged his tray against Henry's. "Hear you're flying left wing to my plane, farm boy. Make sure you keep that formation tight. Close as I dance with village girls at the pub."

"Don't worry, Romeo," said Henry, keeping the tone friendly. "You'll be able to play cards off my wing tip, I'll keep it so close and steady."

Billy nodded and turned to go. Henry reached out to touch his arm. "Be careful out there in the lead, Billy. The shooting gets thick, you know?"

"Yeah." Billy tried to smile. "Thanks, Hank."

Henry sat down with his crew. His food was not inviting. He imagined the warm bacon smell and sizzling sound of his ma's frying pan as she cooked breakfast. She always hummed something as she cooked. What was it? *Amazing Grace*, that was it.

He checked his watch. 5:20. He thought about home at 5:20 A.M. The old man would be back in the house after feeding the chickens. Henry could smell Clayton's cup of acid-strong coffee, hear him dump a spoonful of sugar and stir it rapidly. He'd be clinking the teaspoon against the cup loudly until Lilly gently reached over to still his hand.

Henry thought about Patsy. At 5:20, Patsy would be getting up. Henry wondered how she did, walking to school on her own in the dawning light. They had always quizzed each other on spelling and math as they walked. Who did that for her now? Her parents never had time for that.

Stop thinking, Henry told himself. He forced down the rest of his breakfast and got up from the table. "Gotta get in line for the escape kits. I'll see y'all at the plane."

That was one of Henry's duties as copilot, to pick up and distribute the small packages meant to help fliers survive behind enemy lines if they had to bail out. The contents included: one candy bar, one can of food, three syringes of morphine, a compass, a silk map of France, bandages, pills for sterilizing water, and a little French money. There was also a pamphlet with a list of English phrases translated into French, Dutch, Spanish, and German. *I am in a hurry* and *Heil Hitler* were repeated across all four columns. Not much to protect you against the Third Reich, thought Henry.

He waved off a ride in a jeep already overflowing

with fliers. He preferred to walk to the landing field and get his head straight. "'We did it before and we can do it again,'" Henry sang. It was a song that had come out right after the Japanese bombed Pearl Harbor. We can do it again. Just another bomb run, Henry. No big deal.

"Got any gum, chum?" asked a small voice.

Henry turned around to see a young boy who lived on the farm next door. The base's runways had been sliced right into the farm's fields. The boy was constantly asking fliers for gum. Food was rationed in England. Meat went to the American and British fliers first. Gum helped trick civilian stomachs to stop rumbling.

Henry knew what it was like to be a child feeling hungry. There had been many days he'd eaten nothing but boiled eggs and bread after the stock market crashed and crushed farm prices. His father and mother had such a hard time making their mortgage payments during the first year of the Depression, they'd only kill a chicken for Sunday dinner, and then only after she'd gotten too old to lay eggs for them to sell.

Henry handed the English boy a stick of gum. "You're not supposed to be on base, you know," he said.

"You going to tell on me, Yank?" said the boy with a mischievous grin. Henry watched him dart across the fence. The boy's grandfather was already out trying to plow a field with his old cart horse.

Henry reached their B-24 ahead of his crew. He stopped to look her over. The ground crews had patched the baseball-sized holes left by flak on their last run. The olive-colored Liberator looked clean and ready. *Out of the*

Blue was her name. Henry loved the picture painted on her: a fiery red-haired woman dressed in blue sitting atop a cloud and holding a bomb by the tail.

When he had gone on a pass to London, Henry met a lot of B-17 pilots. They made fun of the B-24's odd tail, the two fins popping up off a crossbeam. But the Liberator's slim wing had better aerodynamics than the B-17s. A B-24 could fly faster and higher, with a heavier load of bombs. What Henry and other B-24 pilots didn't like to admit, though, was that the wing's design gave the Liberator a tendency to stall and spin. B-17s, the Flying Fortresses, held up better under battle damage, too. They could even make it back to base on just one of their four engines. If a B-24's wing was hit, the plane went down fast.

Henry reached up to grab the edge of the hatch in the plane's nose. He swung himself up, feet first. He squeezed through the compartment where the engineer operated the turret guns. Then he shimmied into the cockpit's right-hand seat. He had already checked most of the controls when Dan squashed himself in behind the left control wheel.

They began their preflight ritual, crucial to safety, crucial to nerves. Henry followed a procedures list. But the two could have done it in their sleep.

"Set on preflight?" asked Dan.

"Roger," confirmed Henry.

"Weight and balance?"

"Check."

"Fuel-boost pumps, valves, switches?"

"Roger, set."

Chapter Two

Following Dan, Henry continued down the list, checking the brakes, and the electrical and hydraulic systems. They tested flaps, throttles, gears, deicers, and generators. Henry flicked a dozen handles and switches on and off, on and off. He verified the oxygen supplies.

Finally, Dan sang out: "All set to fire up?"

"Roger."

Dan radioed the tower, "All set. Crew, check-in."

A chorus of checking in followed: Fred and Paul directly below them in the glass cage of the plane's nose; the engineer right behind. Then the radio operator, two waist gunners, ball-turret gunner, and tail gunner. There were ten crew members in all.

Henry and Dan went through more last-minute checks. Then Dan uttered the final question: "Fuel supply and quantity?"

"Check," answered Henry.

"Start engines."

Henry pulled the generators. The starter engine popped.

"Mesh!" said Dan.

The number three engine swirled slowly, then faster and faster, until it was a whir. *Out of the Blue* began to wiggle, like a racehorse twitching at the start gate.

"Number two," called Dan.

The left inside engine snorted blue smoke and spun into action. The plane hummed and rattled.

Dan and Henry let the plane creep out to the take-off point to join the twenty-three other planes. They bucked against their brakes, ready to hurtle down the runway. Dan fired engine one, then engine four.

Henry watched for the flare from Flying Control. If he saw a green-red combination that meant the mission was a go, but they weren't cleared yet for takeoff. If it was red-red, the raid was called off. If it was green-green, they were on their way to Germany.

A sequence of green-green balls of light spit over the runway.

"Okay, crew," Dan said over the intercom. "Ready for takeoff."

He and Henry pushed all four throttles forward. Overloaded with 500-pound bombs and almost 3,000 gallons of fuel, *Out of the Blue* shuddered and convulsed as she roared along the airstrip. There was just barely enough pavement to get her up into the air and over the oak trees that stood at the end of the runway. They could easily smash into those trees and explode.

"Come on, baby, come on," whispered Henry.

Right behind them was another bomb-filled plane, due to take off a mere thirty seconds after they did. There was absolutely no room for error. Henry glanced over at Dan and saw his jaw muscles twitching.

The plane needed a speed of at least 120 miles per hour to take off and not stall. "Hundred 'n' five . . . hundred 'n' ten," Henry counted off as he watched the air speed indicator. "Come on," he said again, more urgently. They were almost to the trees.

"Saint-Paddy, please," muttered Dan.

"Hundred 'n' twenty!" shouted Henry. "Yes! I love you, Blue."

Dan and Henry pulled back on the control wheels to tilt up the plane's nose.

Out of the Blue hopped up and down off the pavement like a stone skipping across water. *Bounce, bounce, bounce.* She heaved herself up just in time.

Snap, swish.

Out of the Blue's landing wheels skimmed along the treetops as they slowly lifted up into their compartments.

"We're off," Dan said. He patted the plane's control board lovingly.

Off on a seven- to nine-hour flight. Off to a land where people who feared and hated them pointed thousands of guns skyward. Off to deliver death or meet it themselves.

Chapter Three

"**K**eep a look-out for planes," said Dan.

"Roger that," Henry answered. They were climbing through clouds and could see only mountains of gray. But both pilots knew there were already a dozen B-24s circling the very same air space they were. A dozen more were coming up fast. Henry anxiously scanned the sky for a glint of metal. He knew of two crews who had died in midair collisions while the group tried to assemble itself.

"Didn't the weather officer say we'd clear at 2,500 feet?" Dan complained.

Wisps of clouds skimmed along the cockpit like thick cotton candy. Henry couldn't see a thing.

Four thousand feet. The clouds were aglow now with pink light.

"See anything?" asked Dan.

Chapter Three

Henry strained his eyes left and right. "No." Then he glanced up and shouted, "Look out!"

"Jesus, Mary, and Joseph!" Dan jammed in the control wheel to make the plane drop like a stone. They'd come up right underneath the belly of Billy White's plane, *Battling Queen.*

The radio crackled and Henry heard, "You awake, farm boy?"

"I am now," Henry radioed back.

Billy's pilot broke in. He was all business. His plane was group leader that day. The Luftwaffe might pick up any radio signals between their planes. "No more radio chatter," Billy's captain ordered. The radio clicked to silence.

At 6,000 feet the planes bobbed up into blue heaven, with a sea of fleecy white below. Henry blinked in the bright sun.

The top turret operator in *Battling Queen* fired off yellow-green flares, signaling the bombers to pull into tight Vs. Three planes formed a V, or element. That was the building block of any large formation. A second element of three planes would pull in about fifty feet behind, above, and to the left, of the first, lead V. Six planes total made up a squadron.

Today Henry's bomb group would fly in a diamond shape. That meant a lead squadron in front, a high squadron slightly above and to its side. A third, low squadron would be on the opposite side. And a fourth squadron would bring up the rear, in the slot position. Twenty-four bombers total.

Henry's hands trembled slightly. The air was thick with B-24s flying at 180 m.p.h., all trying to pull within a few yards of one another. Dan fought to keep *Out of the Blue* level as it flopped around in the prop wash of the other planes.

Dan pulled up to the left of *Battling Queen*. Because the copilot's seat was on the right of the cockpit, Henry could see *Battling Queen* better. "Controls are yours, Hank. Tuck her in."

Slowly, Henry pushed the floor pedal forward to turn the B-24's black-and-white striped tail rudder. Easy, he thought to himself. If he pushed the pedal too far the plane could veer sharply into *Battling Queen*, killing them all.

"A little more," Dan urged.

Henry pressed his foot forward another half inch. The very tip of his wing was about six feet over, six feet back from *Battling Queen*'s.

"Nice," said Dan. "I'll take a nap now. Tell me when we're in Krautville," he joked.

Henry laughed. He appreciated Dan's ease with compliments. His dad had been so stingy with them. Dan will be a good father, thought Henry.

"We have a 6:15 A.M. rally point at Great Yarmouth right before the North Sea," said Dan. "That's where we'll link up with the other bomb groups."

"Roger," said Henry.

They flew in silence. Henry kept checking his position. He had to react to crosswinds and turbulence that bumped his plane too close or too far away from *Battling*

Queen. Keeping the pedal pressure just right on the tail's rudders took a lot of thigh strength. Henry often felt as if he were bicycling across Europe instead of flying, his legs were so sore after a mission.

"Ten thousand feet. Turn on your oxygen," Henry called through the plane's intercom. He heard the crew grumble as they latched the rubber masks onto their faces. They all hated wearing them. They smelled horrible and the tubing got in their way.

"We're going to be flying at twenty thousand feet today, y'all," Henry reminded them. "So don't forget to check your lines for ice." At such high attitudes, their saliva would freeze. During the flight, Henry would constantly have to crush his mask to break up the ice. If he didn't, his oxygen supply would be cut. He could pass out at the wheel.

"There they are," said Dan. Two diamonds made up of twenty-four bombers each were coming in from the west. Two more diamonds approached from the south, a third from the north.

That was only part of the American armada flying that day. One member of the ground crew had told Henry that today's mission was a maximum effort, involving almost every base in England. "Heard tell there were eight hundred bombers and fighters prepped last night, Lieutenant. That should keep you safe."

For forty-five precious minutes they flew in peace. Nothing but water below and sky above—a mirrored world of soft blues. The ocean's white caps looked like small clouds. This is what Henry had thought flying would be like. For a few wondrous minutes, he was filled with an awed happiness.

But his peace didn't last.

"Flak." Dan pointed.

Little black puffs of smoke dotted the sky ahead of them. It looked harmless, but Henry knew each burst threw countless pieces of jagged, burning metal into the air. A direct hit could cripple their plane or tear his flesh wide open. The Reich had lined the European coast with flak guns. One flak battery at the southern tip of Holland was so deadly accurate the fliers had nicknamed its German commander Daniel Boone after the frontier marks-man.

Boom, boom, boom, boom.

Flak came in bursts of four. Each explosion sounded like a huge door slamming. The first shot generally gauged the bombers' altitude for the gunners down below; the second shot measured air speed. The third and fourth usually hit dead on or close to it.

Ping, ping, ping.

Shrapnel fragments skittered along the bottom of *Out of the Blue*, like gravel hitting a truck's underside. The plane shuddered.

"Any damage?" Dan called to the crew.

"No, sir," was the answer. "They're having an off day, Captain."

Henry hunkered down in his seat. He glued his eyes to *Battling Queen*'s wing. This barrage would only last a few miles. The real flak would hit when they were over the target. What they really had to worry about now were the fighters. They were due to show up any second.

"Keep sharp for bogeys," warned Dan.

Out of the glaring sun zoomed a swarm of single-engine fighters. They fanned out into pairs and *swooshed* in, closing at a rate of two hundred yards a second.

"Bandits! Two of them, two o'clock high," called Henry's top-turret gunner.

"Fighters low at ten o'clock, climbing fast," shouted the ball-turret gunner.

Rat-tat-tat-tat-tat-tat.

Firing their 20-mm cannons, the Luftwaffe fighters whooshed by the cockpit. Henry recognized the yellow noses of Focke-Wulf 190s. "Abbeville kids." Henry muttered a curse. Fw 190s were based in Abbeville, France, just inland from the coast. They were Air Marshal Hermann Goering's most elite Luftwaffe squadron. They were absolutely the worst fighters to encounter—precise and relentless.

"Where are our guys?" Henry asked Dan.

"Little friends, little friends, we could use some help here," Dan radioed for American fighters.

"Look out! They're coming in again."

Six Fw 190s buzzed by the cockpit, arcing up into the clouds. They doubled back and rushed in from behind, where only the tail gunner had a clear shot at them. Henry held his breath and thought about their tail gunner, Jim Wilkinson. He was a little guy with a big grin. Henry always wondered how he could stand the tail's cramped compartment—he was so vulnerable to being shot to pieces.

Out of the Blue reverberated with Jim's frantic shooting. *Rat-tat-tat-tat-tat.* Jim was breathing like a horse over the intercom.

BOOM!

One of the Focke-Wulf fighters burst into flames and exploded. The others veered off to avoid colliding with the debris.

"I got him, I got him!"

"Way to go, Jimmy-boy!" yelled Dan.

The fighters disappeared.

"Where'd they go?" asked Henry.

Dan pointed ahead. Their group was in the huge formation's second combat wing. The Luftwaffe was going after the lead plane, in the lead group.

A dozen Fw 190s swarmed it. One after another, the Germans raced out to a few thousand yards ahead of the formation's point, then U-turned and charged back, head-on, rolling. Henry could see their guns blinking. Their tracer fire singed the sky.

"Move, you guys," Henry whispered.

The bomb group took evasive action. It swung itself in the opposite direction from the fighters' roll, hoping the maneuver would throw them off target momentarily. But the well-trained Luftwaffe pilots anticipated the move. Their bullets tore the lead bomber's wings open. One of its engines exploded, sending fire ripping toward the B-24's cabin.

The plane seemed to crumple. Then it exploded. Huge

pieces of metal hurtled through the air. Half of a wing spun viciously through the group of B-24s. It hit a bomber one squadron back and sliced off its tail. One second, two seconds, three seconds—*BOOM!* The second bomber plane exploded, too. No chutes from either B-24. No survivors.

Two bombers and their deadly cargo destroyed. Twenty American boys dead instantly. It was just the domino effect the German fighters were after. Henry shuddered.

The Fw 190s whirred back to the B-24 bomber that had moved up the line to take the formation's lead position.

Rat-tat-tat-tat-tat-tat.

That B-24 plummeted.

At this rate, no lead plane would survive. "Just like foxes in a chicken coop," swore Henry. "Where are our guys?"

Another *WHOOSH* on the left wing of *Out of the Blue.* A flash of silver wings, red-and-yellow checkers. It was a squadron of American fighters, P-51 Mustangs, on its way to protect the front combat wing.

The men of *Out of the Blue* cheered.

To the west Henry spotted another set of small black dots. They grew larger and larger as they approached. Enemy aircraft or Americans? Henry could feel himself sweat inside his flight suit, even as his face and breath froze in the subzero air. Finally, Henry could make out the colors of olive drab and yellow. Thank God, P-47 Thunderbolts.

"Glad to see you, Little Friends," Dan radioed.

"Little Friends to Big Friend," the Thunderbolt leader radioed back, "weather delayed us. The party will start now."

German fighters broke off their attack on the bombers to face down the American Thunderbolts and Mustangs. Like falcons twisting and diving, the fighter planes went after each other. The sky lit up with orange explosions as the fighters' gas tanks burst into flames when they were hit.

Dan and Henry had to jerk their plane around repeatedly to avoid crashing into smoking, spinning debris. Then a pilot's body slammed into the glass window below the cockpit where Fred and Paul crouched.

"God Almighty," Paul sobbed over the intercom. "That guy's eyes were open. He looked right at me."

The air battle bled on. Each time a bomber or American fighter fell from the sky, the crew of *Out of the Blue* searched for parachutes.

"See any?" Dan would call.

Two here. Four there. One alone. Never all ten of a bomber crew.

Several planes near them were hit severely enough to drastically slow their engines or hobble their navigation. Unable to keep up their altitude or speed, they drifted out of the protection of the formation. In friendly territory they would be able to do a controlled crash landing, but here they became sitting ducks.

"The bogeyman is gonna get them," muttered Dan.

"The Alps are ahead," Fred called over the intercom.

"Maybe those guys can make it into Switzerland."

Switzerland was neutral. The Swiss interned Allied and German crews alike who landed there. But they were safe, in one piece. Henry kept his eyes on the disabled planes as long as he could until they disappeared into clouds below. He could only imagine how terrifying it would be to be left behind all alone in a sky full of German fighters.

"Let's hope they do, Fred," answered Dan. "But right now we've got other things to worry about."

More fighters had soared up from German bases below: speckled green-blue Messerschmitts and sand-brown Junkers with huge black Swastikas on their tails. There was also something Henry had never seen before: a group of four-engine, two-finned fighters. They hurtled past *Out of the Blue* on their way to the front of the bomber formation.

"What the heck are those?" asked Dan.

"No idea," Henry answered. "Look how they rip past the Junkers."

"Remember to report that at debriefing," said Dan.

But the pilots had little time to think about Hitler's new planes. The Junkers and Messerschmitts were now concentrating their firepower on the outer ribs of the American bomber formation—on them and *Battling Queen*.

Chapter Four

"Pull in snug, Hank," Dan spoke sharply. "They're coming for us."

Rat-tat-tat-tat-tat.

The Junkers spun and came at them, hurling lead. Most of the bullets bounced off, but one broke through the cockpit's Plexiglas armor. *Zing, zing, zing, zing.* It rattled around and around until it found its mark: Dan's leg.

Dan screamed and slumped over, breathing hard. "Sweet Jesus!" He grabbed his calf.

"Dan!" Henry reached toward his captain.

"Keep your hands on the wheel, Lieutenant." Dan snarled. He groaned as he straightened himself. "I'm all right. It's not deep enough for me to bleed to death. Focus, Hank. They'll be back any second."

On this swing, the Luftwaffe targeted *Battling Queen.* Four fighters veered toward her, guns blinking.

Then they loosed something else Dan and Henry had never seen before. A small rocket shot out from under one of the Junkers' wings.

BOOM!

The rocket hit *Battling Queen's* number three engine. The bomber lurched wildly, but somehow Billy and Dick kept the B-24 level. Henry knew, though, that a number-three explosion meant that Billy had lost his hydraulic system. The electrical was probably out, too. *Battling Queen* had no chance of making it home now.

The wounded bomber slid out and away from the squadron. Smoke trailed out of its blackened engine and the number-two propeller swung around uselessly. The bomb bay door opened. One, two, three crewmembers jumped out. Then another two. Five little white chutes popped open and were scattered by the wind. Clouds swallowed them.

Did Billy make it out? Lord, I know he can be a jerk, Henry prayed silently. *But look after him now.*

Empty of her crew, *Battling Queen* seemed to just hang there for a moment, dead in the air. Then it burst into flames and—*BOOM!*—blew up.

"Hold on!" shouted Dan. He and Henry gripped their wheels as debris clattered across the shell of their plane. *Out of the Blue* pitched around violently in the explosion's wake.

"They'll be on us now," Dan warned.

Henry nodded grimly and locked onto his control wheel even tighter. He placed his life in the hands of his gunners. "Get me a bird, guys," he called through the intercom.

It all happened faster than Henry expected. Just as Dan radioed: "Little Friends, Little Friends, we've got a bee's nest back here," Messerschmitts swarmed them. Four whirled around, looped up over *Out of the Blue* and came back, straight on, rolling.

Rat-tat-tat-tat-tat.

Another bullet pierced the cockpit window.

Zing, zing, zing.

Henry felt it whiz by his ear to lodge somewhere behind him.

CRRRRACK.

Glass shattered. A scream of pain came from the bombardier's compartment below.

"God, oh God," Paul cried out over the intercom. "Fred's hit! There's blood everywhere! Oh, God."

Other cries of agony shrieked through the intercom. Henry started to lift himself out of his chair to help.

"Sit down! They're coming around again, Hank." Dan steadied Henry with his commanding voice.

A thousand yards ahead, Henry could see American Mustangs closing in. "Come on, boys," he urged.

A Messerschmitt streaked by the cockpit.

BANG, BANG, BANG.

Henry heard the sound of bullets puncturing metal, of engine gears grinding and cracking. *Out of the Blue* quaked and dipped. Its number two-engine was on fire. The edge of its left wing was sheered off.

BANG!

Henry looked to the right. Their number three-engine sputtered and shook. Its propeller grated to a stop.

"Dan!" Henry cried.

"I know. We're cooked." Dan called to the crew, "Bail out. Everybody out NOW!"

Out of the Blue began to whine and drift away from the formation, falling like a leaf on a strong wind. Henry knew it was only a matter of a minute, seconds maybe, before her nose would go down. Then she'd start spin-ning, generating a centrifugal force that would lock all of them inside until she exploded. But he and Dan clung to the controls for a few more moments to give the crew—whoever was still alive—a chance to get out.

"Now you," Dan ordered Henry. "I'm right behind you." The entire left wing was ablaze.

Henry pushed himself up, fighting the plane's wild bucking. He glanced down at Dan's leg. It was drenched in blood. Dan would never get himself out with that wound. "I'm not leaving without you, Captain."

"Go on!" shouted Dan. "That's an order!"

Henry had disconnected himself from his oxygen supply to get out. He could feel himself getting lightheaded. Hurry, he told himself. Hurry!

He started out of the cockpit, following orders. Then he looked at Dan's leg again. This man had saved his skin plenty of times. Henry couldn't leave him behind. He grabbed Dan by the arm and yanked him up. "Sorry, Captain. You're coming."

Waddling in his fat, fleece-lined suit, Henry dragged the two of them out of the cockpit. He could hear the wings tearing apart. The plane rocked like an earthquake. Dan cried out with each step.

Somehow, Henry got them to the bomb bay. He lowered Dan into the opening. Clouds rushed below. Dan clutched Henry's collar. It was the first time Henry had seen fear on Dan's face.

"Thanks, Hank," he said. Then Dan let go and dropped into the sky.

Henry wriggled down among the four 500-pound bombs. He squeezed his way through and fell into the blue.

Henry waited before pulling the parachute's red handle. Pull the release cord too soon and the chute might snag on the plane's tail.

One one thousand, two one thousand . . . In flight training, Henry had been taught to count to ten by thousands before pulling. If he let his freefall go long enough, the friction of his body against air would slow his descent, making the chute's snapping open more merciful. Many an airman had broken ribs, collarbones, and even their necks from the jolt of the chute surging open.

Three one thousand, four one thousand, five . . .

Henry couldn't see much but mist.

Six one thousand, seven one thousand, eight one thousand . . .

His ears felt like they would explode from the changing air pressure.

Nine one thousand, ten.

Henry pulled the cord. His chute billowed open and jerked him up into a float. He was cocooned in a cloud. He couldn't hear the battle's explosions, the roar of planes, the screams of men. Nothing. For a blissful moment, Henry felt like a hawk skating on the winds above his farm.

When he was blown clear of the cloudbank, he looked down. If he were over a town, or a river, or a forest, he'd be in trouble. His parachute could drag him under water and drown him; trees and church spires could lynch him.

Below stretched a hilly landscape of snow.

Snow? Maybe he was in Switzerland. Henry scanned the sky. In the distance, he could just make out another chute. That had to be Dan.

Something black was zeroing in on his captain. "Oh, no!" Henry cupped his hands to his mouth and shouted from his belly, "Dan! Look out!"

They'd been warned that German fighters, sensing the Allies' momentum, sometimes strafed fliers drifting to safety in parachutes. One began circling Dan, like a buzzard looping over a hurt animal.

Henry could hear a faint popping sound as the Messerschmitt fired. He strained to see. He couldn't believe the fighter would go after a man hanging helpless in a parachute. With horror, Henry watched Dan twist and swing back and forth, desperately trying to make himself a moving target.

The fighter took a final, razor-close pass. Dan's parachute turned inside out, blown by the backwash of the Messerschmitt. Instantly, Dan plunged toward earth, a worthless plume of white canvas streaming above him.

"NOOOOOOOOO!" Henry screamed. They had to be a mile up in the air. When he hit ground, Dan's body would shatter like a glass hitting pavement. Henry covered his eyes and heaved wrenching sobs. He thought of the baby pictures that Dan had shown him dozens of times. Baby Colleen.

Then he heard it—the whine of a plane closing in. The Messerschmitt was coming after him.

"You've got to be kidding!" Henry wrestled his pistol free and pointed it at the dark smudge that was getting bigger and louder by the second. "Come on!" he yelled. "This is for Dan."

Blinded by anger and grief, Henry didn't think about the futility of trying to shoot down a plane moving at such speed with a handgun. He sucked in the freezing air to clear his vision. He thought of how his Dad had taught him to shoot a quail: Never take your eye off it. Track the bird, then squeeze the trigger gently so your hand doesn't jerk and spoil your aim.

Henry lined up the pistol's nose with the fighter's oncoming cockpit. "I've got you," he muttered.

Pop, pop. Henry squeezed the trigger. The .45 spit uselessly at the gleaming, roaring machine. *Pop, pop.*

Rat-tat-tat-tat-tat-tat.

The Messerschmitt's machine guns thundered back at him.

Chapter Four

Henry could feel bullets zinging past him. He aimed again. *Pop, pop.*

Six shots. He was out of ammunition. Henry helplessly threw the pistol toward the Messerschmitt and watched it tumble aimlessly through heaven. He faced the oncoming machine, naked.

Rat-tat-tat-tat-tat-tat.

The fighter's machine gun bullets ripped through Henry's parachute. He felt the chute dip, felt the air rushing faster up his body to his face. He looked up and saw holes peppering the chute's canvas.

Henry looked down and saw the earth roaring up to meet him. The chute's pinholes were tearing open. Would it hold long enough to get him to the ground? The snow might cushion his landing.

"Please, God, please." Henry braced himself for impact.

Ka-thump. A snowdrift swallowed him. Searing pain ripped up his left leg. Henry pulled the chute down over him and didn't move, hardly breathed, as he listened to the sound of other planes buzzing by overhead.

At last it was quiet. Still Henry waited until he was shivering inside all that fleece before kicking himself free of the wet, melting snowdrift. It was twilight and the rose-washed countryside looked oddly serene. Bury the chute, he remembered, bury it so it can't be seen. He staggered to a bramble, stuffed the chute into its roots, and covered it with muddy snow.

Henry sat down. His left ankle was already swelling

and straining his boot. Sprained? Broken, maybe. Could he walk on it?

Henry opened the escape kit and pulled out one of its three morphine syringes. Taking a deep breath, he injected the painkiller into his leg. Then he crammed part of the kit's C-rations into his mouth. It tasted awful. He had no appetite. But Henry knew he wouldn't get far without something in his stomach. He hadn't had anything to eat since 5:30 that morning.

Henry stood, winced, and began limping west, toward the sunset. He had no idea whether he was in Germany, France, or Switzerland. All he knew was that west was the way home.

Chapter Five

Henry clenched his fists to keep from crying out as he skidded down the hillsides. He swore he could feel the bones of his left ankle scraping together with each step. Whenever he came to level ground he hopped on his right foot. But he certainly couldn't outrun any Nazis this way.

He scanned the horizon to see if he could spot another American limping along. Could any of his crew be alive? Did they need help? Could they help him?

He saw no one. He was completely on his own.

Move on, boy. They'll be out looking for you.

Henry came to the edge of a pine forest and picked up a fallen limb to use as a crutch. But it was heavy to drag and soon his vision began to blur with exhaustion. Finally, he found the beginnings of a road. It was narrow and muddy from the March thaw. He followed it, not knowing what else to do. He berated himself for throwing away his .45. What a hothead, what an idiot. If he still had his gun he could at least put up a real fight. Now all he could do was hide.

At a crossroad, a wooden sign of arrows pointed the way to several towns: STRASBOURG, NEUF-BRISACH, GUEB-WILLER, MULHOUSE. Henry was not reassured by the names. Strasbourg and Guebwiller sounded distinctly German. He couldn't tell about Mulhouse. Of the four, Neuf-Brisach was the only one that sounded French. He clung to his hope that if he was not in France, he was in Switzerland. He knew that both German and French were spoken in that country. He chose the path to Neuf-Brisach.

Within a few minutes Henry saw a scattering of houses. They were half-timbered, held together with mortar and a latticework of wooden beams that made diamond patterns. They looked just like gingerbread houses pictured in a book of fairy tales his mother used to read him.

He thought of Lilly reading books at bedtime, and the way the moon shone through his curtains. Henry's eyes welled up with tears. How was he ever going to get out of this mess? He could barely walk.

As he stood worrying, Henry spotted a solitary bicyclist. It was hard to make out the rider in the spreading gloom of nightfall. But the sharp lines of a rifle didn't break the silhouette. He pedaled stiffly, as if he were old. The man had to be civilian. Maybe he'd help. But then again, if he was in Germany, could Henry really expect a German to aid an American flier?

Henry stood his ground. He had no other options. It was obvious that his ankle needed tending. And clearly the cyclist had already seen him, standing there in a flight suit. Even if Henry struggled into the forest to hide, it would be a simple matter for the man to alert police to his whereabouts.

As the bicyclist neared, Henry racked his brain for the French word for help. He'd had four years of French in high school and been one of Miss Dixon's prize students. Not many of the farm boys attending his tiny, rural high school had thought much of learning a sissy-sounding foreign language. But Henry had wanted to travel the world. He loved French. He'd worked hard to conjugate verbs correctly. He memorized whether words were feminine, needing *la* in front of them, or masculine, requiring *le*. Whenever he wanted to impress Patsy he'd throw some French at her. He'd do Miss Dixon proud—*if* this man spoke French.

A few yards short of Henry, the bicyclist dragged his foot along the road to stop. He was small, gray-haired, with spectacles atop a rather long nose. A black French beret on his head gave Henry hope he was in the right country. He took a deep breath to slow down the wild thumping of his heart.

"Bonjour, monsieur," said Henry.

The old man made no reply.

Henry thought a moment and decided to say that he was American and hungry. He couldn't remember the word for hurt. *"J'aime American. Je suis femme."*

The man still said nothing. He just studied Henry.

Henry repeated himself, not realizing that in his nervousness he was mixing up his words.

The man looked at the ground and shook his head.

Then he sighed and said in excellent English, "I guess I must help you. What is the matter with you? You like America, yes, but you do not look like a woman to me."

Henry caught his breath with relief. "Is this France or Switzerland?"

"You are in Alsace," the man informed him. "Do you know what that is?"

Henry wasn't sure.

"Do they not teach you history in America? This is a French province Germany has invaded over and over again. Most people here have some German blood in them, but not by choice. There is much hatred between us. Even so, when Hitler annexed Alsace four years ago, many people welcomed the Germans' return. They are impressed with the Nazis. So disciplined, they say. To me the Germans are *les boches*—swine."

Henry shifted uncomfortably. Did they really have time for a political history lesson right now?

The Frenchman smiled. "I forget myself. I am a teacher. *Was* a teacher. The Nazis took my students for their army. They went to the Russian front. I think they must be dead." He scanned the horizon nervously. "Come." He gestured to Henry to follow him.

The teacher set off on his bicycle. Henry staggered to keep up. "Pah," the teacher grunted in irritation. "You are hurt?"

"Yes. My parachute was shot. I hit the ground too hard. Sorry." Henry realized his injury endangered the old man even more.

"Get on the bicycle. *Vite, vite.*" The teacher patted

the handlebars. Henry braced himself as the Frenchman pedaled, struggling with the weight. It was a slow, bumpy, painful ride. The wheels were wooden. The German army had confiscated all rubber for their tires.

"We go to my school. It is outside the village. If we meet someone, take bicycle and go to forest. I do not know what the townspeople would do if they caught you. Americans bombed Mulhouse very badly. People are sick of the fighting."

On base, Henry and his fellow airmen had always thought of beating the Luftwaffe, knocking them and their guns out of the sky. They saw it as a constant, brutal cock-fight between plane crews. He'd never really thought much about the people they were trying to liberate, or what their struggles must be on the ground under a war-torn sky.

"We're coming, *monsieur*. Soon, I promise."

"Ah, yes," the man nodded and smiled sadly. "But can you bring back my students?"

It was so dark by the time Henry and the teacher made it to the schoolhouse that they didn't see the huge black pigs until they crashed into them. Henry hit the ground on his bad ankle, in a tangle of hooves, muck, and wheels. Frightened, the pigs squealed, trampled him, and pinned him beneath the bicycle.

"God Almighty," Henry cried out and clutched his shin. "Get off! Get off!" he screamed.

"SHHHH!" the teacher hissed at him. *"Ferme-la!"*

But Henry was already silent. He had passed out from the pain.

When he opened his eyes, Henry saw a huge bell hanging over his head. He strained to focus. The room had many windows and was lit only by starlight. Was he in a bell tower?

He struggled to get up. Poker-hot pain ripped up his left side and slapped his brain into remembering. The air battle, his plane, Dan, the Messerschmitt, his mangled ankle all rushed back on him. Henry buried his face into the blanket he lay on. "Let it be a bad dream, Lord."

"It is not," said a voice from the shadows. The school-teacher arose. "I hide you in my school. Foot is bad. Perhaps broken. Our doctor was commandeered into the Nazi army. The Gestapo has arrested the only man who might have helped you. I think I must get you to a hospital. I worry the leg will grow an infection."

"What hospital?" Henry asked. He looked down at his ankle. The skin was streaked blue and purple.

"Bern is closest and safest. And your government has a presence there."

"Switzerland?"

"*Oui.*"

"How will I get there?" Henry knew the borders were closed, guarded by Germans on one side and Swiss on the other. The Swiss were adamant about maintaining their neutrality, sometimes even shooting down American bombers flying over their country. Would they really let him in?

"I am not certain. I have never done this before," said the teacher. "But it is time for me to take action. I watched them take my students and did nothing. An old man's fear. Tomorrow I will know how to proceed. Now you eat."

The teacher handed Henry a plate of food—fried carp, sauerkraut (the Frenchman called it *"choucroute"*), and pale-yellow cheese. The food was ice-cold. Henry realized that he must have lain unconscious a long time while the teacher kept watch over him. *"Merci, monsieur,"* said Henry.

The schoolteacher grimaced at Henry's Tidewater drawl. "Try not to speak." He opened the bell tower's trap door and disappeared.

Henry pulled out his survival kit and found a second syringe of morphine. He injected the medicine and choked down the Frenchman's food.

His ma would be getting a telegram in a few days. Missing in action, it would say. Missing, lost, maimed. With no one to help him but a wizened old teacher who couldn't stop talking history. What did history matter these days?

Panic kept the words swirling in Henry's head: *Missing in action.* Henry imagined his father's snarl: *I told you, Lilly. I knew he'd never make it. You gentled him too much. Never let me make a man of him.*

Henry clamped his hands over his ears. He'd spent his life trying to prove himself to Clayton, to seem worthy of his respect even if he couldn't win his father's love. He'd thought joining the Air Corps would do it. But Clayton had shouted at him: "Boy, you gonna throw away that scholarship to the university because a bunch of foreigners are fighting *again?* People who don't have anything to do with this family, this farm? They don't even speak English, most of 'em."

Henry had simply nodded his head, yes.

"Then you haven't learned anything from me," Clayton had snapped, and stormed out the back door.

Lilly had tried to ease the rejection. "I'm real proud of you, honeybunch," she'd said.

Henry rolled over and pushed the blanket around in an attempt to make it a better buffer between him and the wooden floor. "I will make it, you old buzzard. I'll show you."

Henry longed for his uncomfortable cot back in England, even the stench of wet socks. His bunkmates would be checking his footlocker now. They'd be divvying up his long johns and extra T-shirts. He hoped someone would mail the letter he'd almost finished to Patsy. Maybe Sarge would. He should have left a note somewhere in his trunk asking that Patsy's letters be sent back to her to keep, just in case, in case he didn't . . . well, just in case it took him a while to get back.

He saw Billy's face, Paul's, Jimmy's. He had no idea how many of his crew had made it out of the plane. He'd seen Fred's lifeless body as he and Dan struggled to the bomb bay, but no one else. "Please, Lord, let some of them have made it to the ground alive."

He couldn't bear to think of Dan and pretty baby Colleen. How would Rose raise her alone?

Henry's leg was aquiver with pain. But the morphine was taking effect. He couldn't hold his eyes open. Henry slid into sleep, seeing pilots who had made it back from their mission, gathered around the piano in the officers' club, singing: "'We are poor little lambs, who have lost our way.'"

Chapter Six

Henry awoke to the sound of fluttering wings. He squinted against the brilliant morning light that flooded the bell-tower. Hovering over him in the window directly above his head was a pair of huge, creamy white wings. They stretched out six feet from tip to tip, and were backlit by a halo of golden light.

"Am I dead?" Henry rubbed his eyes.

The wings fluttered once more, making a soft rustling sound. Henry propped himself up on his elbows to gaze at what had to be an angel. It had a long downy neck and great, black, soulful eyes. "If God will give me wings like that I won't mind dying so much," Henry whispered.

"*Clack,*" the angel squawked at him.

"Excuse me?"

The angel swung his head all the way round to face Henry. "*Clack, click, click, clack.*"

Henry stared. The angel had a strange, long, orange

nose. Henry rubbed his eyes again, then shaded them against the blinding shafts of light that spilled around the angel.

The nose was a beak. The angel was a bird, a huge white bird.

Laughing, Henry fell back onto his blanket. His laughter tripped into a sob and then into a strange, anxious wrenching.

The trap door of the bell tower swung open. "Shhhh," hissed the schoolteacher. "Are you delirious?"

Henry shook his head and pointed to the window. But the bird had jumped off the sill to the roof immediately below.

The teacher rushed to the window. "She is back! My stork. *Bienvenue, ma belle!*" He turned to Henry. "This is a very good omen. Always this stork has migrated from Africa to nest on my school's chimney. But for two years she and her mate have not come. I feared soldiers shot them or that they stayed away because they knew France had gone mad. Perhaps her coming foretells the beginning of the end for Hitler."

He eased himself down to the floor beside Henry. "We must take courage from her. Birds know when the season is turning." He looked at Henry's ankle. "We have a long way to travel. Do you have the strength?"

Henry sat up. His leg throbbed. He was sick to his stomach and sweaty. He felt like crying. Did he have the strength? Not really. But Henry knew that wasn't the right answer. He thought back to the time he'd been plowing the fields by the creek and a water moccasin had bitten him, right above his high-top boot. If he hadn't fought his fear and nausea and ridden the mule up to the farmhouse for help, he'd have died at fourteen from a snakebite. It'd been the one time Clayton had admitted that Henry had some sense.

Henry could tell this situation was the same. This old man was risking his life to help him. The least he could do was hold himself together. Henry straightened his back. "I do if you do, *monsieur*."

The teacher nodded in approval. Then he unwrapped the bandage he had put on Henry the night before. Henry bit back a shriek of pain.

"I think the bone sticks out here," said the teacher, pointing to a nasty bulge beside Henry's anklebone. He rewrapped Henry's ankle with a rough-hewn splint and a clean cloth. "There is no way you can walk. We cannot take the bicycle. Too slow. Too obvious." He took out a small loaf of bread from his pocket and broke it. He handed half to Henry and slowly ate the other himself.

"Perhaps there is a better way, yes? The Grand Canal d'Alsace passes here and goes into Basel, a city just inside Switzerland. I have a cousin who fled Alsace for Basel when the Nazis invaded us. Back then the Swiss still honored the *Niederlassungsvertrag*—the agreement between our countries that said French and Swiss people could be citizens in either land. The agreement dates to the French Revolution," said the old man, again playing teacher.

"But we must be careful. The Swiss attitude has changed. They are afraid Hitler will invade them. The Swiss government does nothing to look as if the country favors the Allies. My cousin writes that some of them agree with Hitler's racist ideas. They have put up barbed wire along much of the border. At first, when the Nazis started deporting French Jews, Switzerland let them enter as refugees. But it is a small country. So many came, now they may enter only when Jewish groups already inside can pay money to support them. Their justice minister said, *'Das Boot ist voll.'* The lifeboat is full."

He shook his head sadly. "If you had come down in Switzerland you would be in no danger. But if you surrender to the border guards they might turn you over to the Germans. No, we must slip past the border guards somehow. In Basel, my cousin will shelter us. And then from Basel, we must find a way to Bern. But first I must get a boat, without being arrested." He smiled ruefully at Henry.

Henry looked at the frail, mild man. He was obviously afraid. Henry's face burned with embarrassment. He'd learned a fierce independence from his parents. He didn't like asking for help, especially since it meant endangering a kindhearted old man. "I am sorry for the trouble, *monsieur*," Henry mumbled.

"The world is a troubled place, young man." The old schoolteacher stood up stiffly. "But the storks are back. There is hope."

The teacher didn't return until twilight. Henry had slipped in and out of consciousness all day long. He was feverish, first burning hot, then teeth-chattering cold.

"You are worse," grunted the old teacher. "The skin color is very bad. We must go."

He handed Henry a change of clothes. "You cannot travel in your uniform." Henry was loath to give up his warm flight jacket for the scratchy sweater and pants. But he put them on, carefully tucking his lucky marble into a pocket.

As Henry struggled with the pants, the teacher called down the staircase: *"Entrez."*

A thick, sturdy man heaved himself up through the trap door into the tower, just missing the bell as he stood.

"Who is that?" Henry asked. He knew he could trust the teacher, but what about this fellow?

"This is the father of my best student. He has papers to carry goods on the canal in his boat. He can carry us."

"Do you trust him?"

"When I told him I needed to go to Basel, he asked if I was in trouble. I told him I was. He said he needed to know what kind of trouble. I told him." The teacher paused and put his hand on the man's shoulder. "He said he would help, *'pour François.'* François was his son."

The large man nodded and echoed: *"Pour François."*

He scooped Henry up and carried him down the narrow staircase. He and the teacher whispered back and forth in French. Henry searched their faces in the flickering light of the candle the teacher held. He could only understand individual words here and there. He could make no sense of their context.

"Allemands . . . soldats . . . pots de vin . . ." Did they mean they'd have to bribe German soldiers with money or

did they mean they'd make money by turning him over to the soldiers? Henry trembled with uncertainty.

The boat master laid Henry in a wheelbarrow and patted him on the head as if he were a toddler. The tenderness of the huge man quieted Henry. Without another word the trio bumped its way down the dark forest path.

Henry caught the sweet, cool nighttime scent of water a few hundred yards before they came to a small dock. Spring frogs newly emerged from the thawing mud were peeping. A long, flat-bottomed boat bobbed on the water. It was heavily loaded with crates of red and white cabbages.

Henry hobbled on and squeezed himself down among the crates. The teacher sat beside him as the boat master pushed off with a long pole. He would punt the boat down the narrow canal.

"Basel is about sixty kilometers south," explained the teacher. "We will reach it in morning. We must be silent. Near Basel you must crawl under here." He pointed to a tiny cavern visible only from where Henry lay, built by carefully stacking the crates along their edges. "Sainte-Odile, Alsace's patron saint, escaped her father's cruelty by slipping into a hole miraculously opened in the rocks for her. We will try to be like Odile when the time comes, yes?"

Henry nodded.

The teacher handed him a large pretzel. Henry had little appetite, but he ate, looking up at the stars. It was a clear night. He knew the British would be up flying a mission. American crews would follow at daybreak.

Under any other circumstances, Henry would have enjoyed the ride along the still, quiet waters. They passed ancient dairy farms, gaggles of geese asleep in tall grass along the canal banks, and fields just beginning to sprout. His own father would be planting soon if the Richmond weather was good. Henry walked the farm in his mind to keep himself from worrying.

But after two hours, Henry could no longer stomach the constant pulse of pain up his leg. He injected his final syringe of morphine. If all went well he'd be in a hospital by the next night. Henry reassured himself his ankle would feel much better once it was properly set and immobilized. Rocked by the boat, lulled by the steady, soft *lap-lap-lap* of water against its hull, Henry passed into oblivion once more.

Slap-flop-flop-flop.

Henry was startled awake as the teacher dropped a freshly caught eel into a bucket right beside his head. The eel squirmed and writhed and set off the fish already swimming around the bucket. There must have been a dozen eels and fish in there. They made quite a commotion.

"Protection," said the teacher with a smile.

Before Henry could ask what he meant, he heard dogs barking and shouts in German. "Quickly," the teacher whispered, smiling a frozen, made-for-show smile.

Henry shimmied into the hiding place among the

crates, careful not to topple any. As his feet disappeared, the teacher wedged a final crate into the hole, sealing Henry in.

Beneath the big, round heads of cabbage, he could not hear well. But Henry felt the barge turn toward the side of the canal after soldiers yelled several commands in German. The sound of his enemy's language sent chills through Henry.

With growing horror, he realized the soldiers were going to board the boat with the dogs. They'd sniff him out in an instant. Henry started to panic, feeling trapped, like a scared rabbit down a hole. He swallowed hard and tried to dispel the image of how hunting dogs back home tore apart a rabbit when they caught it.

Stamp, stamp. The boat tipped and rocked. The soldiers had boarded. Henry heard panting and the hot, heavy breathing of dogs excited by new smells. But so far, they were held back on leashes.

"Wohin gehen Sie?" one soldier demanded.

"Au marché à Bâle." The boatman answered in French that he was heading to market in Basel.

The soldier switched to French himself: *"Pourquoi est-ce que vous ne vendez pas les choux dans votre village?"*

"Personne n'a de l'argent pour acheter des legumes." The teacher truthfully told the soldiers his neighbors were too poor to buy the cabbages.

"Ah, oui?" the soldier asked sarcastically.

Without warning—*SLASH!*—a bayonet jabbed through a cabbage and down through a slat in the crates. Its point stopped just inches above Henry's heart. The steel tip withdrew. Henry held his breath, bracing for another stab.

SLASH!

The bayonet ripped through the cabbages again, this time just missing Henry's eye.

"Quelque chose en-dessous?" the soldier snarled. *"Des Juifs, peut-être?"*

His companion grabbed a crate and threw it into the water, splashing the teacher. The two soldiers laughed. The boat rocked. The dogs barked ferociously.

SLASH!

The bayonet rammed down next to Henry's knee.

Henry glared at the bottom of the crates above his head. They were going to tear apart the boat. What did they suspect? *Juif*—was that the word for Jew? Henry glimpsed the soldiers' boots circle the crates, saw their fingers reach through the top rung of the top tier of crates. They'd only need to lift one or two more before they could spot him through the cabbages.

Henry clenched his fists, holding them up in front of his face like a boxer—the way his Dad had taught him to fight. At least they wouldn't get him easy.

Henry heard the teacher offer to help move the crates so the soldiers wouldn't destroy the cabbages in their search. The teacher shuffled and clumsily lifted a crate himself. What are you doing, old man? Henry anxiously wondered.

Then Henry heard him trip and stumble into one of the soldiers.

SLOSH.

The bucket of fish toppled over, too, spilling water and eels everywhere.

"Oh, pardonnez-moi," the teacher cried.

The dogs went berserk, barking and jumping and snapping at the fish that flopped about the boat. In the mayhem, the dogs' leashes wrapped round and round the soldiers' legs.

"Verfluchen!" The soldiers cursed and reeled, yanked around by the crazed dogs. They hit and kicked at them, finally heaving the dogs off the boat onto the dock.

The boat almost pitched over as the soldiers jumped out as well.

"Avance, vieux idiot! Vas vendre tes sales choux ailleurs!"

The teacher ignored the insult and followed their orders to shove off. *"Merci, messieurs!"* he called innocently and waved as the boat swung out into the water.

Henry felt the boat jerk forward with great heaves as the boatman pushed with the pole. The boat skimmed quickly along the water. Gradually, Henry's heart stopped knocking in his ears.

After ten minutes, the teacher whispered, "We are all right. We are past sight. But remain under until I tell you."

"Will you have the same trouble with the Swiss border guards that you did with those Germans?" Henry whispered back.

"Germans? Those were not Germans. Those were Swiss soldiers. They thought we hid Jews. *Certainement,* some of them are as bad as the Nazis."

Chapter Seven

Henry and the boatman waited at a pier for a long time, bobbing among many other barges. The school-teacher had walked to his cousin's house.

Henry remained tucked under the cabbages, hungry, hurting, hot. He felt like he couldn't breathe. His only view of the world was through the slats of the crates. Repeatedly, he heard voices nearing, nearing, and then receding. German voices, completely incomprehensible to him.

To keep still, Henry tried mentally reciting snippets of history: *In 1400 and 92, Columbus sailed the ocean blue.* . . . He worked through the table of elements his chemistry teacher had drilled into him the previous spring: *Aluminum, Al, thirteen atoms. Calcium, Ca, twenty atoms.* . . . He even traveled back to third grade to work through the multiplication tables: *9 x 10 is 90; 9 x 11 is 99; 9 x 12 is 108.* . . . Anything to keep himself quiet, sane, less aware of his dangerous circumstances.

Finally, when he thought he would scream from anxiety and the pulsating throb up his leg, the old teacher reappeared, carrying a basket. He was alone.

"Quitte le quai," he told the boatman.

When they were back on the canal, floating south, he explained, "My cousin was afraid to help, afraid he could be deported if caught. But he gave me food. He said to stay on the water. Down the Rhein to the Aare. Then the Aare canal into Bern. It will take a day. Have you more medicine?"

"No," Henry answered. He knew he was in trouble. If his ankle wasn't set correctly soon, his foot might never be normal again. He couldn't bear the thought of hobbling the rest of his life.

"I am sorry. You must have courage, *oui?*" He passed Henry a bottle. "Drink. It may ease the pain."

It was a fruity brandy. Henry gasped as the liquor ripped down his throat. He'd never drunk much of anything alcoholic before the Air Corps since he was underage. He didn't much like the way it made people stupid-sounding either. Tonight, however, Henry gulped the liquor to numb the ache and ease the claustrophobia of his cage of crates. The brandy quickly lulled him into a stupor. The boat rocked, Henry's head whirled, and the night slipped by.

Henry came to, standing. He was between the boatman and schoolteacher, his arms across their shoulders; theirs around his waist. They were trying to walk him forward. It was still dark, dark and foggy.

Chapter Seven

"The hospital is near," whispered the schoolteacher.

Hospital? Henry tried to focus on the old man's face. Hospital? Why did he need a hospital? Henry took a step and felt his leg on fire. His stomach turned viciously. The world spun.

"*Leve-le,*" the teacher told the boatman. "*Vite, vite.*"

Henry felt himself hoisted, cradled like a baby, jostled, hurried. He tried to look about him. Tall buildings with ornate stone facades leaped up into the night sky. He heard a bell chime the hour. Twisting his head around he saw life-size bears and a knight marching in front of a ghoulish-looking clock face. "This has got to be a nightmare," Henry steadied himself.

"Be still," hissed the teacher.

Suddenly, they stopped. Henry was lowered and propped up against a column.

"Stay," the teacher said. "*Bonne chance.*"

"Wait," Henry called out. "Where am I?" But there was no answer. The old man and his giant companion had vanished.

Click, click, click, click. Something was coming. What was it? Henry peered into the fog.

Click, click, click, click. Voices droned.

Henry searched the swirl of mist. No bodies that he could see.

Click, click, click, click.

Henry used his good leg to shove himself up the stone column. Whatever it was, he'd face it standing.

Out of the mist drifted two figures in white. White

veils fluttered about their heads. Henry rubbed his eyes and looked again. There were red crosses on the brims of their veils. Red crosses. Could they be nurses? The old man had said *hospital.*

The figures—one young, one old—drew near, heels clicking along the stone pavement. The young one noticed him first. She stopped her companion abruptly with her arm. The old nurse shrugged her off.

She asked Henry something gruffly in an unfamiliar language.

Henry forced himself to think calmly. What should he do? Pretend to be a French-speaking Swiss?

The old nurse repeated her question in French: *"Qui êtes-vous?"* Who are you? she asked.

Henry couldn't pretend to be French with her. Be honest, Henry. Hope for the best. He fumbled around his collar to pull out the metal chain of his dog tags. "American flier," he muttered. His voice sounded miles away. "Plane down. Hurt leg. Serial number 092 . . ."

With that, he crumbled to the ground and lost consciousness.

"Make sure you drain that foot. The nurse told me the break wasn't bad. It's just the possibility of gangrene to worry over. Give him penicillin. If you don't have any, I can get some into the country. President Roosevelt will be most unhappy if an American boy loses his foot when you can easily save it. So would your chief of surgery. He and our ambassador are very good friends. Do you understand?"

Chapter Seven

A woman's voice translated in German. Henry heard the crisp crinkle of new money.

He forced his eyes open against the glare of hot lights. He found himself in a starched white world. White walls, white sheets, white lights. A face popped into his vision—a pale, bald, and flaccid face with reflective glasses. Henry couldn't make out the eyes behind them.

"Hello, son," said the face. The voice was kind. "Don't worry about a thing. Uncle Sam's here."

Henry felt himself rolling. "They're taking you to surgery. Nurse Weir tells me the fracture is a clean break. That's excellent news. But they need to drain your ankle of blood and puss. Nasty wound, son." The round face came within an inch of Henry's and whispered, "How did you get here?"

Henry looked at the bespectacled face, looked at the white masks blocking the faces of the other people surrounding the gurney. Instinct told him never to reveal the old schoolteacher, not even to another American. "I flew, sir," Henry answered.

The round face smiled. "Good man. You remember that, son. I'll be waiting for you when you get out."

Huge white doors slammed behind Henry's gurney and shut the American voice out. A rubber mask came down over Henry's face and gassed him to sleep.

Henry awoke in a cold, stark ward that reeked of antiseptic. In twenty other beds men slept, groaned, or played solitaire. There was a man sitting in a white iron chair beside him. A briefcase was on his lap. He sifted through a huge pile of papers, which kept cascading to the floor. The sound crashed through the ward.

"Ah, Lieutenant Forester. Feeling better?"

Henry was groggy, but the fever was gone and his head was clear. He propped himself up on his elbows to check the bottom of his bed for the lump of two feet. His left leg swung above the sheets in a sling. A cast reached up his shin. Thank God. Only then did Henry turn to the man. "Do I know you, sir?"

"We've met, son. Saw you as they wheeled you into surgery. Your dog tags let me trace your name. My name's Samuel Watson. Special assistant to the U.S. Ambassador here in Bern. But most of the fliers call me Uncle Sam."

He tucked his papers together. "We'll only have a few moments to talk. Do you want to get home, son?"

"Of course, sir."

"Then let me tell you a few things. Officially, the Swiss are neutral. American and German fliers are equally safe here. The Americans are interned in Adelboden. There are about five hundred Americans in the camp there now. It's a good deal—in the mountains, beautiful. You can play baseball, tennis, even attend college classes until the war ends."

Watson scooted his chair closer.

"But here's the thing. We've learned a lot in Bern. Everyone has a consulate here—Germans, Italians, Spanish, Russians. It's a real hotbed of gossip. I work with Allen Dulles, sent here by OSS, our office of strategic services. Mr. Dulles is quite talented at gleaning information. Can't get into all the details, mind you, but we worry that the neutrality of Switzerland's government may be somewhat questionable. Nazi trains pass through Switzerland on its rail lines, transporting coal through the Simplon Tunnel into Italy. In Milan and Turin the coal's used in Nazi-controlled war plants to build tanks, which are then returned through Switzerland to Germany to be used against the Allies. Even though we've got the toe of Italy's boot now, it's going to take a while for the Allies to reach northern Italy. We don't know what Hitler will do as we move in or when Eisenhower eventually invades Europe. It would be very easy for Hitler to take over Switzerland. What would happen to our boys in Adelboden then?" He shrugged, leaving the question ominously unanswered.

"You've got an advantage, Lieutenant. Because you just showed up on the hospital's doorstep, you're not yet classified as a prisoner of war. You can wear civilian clothes as they transport you to Adelboden. It'd be easy for you to get misplaced on a train. Catch my drift?"

"Yes, sir. But what would I do then?"

"I'll have to work out the details of how, but we'd get you into France. We've done it before. The Swiss people are far more pro-Allies than the country's official economic actions might suggest. We have a good network here. They'd get you into France and hooked up with French resistance fighters, who'd get you to Spain. From there you'd head to Portugal to find a boat bound for England."

Henry shook his head, trying to connect all the dots. "Boy, that's complicated, sir. Anyone ever made it?"

Watson sat back in his chair and pursed his lips.

"Honest? About half of our interned boys have been willing to try it. Most are still in transit somewhere. A handful of them have made it all the way back to England. Some were caught before crossing the Swiss border and sent to a pretty tough prison camp called Wauwilermoos. But it's not like Americans to just sit out a fight if they can escape and help, now is it? We'd hope all officers would at least make the attempt. We need all the good pilots we've got. You game?"

Henry tried to size up Watson. Easy for him to shuffle his papers and encourage a guy to walk across France. He'd bet those soft leather shoes hadn't ever walked a mile except on the dance floor. Henry had had a taste of hiding and giving up his life to strangers and pure luck. It wasn't fun. And hadn't he flown enough missions through hell? Hadn't he seen enough blood and explosions? Tennis and starting his college education sounded pretty darn good.

Henry crossed his arms and frowned. Watson just waited, watching him.

But he'd be a coward, wouldn't he, if he didn't try this. Henry shifted uncomfortably. What would Ma want him to do? Probably be safe. But she also taught him to help everybody that he could. How many times had she endangered herself taking food and nursing people sick with polio, typhus, TB? Patsy would do it. She always took a dare, even diving off a quarry cliff into water twenty feet below. And what about his old man? What about Clayton? Escaping would be one way to impress that old jerk.

Chapter Seven

Finally, Henry thought of Dan. Dan would do it. Dan was willing to explode with his plane to give every living member of his crew a chance to bail out.

Henry could feel himself making a decision. This way he'd get home faster, right? Who knew how long the war might drag on, how long those guys would be sitting, waiting, in Adelboden? It could be years. How long could it take to get to Portugal, anyway? A month? He'd made it into Switzerland within a few days.

Henry sighed. "Okay, sir. Tell me what to do."

Watson smiled. "I'll be in touch."

He started to get up, then sat down, spilling papers again. As he leaned over to pick them up, he whispered, "One other thing. You can't write your parents. We can't notify them. If we do, and the Gestapo catches you, you'll be classified as an escaped prisoner. Then they're free to shoot you. If your whereabouts, your very existence, remain a mystery, there's a chance that they'll assume you've been wandering around by yourself if they do pick you up. Then you should be sent to a P.O.W. camp. The Red Cross keeps tabs on whether P.O.W. camps abide by the Geneva Convention. Most do. Our only risk will be Swiss records. There will be one about your being here. But hopefully that won't matter."

"You mean Ma can't know I'm alive?"

"No. She'll only know that you're missing in action. She can hope."

Henry was filled with pity. It would be so awful for her. But he held by his decision.

"Then I guess we'd just better hurry, sir."

Chapter Eight

Four weeks later, Henry sat, rattling, on a train to Adelboden. The doctors had cut off his cast the previous morning. His ankle was paper white, his calf thin, but his leg had held his weight. It was stiff, but solid. They'd ordered him to internment.

Next to Henry sat his escort, an aging Swiss soldier, reading. He seemed to Henry to be studiously inattentive. All that identified Henry as a transporting prisoner was a white tag around his wrist. He wore a civilian suit of clothes that had arrived at the hospital from the American consulate. But Henry hadn't talked again with Uncle Sam about his escape. He had no idea what he was supposed to do. The train had just passed through the city of Thun. Adelboden was only two stops away, at most an hour's worth of travel, maybe two. Henry wiped beads of sweat from his upper lip.

A crowd of passengers had boarded at Thun and

elbowed their way down the aisle, looking for seats. All were already taken. One after another, people lined up, squared their legs to brace against the train's swinging, and opened their newspapers. Henry noticed a delicate pregnant woman enter the car, lugging a hatbox and small suitcase. She sighed and shielded her round tummy as she tried to slip past the standing passengers, their newspapers, and bags.

What kind of men are they, thought Henry, who wouldn't give up their seat to this woman? She obviously didn't feel well. Henry stood and motioned to her. He looked down at the soldier, who assessed the woman, and then nodded to Henry. The woman smiled gratefully.

It took her a moment to wade through the passengers to him. *"Danken,"* she said. As she brushed past him to the seat, she seemed to stagger. She clutched Henry's sleeve and whispered in his ear, "Leave your crutches. Go to the toilet one car back." Then the woman sat down with a plop and *"Tut mir leid,"* to the Swiss soldier.

Had Henry heard right? The words had been breathed so quietly. Had he imagined it? He stood, hesitant, swaying with the motion of the train. A small foot began to nudge his. He looked down. It was the woman's. He must have heard right.

Henry leaned over and said to the soldier, "Toilet?" He pointed to the back of the car.

The soldier grunted, annoyed, and closed his book. As he started to get up, the woman piled her hatbox and suitcase onto her knees. The soldier would practically have to pole vault to get out into the aisle. He scowled and waved Henry on. *"Schnell,"* he ordered.

Henry nodded. He'd hurry, all right.

Henry lurched down the aisle to the back door of the train car. He opened it to wind and racket. He watched trees and scrub whisk past. He'd break his leg all over again if he tried to jump. He opened the next car door, passed a row of private sleeping compartments, and found a narrow toilet door at the very end of the car.

It was open just a crack. As Henry approached, the door swung open. A fat, middle-aged man pressed past.

Henry slipped into the tiny bathroom. He only had to wait a moment before an envelope slid under the door. Hands shaking, Henry opened it. Inside was a ticket to Montreux plus a note. It read: *The train will stop in ten minutes. Remain in the toilet until you feel the brakes. Step off the train quickly. Walk into the station. Cross the street to Café Spiez. Destroy this note.*

Henry reread it three times, memorizing the sparse thirty-four words. He tore the note into bits, ripped off his wrist tag, and flushed them down the toilet. He crammed the ticket into his pants pocket.

SQUEEEEEEEAKKKK!

Henry fell against the bathroom wall as the train began to brake. He took a deep breath and walked out. People were crowding out the back door onto the black steps between train cars. Henry lost himself among them and quickly hopped to the ground as the train stopped moving.

Keep your head, now, Henry steadied himself. Don't

look around like you're lost. Walk like you know exactly where you're going.

He spotted a pair of Swiss soldiers idly propped up against the wall, watching the push and hurry of passengers. Henry stepped beside an older couple to block himself from view. He entered the small station through ornate doors, passed rows of wooden benches, and emerged on the other side. Across the way was Café Spiez, its door open to the warming spring air. Waiters were setting tables outside for lunch.

Henry's heart was pounding in his head. But so far, so good. He checked for traffic and jogged across the street, limping only slightly. Where to now?

A waiter looked up as he smoothed out a tablecloth and fussed at Henry. *"Schon wieder spät! Ab in die Küche. Schnell!"*

Henry had no idea what the man was saying. But he could tell it was part of some playacting. He fought the instinct to look back over his shoulder to make sure the waiter wasn't really talking to someone else.

Henry skittered into the café. There was a huge curved bar inside, its wooden grain carefully polished and shining. On the back wall, large beveled mirrors reflected the scene outdoors. A thick, bald man stood behind the bar. Several people sat at the scattered tables. At the sight of Henry, the bartender slammed his fist to the counter and threw up his hands. He hurled a torrent of angry words at Henry, *"Noch einmal und du bist deiner Stelle los! Ab in die Küche!"*

He came out from behind the bar to hustle Henry through swinging doors to the kitchen. Hastily the man yanked off Henry's coat and wrapped a huge white apron around him. "Off tie," he whispered to Henry. "Up sleeves." Henry ripped off his tie and handed it to the man. He rolled up his sleeves.

When the man shoved him toward a huge sink, full of steaming water, Henry understood. He was to appear as if he were kitchen help, late arriving. He must need to blend in for a while before catching the train to Montreux. Henry nodded. He stuck his arms deep into the soapy water and began scrubbing.

"No speak," was the man's final gruff instruction before disappearing.

Henry could feel the eyes of two old cooks on him. He tried not to look back. Waiters began to drift in and out, pinning scraps of paper on a board, and barking orders at the cooks. The griddle sizzled with fat sausage.

With a heartstopping thump, the doors into the kitchen flew open and crashed against the walls. The soldiers Henry had seen at the train station entered and slowly scanned the room. His hospital escort accompanied them.

Henry stared down into the soapsuds and tried not to panic. Surely the old guard would recognize him. He stepped away from the sink, and rubbed his face with his hands to shield it. Maybe he could slip out the back. Was there a back door?

Henry bumped into one of the waiters who shoved him brusquely toward the sink and yelled at him. *"Zurück zur Arbeit!"*

78

Henry gaped at the man. Did he really expect an answer? Henry had no idea what he was saying. The man shook his head and continued angrily, *"Dummkopf!"* He shoved Henry's hands back into the water.

Every inch of Henry screamed for him to run, to fly. But there was something about the waiter's urgency. *It's part of the ruse, Henry. Get a grip.* Henry nodded, trying to look as subservient and stupid as possible. He kept his hands in the water, to hide their shaking.

The soldiers began to circle the room. They paused by each man, waiting for the hospital escort to look him over and shake his head no, *nein.* They were getting closer. Closer. Henry quivered from head to foot.

"Guten Tag." The soldiers stood beside him.

Henry bit his lip to keep from answering. He simply bowed his head to these army superiors and continued washing dishes as if his life depended on it.

The waiter who had shoved Henry bellied up again to talk to the soldiers. He pointed at Henry and unleashed another flood of abuse. *"Ein idiot"* the man called him. His voice was loud, agitated, dismissive. The soldiers smirked and laughed. They strolled away.

Only his train escort lingered beside the sink. Henry couldn't help it. He looked up and caught the old guard's eye. The guard gave a slight nod of his head and then just walked away.

"Nein, nein. Nichts," he said to the soldiers, holding his arms up in a shrug.

So his train escort had been in on his escape all along! Relief made Henry's vision grow black, speckled with dancing white dots as the soldiers left the kitchen.

An arm steadied him. The bartender had appeared with a tray full of dirty dishes. "Wash," he muttered. "One hour."

The hour felt like a day. Finally, the lunch dishes stopped appearing and the cooks took a break. Only then did the bartender reappear. He motioned Henry to follow him to the men's room. Henry was given an elegant double-breasted tweed suit, hat, and well-polished shoes. He was also handed a copy of Jean-Jacques Rousseau's *La Nouvelle Héloïse*. The bartender opened the book to page 100. False identity papers were tucked between the pages. Henry was to be Gaston Sieber, a student of the University of Geneva.

A girl awaited Henry in the café. When she smiled, Henry recognized her as the pregnant woman, no longer pregnant. She too was clad in a sophisticated suit. *"Viens, chéri."* She continued in French—something about saying good-bye. *"Nous devons dire nos adieux."*

She slipped her arm through his and sauntered toward the train station. As a bus blew by on the street, belching smoke and backfiring, she whispered in English, "Board the train. Stay on the aisle where you can move if you need to. You will be met in Montreux. Once there, make sure the book is visible."

The very same guards who had searched the café loitered by the awaiting train. Now she spoke to Henry in German, something about his journey. They reached the platform. As he pulled out his ticket and papers to show the conductor, the girl embraced him passionately. Her lips caught his for a long, insistent kiss. Then just as abruptly she shoved him away and slapped him playfully with her white gloves, saying, *"Auf, geh heim."* She turned to walk flirtatiously toward the soldiers, who had begun to approach Henry.

He hurried up the steps, passed the inspection of the conductor, and threw himself into a seat just as the train began to roll away from the station. Through a window, he could see the girl laughing and talking with the soldiers.

Henry felt breathless from the secretive whirlwind of the day's events, the multitude of unannounced players. He'd been handled, just like a hot potato. He was a package no one wanted to be caught holding.

Chapter Nine

On the train to Montreux, Henry alternated between gazing out the window, avoiding eye contact, and burying his head in the Rousseau novel. He worked on recognizing as many French phrases as he could. But he couldn't understand as much as he'd hoped. Individual words popped out at him, but each page remained a jig-saw puzzle with only half of its pieces in place. He could make out, however, that the novel was set in Montreux, which explained why he carried it. The book would be a clear signal to whoever was watching for him.

The train chugged over an ocean of cliffs, swelling into the sky, cresting in rock and snow. Occasionally long streaks of smooth green sliced down the mountains' alpine forests. Ski runs, Henry reckoned, even though he'd never seen any before. The pell-mell slopes impressed him. And they called pilots daredevils.

As the train began consistently chugging down, rather

than up, the conductor passed through the cars announc-
ing that Montreux was the next stop. *"Montreux,
Montreux, prochain arrêt,"* he called.

French had replaced German as the public language.
Henry felt safer. But what was he to do? Getting off the
train was obvious, but then what? Wait by the platform?
Walk through the station? What if no one claimed him?

It ended up being worse than Henry had feared. No
one met him at the terminal. No one signaled him inside
the station's vaulted waiting room. There was no one in
the men's room, no one in the coffee shop, no one by the
newsstand—absolutely no one.

Dinnertime came and the crowds dissipated. A thin
farmboy in a man's suit, wandering about aimlessly,
became more and more obvious. Only the number of soldiers pacing through the station remained constant.

Sit down, Forester, Henry berated himself. Sit down
by the door and read your stupid book. Henry sat, forced
his foot to stop tapping, forced his eyes to scan the pages,
forced his fingers to turn them at appropriate intervals.

Another half hour passed. Henry's stomach began to
grumble loudly. He was now the only person sitting on
his long bench. Brisk steps thundered into the emptied,
marble-floored lounge. A half dozen new soldiers arrived
to replace the others. Great, thought Henry, fresh
eyes.

Just as the off-duty soldiers exited through the front
doors, a woman fluttered in. She was middle-aged and
chic, still capable of turning heads. Her glossy dark hair

was swept up under a mocha-colored cap, festooned with pheasant feathers. Her brown suit was cut long and close, her shoes were suede and high. A diamond brooch glittered on her lapel and a long, silk scarf draped her right shoulder. In her left hand, she carried a tiny, fluffy dog against her heart. A chauffeur shadowed her.

For a brief moment the grande dame scanned the room before squealing, *"Chéri!"* She rushed to Henry with open arms.

Henry was too startled to respond. The woman embraced him, enveloping him in flowery perfume, silk, scratchy tweed, and squirming poodle. She whispered: "You are my nephew, visiting from school."

She pulled him to his feet and made a fuss over kissing him on both cheeks, then wiping off the lipstick imprints with a lace handkerchief. She burbled in a breathy voice, something about being late, having a chocolate *soufflé* with a talkative cousin that Henry was supposed to remember: *"Je m'excuse d'être en retard. J'étais prise au restaurant avec ton cousin Ernst, tu te rappelles de lui? Il est tellement bavard! En plus, le chef a préparé un soufflé au chocolat tout à fait superbe. . . ."*

As she prattled on, the woman thrust the dog into Henry's hands, put her arm through his, and led him toward the door. Henry tried to bolster her charade. He nodded and smiled, nodded and smiled, as he'd always done with his chatterbox Aunt Barbara.

"Bonsoir, messieurs," the woman greeted the soldiers with a broad smile and a flood of praise about their protecting the country. *"Mais qu'est-ce qu'on deviendrait*

sans la protection des jeunes hommes forts comme vous qui nous gardent sains et saufs . . . ?"

The soldiers preened under her compliments. She and Henry glided through the station, out the entrance, and into the backseat of a Mercedes sedan. Her chauffeur closed their door. They roared away.

Henry still clutched the poodle. The woman smiled and rescued the dog, kissing it on the nose. "I am sorry to be so late, young man. I was not contacted until this afternoon. And there were many arrangements to be made. Your friend Mr. Watson knows me as Madame Gaulloise, but in public you must call me Tante Héloïse, *d'accord?"*

Henry nodded. He assumed *Gaulloise* wasn't her real name, being a brand of French cigarettes. But was *Héloïse?* Probably not either, since that was the name in Rousseau's book.

"How is your French? *Tu parles français?"*

"Un peu, Madame. Je comprends un petit peu. My accent is not great."

She smiled again. It was a generous, warm smile. She must have been breathtaking when she was young, Henry thought fleetingly. "No, my dear, your accent is less than perfect. But perhaps you will pick up a bit? At least this madness can afford you some linguistic education, *non?"*

Henry nodded.

She pulled off her gloves and explained, "We are heading to the Grand Hotel Excelsior for a few days. I live in Annecy, but frequently visit Montreux and Lausanne. My late husband was Swiss. His business was here. I have a kind of courtesy citizenship. So my coming is nothing out of the ordinary. And fortunately, the Swiss are more sympathetic to the French in this region. France is just across the lake, you know." She pointed through the window to a glistening, wide swath of blue that bordered the city. "But it will still be a trick to get you across the border. I plan to visit the casino tonight to see if I can stoke our fortunes in case a bit of persuasion is needed. It usually is."

That night, Madame left Henry. She had managed to talk them into their rooms without his having to so much as nod at anyone. The management and busboys seemed completely accustomed to her drama. But what if someone came to the door looking for her? He supposed he'd just hide in the bathroom and not answer.

Henry circled his room. He'd stayed in hotels twice before—once in New York City before being put on the boat for England, once in London. But they'd been nothing like this.

He flopped onto the big, soft bed and ran his hands over the crisp linen and fluffy duvet covering. They were so much nicer than the coarse cotton sheets and wool blanket at home. Henry reached for a gold-foil circle on his pillow that a maid had left earlier when she'd come to turn the bed down—another thing at which he had marveled.

He opened it now. "Wow, chocolate!" He popped it in his mouth and smiled as it melted in his mouth.

Still antsy, Henry stood up to pace and ended up in the bathroom. His footsteps echoed on the shiny black-and-white tiled floor. He stopped in front of the strange con-traption he'd asked Madame about earlier. It was the size of a toilet, but had a faucet. He'd reckoned it was for washing feet, but Madame had laughed at him and called it a bidet, a bath for his *derrière*, his behind.

Henry snorted. Europeans were just plain different. He wished he could write Patsy about it all. She'd think it was so funny. What was she doing tonight? Ma must have gotten the telegram by now. Would Patsy still be writing letters to him in her head? Would they be as beautiful as the ones she'd sent? She wouldn't stop think-ing about him, would she?

He climbed into the white porcelain tub and stretched his legs all the way out. What a huge tub. Henry picked up delicate pink soaps to sniff them and pulled his head back in surprise. They smelled like strawberries. Wouldn't Patsy love them and this tub? She'd never had anything this nice. Her father had just added a tiny indoor bathroom to their little cottage. Before, her family had always used an outhouse and bathed in a big old tin tub they dragged into the kitchen and filled with boiling water.

When he got home, he was going to buy Patsy some bath soaps like the ones in the hotel and tell her all about Switzerland.

Hearing Madame's dog scratch at the door that connected his room to hers, Henry climbed out of the tub and opened it. The poodle danced around him, begging for attention. "All right, all right," muttered Henry, pick-ing it up. What use was such a little scrap of dog? He couldn't hunt, like Henry's pointer, Speed. And he was nothing like poor old Skip.

Madame's room was round, part of a turret, encircled by French doors that opened onto a wrought-iron balcony. He carried the dog out into the night air. Montreux was lit up, stretching itself out in a twinkling line along Lake Léman. You could almost forget the war here, thought Henry, almost.

It was just past 1 A.M. How much longer would Madame play the tables? She'd left swathed in mink stoles, their tails dangling. She'd donned a great deal of jewelry. Wasn't it dangerous for her to be out this long, by herself? Henry looked to the street, three stories down. Only a few cars rolled along the avenue. An elderly man in a tuxedo arrived at the hotel, a too-young woman on his arm. As Henry watched, Madame's car arrived. Behind it came a car flying tiny German swastika flags!

Out popped a portly German diplomat. He darted to Madame's car, pushing past her chauffeur, to open her door. Had she gotten caught? Was she turning him in? Henry's heart sank. No, he couldn't believe that. She'd been too gracious. Besides, only the Swiss had jurisdiction here. Henry flattened himself against the hotel's wall and watched.

Madame placed her gloved hand into the German's and rose out of the car. He didn't let go, although Henry could tell that Madame was firmly shaking his hand, trying to say good night. Henry could hear no voices. He saw Madame pat the German's chest and step back, shaking her head. But the German persisted. He followed her into the lobby.

Chapter Nine

Henry darted back into the room, dropping the dog, which barked at him angrily. "Shush," he warned it. What should he do? Should he try to surprise the guy? Should he just go into his room and lock the door behind him? That didn't feel right, though. It'd looked pretty clear to Henry that Madame was trying to get rid of the German.

He flipped off the lights and went into his own room. Putting his ear to his door, Henry listened for their approach.

The German was speaking in rough English. Henry guessed he didn't know French and Madame had told Henry earlier that she refused to speak German unless absolutely necessary. "Such a harsh language, unlike French," she'd said, and then added that she didn't much like English for that matter. "Too many words for the same meaning. And too many meanings for the same word."

In the hallway, Madame was chattering: "Really, Herr Schmidt, you have been too kind. I am certainly capable of making my way home. My chauffeur is very reliable. But I do appreciate your concern." She made a great rat-tling with her room key. Was she trying to signal Henry?

"It is pleasure, Madame. When I see you at casino, I knew I take you home. Beautiful ladies need German pro-tection."

"Indeed? Switzerland is a peaceful country, is it not, Herr Schmidt? The war does not exist here. Everyone is safe here, yes?"

"Switzerland would do well to invite German protec-tion. *Der Führer* would make it a better country, more clean. No Jews, no Poles, no Czechs, no Yugoslavs." The

German leaned close to Madame. "But I waste time talking politics to a beautiful woman."

Madame's voice was icy. "Oh, no, not at all. I find it fascinating. But I am tired. It is really time to say *adieu.*"

Again, she rattled her keys loudly. This time her poodle began to yap and throw itself at the door.

"Oh, dear," said Madame. "*Mon pauvre petit.* I have left him shut up way too long." She opened the door and out dashed the little dog, yip-yapping and jumping. It raced round and round the German. In its excitement, it urinated all over his trousers.

"Philippe, you naughty dog." Madame barely suppressed a laugh. "Oh, Herr Schmidt, do forgive him." She scooped up the poodle. "Please send me the bill for cleaning. What a wretched end to a lovely evening." And with that she glided through her door, slammed it shut, and bolted it tight.

The German stomped down the hallway. When all was quiet, Henry knocked lightly on the door connecting their rooms.

"*Chéri,*" Madame greeted him with a sigh of exasperation. "Wasn't that just awful? The Germans have taken over the best cabarets and restaurants, especially in France. The casino here is littered with them. That one has been hounding me all night."

Playfully, she rattled her keys once more. "Isn't it a shame that poor Philippe gets so overwrought and has accidents like that, just at the sound of keys?" She cradled the poodle and petted him. "Such a clever boy." The dog licked her face.

Chapter Nine

Henry laughed. "You are quite an actress, Madame."

"But of course, *chéri*. One must be these days." Her triumphant smile faded. "We leave in the morning. I made only a little money tonight, but we must depart before that bore shows up again. I play a high-society coquette to disarm my enemy and to keep myself a mystery. Women have had to cloak themselves in this way forever. But it is especially useful with the Reich. Nazi Aryans can be such fools for a well-made dress, well-bred manners, and witty cocktail chatter. They all want to be aristocrats. But the price is, they think they know me for something I am not. That man will be back and we must not be here when he returns. I would have a hard time ridding myself of him a second time."

Chapter Ten

"Today, *chéri*, you are my chauffeur," Madame told Henry when he answered her knock at 6 A.M. She held up a gray uniform and cap. "You and my driver will exchange papers. He can make his way across the lake through friends. You will be Robert Messien. You will drive me across the border at Geneva. Dress quickly. Robert will show you the car." As Henry took the clothes, she teased: "You do drive better than you speak French?"

Henry blushed at her playfulness. His mother had teased him, but it'd felt different. Madame looked to be about the same age as Lilly, but while it was clear his ma had once been exquisitely beautiful, this woman still was. He couldn't help but wonder if her life had been easier, if his mother would look more like Madame.

They motored along Lake Léman from Montreux to Lausanne, heading toward Geneva, past promenades lined by palm trees. Henry nearly drove into the back end of another car as he stared at them. How did trees like these grow in Switzerland? Didn't they freeze?

"It is a marvel, isn't it?" Madame said, reading his thoughts. "The lake retains heat and the mountains protect the area from the winds. The weather is quite mild here, far gentler than where you are going."

Henry caught his breath at the sight of several massive magnolias, their huge white blossoms beginning to open. The sight made him think of home, remembering the day he'd cut branches and branches of magnolia blossoms from a tree down by the creek and brought them home to his ma. The flowers were a thank-you for her promise to take him to Boy Scouts. Clayton had refused to drive him to the meetings, said it was foolishness, a waste of work time.

"Oh, Henry," his mother had exclaimed as she buried her face in the blossoms. When she lifted it, her face shone, free of the worry that generally shadowed it. "Isn't the world just a miracle, honey? Can you imagine anything more beautiful than this? I hope to get to heaven someday for sure, but I'm gonna hate leaving the smell of magnolias." She'd caught him for a long, tight hug. "You are my sunshine, Henry."

Henry's grip on the steering wheel tightened, remembering how easy it was to make his ma so happy, and how infrequently she was that relaxed. Lilly always worked so hard to give him a happy, normal childhood, despite the Depression and despite Clayton. There was so much work to do at the farm it would have been easy for Henry to have dissolved into nothing more than a child-size field hand, his spirit completely broken by the weight of the labor. That's what Clayton would have reduced him to, because that's all Clayton himself seemed to be—a body to toil and scratch the dirt, then die.

He could see his ma now, fretting about him, staring out their kitchen window, hoping, frightened, as she made dinner—only Clayton coming in to eat to interrupt her worries about whether Henry was alive or dead. Clayton would be telling her that she was a fool to hope. But Lilly *was* hope. Hang on, Ma, Henry thought. I promise I'll be home as soon as possible. I'm going to waltz up our drive and give you the best surprise of your life.

Henry checked the rearview mirror, afraid Madame might have noticed his sadness. She was staring out the window, unusually silent. Or was that her real personality? Henry assessed her elegant attire. Another well-cut suit buttoned to her throat, with just a hint of a lace blouse at the collar. Once more, she wore a long, sweeping silk scarf, this time draped like a shawl across her shoulders. It had an elaborate design of finely etched flowers and ferns, which accentuated the deep forest-green color of her suit. Wouldn't his mother just love something as pretty as that scarf?

"Is that a special kind of scarf, Madame? Would I be able to find one for my ma back home?"

Madame's eyes met his in the mirror. "It is an Hermès scarf, *chéri*. It is very expensive, I am afraid. Does your *maman* like scarves?"

Henry laughed. "She's never had one. But she loves flowers. She'd love to wear something like that on Sundays."

"Your *maman* is special, yes?"

"Very special, Madame," said Henry quietly. "She is very kind, very loving, very strong, really. She was the county beauty when my dad snared her. She could have married anyone, lived in a fancy house, I bet. But she chose my dad. We do pretty well on the farm, but she sure isn't a lady of leisure, like. . . ." He broke off, embarrassed at his rudeness.

"Like me, *chéri?*" Madame finished his sentence. "That's all right. It is quite true. I have been very fortunate. I have had the best education and traveled to many beautiful places." She leaned forward and patted Henry on the shoulder, "But I can tell you right now, *chéri*, that the best gift you can give your *maman* is not a scarf but your return."

It took two hours to drive to Geneva, then another bone-chilling hour of waiting at the border. A German captain in charge of the checkpoint insisted that Madame have a cup of tea with him before she passed through. Henry pretended to sleep with his chauffeur's cap over his eyes, his feet on the dashboard.

Under the brim of his hat, Henry saw Madame approaching, still dogged by the Nazi officer. Like flies to honey, Henry thought with exasperation. What if this man spoke to him? What should he do?

As the German opened Madame's door, he spoke in perfect French to her, *"J'ai oublié de vérifier les papiers du chauffeur. Est-ce que je peux les voir, s'il vous plaît?"*

Henry caught the words: *papiers* and *chauffeur.* But

before he could reach into his pockets, Madame began berating Henry for sleeping on the job. *"Tu as dormi tout ce temps? Pourquoi n'as-tu pas poli la voiture pendant toute cette attente? Espèce de paresseux!"*

She turned to the German officer to continue a tirade of complaints about Henry's inabilities as a servant. Ending with a pointed comment that the war had robbed her of good help and that she was terribly late, Madame slapped Henry on his shoulder with her gloves and snapped, *"Allez, Robert, vite."* She waved at the German captain and off they drove, leaving behind the barbed wire fence that cut off France from Switzerland.

When the Nazi finally vanished from sight, Madame apologized. "I am sorry to speak to you that way, *chéri*. But I have found that the best way to make people forget about checking papers is to make a fuss about something else. Then you must fly before they regather their wits. That man is useful to me, however. It is through him that I buy black-market petrol. Next time, because of the scene I just made, I can tell him I fired you if he is surprised by a new face."

Next time? "Do you do this often, Madame?"

She smiled at him. "Ask me no questions, young man. It is better for you that way." She leaned back onto the leather seat and closed her eyes for a nap.

They reached Annecy that evening. Madame lived just outside town in a walled mansion overlooking another, smaller lake. Henry had never seen such a grand home. Huge Oriental rugs covered the black-and-white marble floor of the foyer. Portraits and oil paintings lined the walls of the staircase. The house smelled of lemon oil and well-rubbed wood. Madame's butler led him up the grand staircase with a carved banister to a small room on the top floor. He pointed to a suit of clothes on the bed and said, *"Le dîner sera servi a huit heures."*

At eight o'clock, when a half dozen clocks chimed the hour throughout the house, Henry found his way to the drawing room. Madame was sitting on a plush couch, propped up by embroidered and tasseled pillows. Her poodle slept on an open book. *"Ah, chéri."* Madame rose and complimented him. *"Tu es très beau."*

"Merci," Henry answered shyly. "The suit fits perfectly, Madame."

She nodded and straightened the shoulders for him. "I thought you were about his size," she said more to herself than to Henry. Her gaze was distant.

"Who?"

Madame stiffened, her characteristic frivolity gone. "My son."

"Where is your son, Madame?"

"He was captured at the Aisne River when Hitler invaded and Paris fell. He is one of the thousands of French prisoners of war held in Germany. They are hostages really. For each German officer killed by the Resistance— 'terrorists' Hitler calls us—several Frenchmen are taken out and shot. He was still alive six months ago. I have not been able to get word since." She turned away from Henry and headed for the door. "Time for dinner. Come."

*　*　*

Henry remained with Madame a week. Each night they dined together, with her laughing gently over his confusion about salad, dinner, and dessert forks. Henry's family had felt lucky to have ten regular silver forks for Thanksgiving dinners.

She taught him to play bridge. She talked of French philosophers. She played her piano for him—Mozart and Debussy and Chopin, she said. Henry had never heard the pieces before. They were beautiful, airy, and delicate.

On the seventh evening she chose to play a melancholy piece called the "Moonlight Sonata" by Beethoven. Henry was drawn from the sofa to the edge of the grand Steinway piano. While she concentrated on the music, he watched her face. It glowed with a rapt appreciation of the music, making her beauty even more intriguing. She obviously found a peace in the melody like that he found in a quiet sky. And yet he could sense it was a more intellectual, complicated joy than the instinctive pleasure Henry felt in flying. He could tell, too, that she was so engaged, so elevated by creating this moment of musical beauty, she had completely forgotten his presence, forgotten the sorrow of her imprisoned son, forgotten the danger of her clandestine work. It was as if he were witnessing a rebirth, a brand new butterfly shedding ugliness and discovering with some surprise and delight that it had wings.

Captivated, he studied her more closely. It was hard to gauge her age exactly. She had lines around her eyes, but they seemed etched more by laughter than by age. She also wore makeup beyond the simple lipstick that Patsy and his mother applied for church and special outings. Yet it was subtle, like the perfume she wore, simply accentuating a sophisticated femininity that was already there. He watched her hands lilt across the piano's bright white keys—her own fingers long and creamy, unblemished by sunburn or picking crops.

But it wasn't so much her well-preserved beauty that mesmerized him. It was a cultivated intelligence that Henry couldn't quite understand, a completely new world of arts and books and refinement that she represented. She had an aura of knowing sadness that she counterbalanced somehow with a determined generosity and hope for happiness. She seemed so unwavering. He could see why fliers followed her through checkpoints.

That was it, he told himself. It was her strength that fascinated him. Sadness had seemed to forge her, rather than leave her broken, as it had so many of the people he'd seen worn out by the Depression and its deprivations. He didn't detect any of the bitter anger that drove Clayton either.

Just then, Madame's hands began to falter. She paused to look up, the minor-key chord she had struck still resonating in the air. Henry hadn't realized until that moment that he had inched quite close to her, close enough to hear her catch her breath. Her eyes caught his. He could feel his pulse throbbing in his temple.

A slow, thoughtful smile crept onto her face. "You flatter me, *chéri*," she whispered, and looked back down to the keyboard.

Henry waited, trembling slightly, confused, eager but

afraid at the same time for something—he didn't know what—to happen.

The tantalizing silence lasted only moments, but felt like forever.

When Madame looked back up at him, her face was masked with a slightly flirtatious, wry smile that Henry had seen as kind and warm but now recognized as anything but intimate. "Do you know American ragtime, young man? It comes from your area of the country, does it not?" And she kicked the piano into a Scott Joplin jaunt.

Henry went back to the sofa and picked up her little dog.

The next afternoon, Henry wandered the house as he was free to do as long as he never lingered in front of a window. He wanted to get another book from Madame's well-stocked library. Most of the volumes were in French, some were even in Latin, but he'd found about three dozen in English. He'd read two books and even tried making his way through his favorite Jules Verne, untranslated.

He studied the many paintings hanging in her house as he made his way to the library. He'd already discovered several spots on the wall where something had used to hang and no longer did. He speculated this was how she kept herself afloat financially—selling off family heirlooms to the Nazis down the street. The idea made him furious.

During the past week, Madame had identified many of the remaining paintings for him. "That is a Renoir," she'd said, for instance. "My father collected the Impressionists.

Chapter Ten

And this is by Morisot. She was a woman, you know. Just as good as the male Impressionists, don't you agree?"

"Impressionists?" Henry had asked, feeling like an un-educated bumpkin around her. But Madame never patronized him. She seemed to enjoy educating him. Henry sucked in the information, hungry to learn new things, realizing how much he missed school, how much he thrived on someone treating him with respect and fuel-ing his mind.

Running his hand along the shelves, Henry found a volume of English poetry by William Wordsworth. He cracked it open. His eyes fell on the line: "For I have learned to look on nature, not as in the hour of thought-less youth; but hearing often-times the still, sad music of humanity. . . ." The words touched him, reminding him of Madame playing the piano the previous night. Henry took the book into the drawing room, where the piano was, where it was sunniest.

When he opened the door his heart jumped. There was Madame standing in front of a painting, staring at it. It was one he'd puzzled over before. It was very odd. There was a nose here, an elbow beside it, crisscrossed eyes and legs where the head should be. She turned to look at him and her expression seemed full of regret.

"Do you know Picasso?" asked Madame.

Henry shook his head.

"I know Picasso," she said in a low voice and with a bittersweet smile of remembrance.

Henry felt himself blush at the warmth of her voice and the obvious meaning of her comment.

Madame's throaty laugh embarrassed him further. *"Ah, chéri."* She tucked her arm through his. "I didn't mean to shock you. You have not known a woman yet, have you?"

Henry was mortified by the question. He felt his face flame red hot. He looked at his shoes and muttered, "No, ma'am."

She pulled him close to her and said gently, "I hope when it happens, *chéri,* it is as full of passion and love as the time I knew with Pablo. Remember to cherish your lady when you hold her. I can tell that you will love completely when you do." She looked back up to the painting. "Pablo was a monster when he turned on a lover. But before"—she paused—*"il était superbe.* I will always have that."

The butler entered the drawing room. Madame stepped away from Henry's side, and he felt the loss like a cold draft. *"Je dois vous parler, Madame,"* said the man.

"Stay here, *chéri,*" Madame told Henry as she glided out of the room.

That night, as Henry lay in bed, he heard voices outside his room. He peeped through the door and saw the butler ushering a man and woman into another bedroom across the hall. They lugged suitcases, several bundles, and what looked like violin cases—as if they were carrying all the possessions they possibly could. The butler reemerged, holding two coats. On the coats were yellow stars.

Madame met the butler at the top of the stairs. *"Brule-les immédiatement,"* she told him. There was urgency in her voice.

Chapter Ten

Henry opened his door and asked, "Can I help, Madame?"

She put her fingers to her lips and signaled for him to go back into his room. She followed and closed the door behind them. "They must not know you are here, *chéri*," she whispered. "And you must not know they have come." She looked at him meaningfully. *"Tu comprends?"*

Henry nodded.

"The time has come to part. It is too dangerous for you here now. This evening I procured a train ticket and papers for you to travel to Grenoble. You must trust me. Someone will wait for you there. Do exactly as they say, yes?"

Henry nodded again.

She paused. "I have enjoyed our time, *chéri*. Be careful." She kissed his cheeks and left.

Henry did not see Madame the next morning. The chauffeur waited in the foyer to lead him to the train station. Before departing the grand house, Henry took one last look into the drawing room, where he felt he'd received so much education in such a short time.

Picasso's painting was gone.

Chapter Eleven

Henry followed Madame's advice and did exactly as he was told by his new Resistance escorts. They were not as pleasant, not as reassuring as Madame had been by a long shot. They barely spoke to him. As he got off the train in Grenoble, two well-dressed men materialized by his side. They nodded to him and he followed, the three of them working their way through the station crowds.

A few streets away they picked up bicycles, propped up against a World War I memorial. A stone angel with drooping wings held a limp, dead soldier. Below her were inscribed the names of soldiers killed in action. Henry noticed five boys with the same last name, listed one after another—obviously brothers, cousins, perhaps even a father and his sons—an entire generation of a family wiped out. Henry shook his head as he pushed off to pedal the bike. Such waste. Madame had told Henry that more than a million Frenchmen had died in the trenches, blown to shreds or killed by disease during that conflict. That was supposed to have been the war to end all wars, she'd said. World War II had started barely twenty years later.

Would he end up on a memorial back in Virginia, just a name on a list?

Henry struggled to keep up with the two men who hurtled through puddles and barely missed knocking down several pedestrians. Why were they in such a rush? They whipped around the corner and Henry gasped. They were heading straight for a gate in the town wall, where stood two German guards checking papers! Were they planning to pass through there? Did Henry have the right papers? Or were these men planning to turn him over?

Instinctively, he began to brake the bicycle. One of the men looked back and hissed: *"Allez!"*

Do what they say, do what they say, Henry prodded himself. But what if . . . ?

Don't be a coward, boy. Clayton's voice roared in Henry's ear. *Only cowards hesitate.*

Right. Do what they say. Madame said to do what they say. Henry pedaled on.

Suddenly close to ten bicyclists came from all directions, pedaling furiously. Everyone crowded the gate, waving papers, shouting, and jostling the young Germans trying to manage them. Henry rolled into the mess of people. Someone's hand and papers shot under his arm at the guard, he felt a push on his back, and Henry slid through.

They all pedaled down the road as if chased by the

entire Nazi army. Within a few minutes the seemingly spontaneous crowd began to disperse. One by one, they drifted off the road down alleys or into houses. All that remained were Henry and the two men.

They biked for an hour and swung into a small farmhouse. Inside they took Henry's forged papers. He guessed that the next downed flier moved from Annecy by train would need them. They replaced the elegant city clothes Madame had given him with dirty, scratchy woolens that were far too short. He wore a knitted black hat with a tassel that tickled his ear and drove him crazy. The wooden-soled shoes didn't bend at all and pained Henry's bad foot. But he knew the costume was to make him look like a peasant of the region. The men even rubbed soot into his sandy-colored hair to darken it and make him resemble the natives.

One of the men gave him advice, muddling English with French: "Never use *la grande avenue. Évitez les cafés. L'église . . . mmmm.*" He paused, searching for the right translation.

"A church?" asked Henry.

"*Oui, oui.* Church *est* safe. Do not walk in village. Someone will meet you *avant.* If not, go around. Someone will meet you after. If not, hide *jusqu'à la nuit, et* try again. Return *jamais.*"

Henry nodded. Don't double back. If he was being followed he could unwittingly lead the Germans right to the Resistance fighters.

Then the fighter, who called himself a member of "the *maquis,*" handed Henry a knife. "Like zeez, *oui?*" he said, holding the blade a few inches above Henry's throat and pulling it horizontally to show how to slice open a man's artery. Alarmed, Henry took the knife and put it in his shirt pocket, right beside his lucky marble. The man patted the pocket with a nod and a grim smile. *"Pour les Boches."*

Outside, the man and Henry followed a small trail. At the top of a steep decline, the man stopped. He pointed down the gorge. *"Allez là-bas. Continuez à gauche."* He held his hands up in a V and moved the left one forward.

The man's accent was very different from the Parisian pronunciation Henry had been taught and had heard Madame Gaulloise use. Henry wanted to make absolutely sure he understood. "Go left if the path forks?" He repeated the motion with his own hands. *"Gauche?* Left?"

"Oui." The man nodded. He stepped back to light a cigarette.

"Wait," Henry caught at the man's sleeve. "How will I know my contact?"

The man shook his head.

Henry repeated his question.

The man shrugged. *"Je ne comprends pas."* Either he couldn't understand Henry, or he didn't want to answer. He pointed his gun toward the path and said gruffly, *"Allez."*

Henry looked down the path. No village, no farm in sight. "How far?" he said. He searched his memory of high school French. *"Combien—?"* What was the word for far? *"Distance? Combien distance?"*

The *maquis* fighter smirked. Henry realized he must have mangled the pronunciation or used the wrong word again. How was he ever going to survive in this foreign land or pass for a native?

"*Quinze, peut-être vingt kilomètres. ALLEZ!*" The man growled the command.

"*Oui, merci.*" Henry began the climb down.

The man said to walk. So Henry walked. Must have been twenty minutes by now. Henry glanced back over his shoulder again. The man was still up there on the jagged ridge, silhouetted against the moon. Henry could see the black outline of his rifle. Why did he keep standing there? Was it to protect Henry or shoot him down if he did something wrong?

Just keep moving, Henry told himself. He knew the French would never tell him much. He'd learned that well in the last few weeks. That way, if he were caught by the Gestapo, not much information could be beaten out of him.

Henry stumbled in the dark. The road was little more than a goat path, narrow, uneven, strewn with sharp white rocks. It zigzagged down along the edges of the mountains. For at least ten minutes it had been nothing more than a ledge chipped into the cliffs. One misstep and Henry would plummet hundreds of feet, bouncing off wickedly pointed rocks before landing on top of a vast pine forest far below.

Soon he heard the rush of water. A seething waterfall crashed through the gorge to a bottom Henry couldn't see. A hundred steps farther he came to a great heap of rocks that had tumbled down in a crushing avalanche of stone. He scrambled over it, knocking loose a slide of pebbles into the abyss. Henry stopped to catch his breath and calm his heart, racing with thinner air and the precariousness of his perch.

He could tell he was descending the Alps, heading southwest. He had tried to memorize a map of France at Madame's. He was probably in the Vercors—hundreds of miles still from the Pyrenees and the border of Spain. Henry had no idea what his destination was tonight. He had not been told.

Now Henry stood at a barely distinguishable split in the trail. To the right, colorful wildflowers and tall brown grasses pushed their way up among the stones. The path looked less disturbed, less traveled. Henry looked up at the tiny figure on the ridge before taking the left fork. After a few steps, he glanced back again. The man was gone. Henry was on his own.

Henry paused to look at the savage cliffs encircling him. His own Virginia Tidewater farm was so flat, the horizon so monotonous. Here it looked as if furious giants had played with boulders the way Henry had tried as a child to construct tippy-toe-high towers with building blocks. Cliff upon jagged cliff, teetering, lurching—a completely irregular string of mammoth granite peaks scraped the bottom of heaven. Henry had never felt so insignificant, so minuscule. He sucked in great gulps of the cold air to make himself feel bigger, stronger, less alone. It smelled of pine.

Finally, Henry clambered out of the crags to stand on a grassy ridge. He saw what felt like the entire world laid out before him. Far below was an emerald green valley threading itself through the mountains to create a long, thin pocket of softness. In the moonlight, he could make out pinpricks of white, cows clustered in slumber perhaps. Here and there were tiny stamps of red, most likely the tiled roofs of farmhouses.

Henry sighed in relief. He could hear his ma reciting: "The Lord is my shepherd; I shall not want. He maketh me to lie down in green pastures. . . . He restoreth my soul. . . ."

Henry's face felt wet. A wispy cloud passed over him. He held his hands up, closed his eyes and thrilled to the feel of clouds at his fingertips.

Henry enjoyed the next hour's walk. But it didn't feel like those tiny squares of red and pricks of white were getting much closer.

Vingt, the man had said. Was that twenty kilometers? How long is a kilometer, Henry wondered. He had no idea. But he had walked two miles to school each morning, two miles back. Henry knew he could make that one-way distance in about forty minutes, no problem. That meant he could cover twenty miles in a night if he had to.

Another hour passed. Henry began to feel vulnerable. *Crunch, crunch*, his hard-soled shoes ground pebble against pebble. In the still, clean air, the crackle of each step seemed to boom down the foothills: *Here's a lost American. Shoot him.*

Henry had often tended his family's chickens, and their milk cows by the light of the stars. But now the night seemed dangerous, hostile. The moon's pearly sheen illuminated only the tops of the trees and bushes. Within the eerie recesses of the plants' shadows, anything could be hiding. His own body, backlit by the moonlight, cast a long, giveaway shadow of its own.

Henry wet his lips to whistle but stopped abruptly. Idiot, he berated himself. Why don't you just light a firecracker to announce yourself?

More time crept by. The moon was sinking. The path leveled out and Henry came to a tiny village that wound itself around a church. The church had a castle-like tower, with a huge clock face. Its hands pointed to half past four. Was that the right time? Dawn would break soon. Should he go through the town? The *maquis* had told him not to, but what if that was where he was supposed to make contact? Maybe he was supposed to go to the church. The man had said churches were safe.

Henry tried to become a soundless shadow. He slid by one house, another, and another. Then he realized he was trapped in a maze. The small, two-story houses opened out onto the narrow lane, making a solidly connected flank of ancient stone facades. If someone appeared, there was no place to hide except in a doorway. What good was that?

What should he do? Go back? Go ahead?

Henry hated being so afraid. Hated his knees feeling wobbly. Hated waiting for a savior, completely unknown, to drop into his path.

He passed another dozen houses. Would there be a checkpoint around the corner?

Henry forced his feet to walk calmly, as if he belonged

in the town. Don't run. They'll hear these stupid shoes clatter. What if a dog starts barking? A good dog will smell me passing, even if I don't make a sound. Speed would, for sure.

Henry's breathing was so labored, he was certain it was loud enough to wake the whole town.

He made it to the church. Carved stone faces glared down at him. Henry tried the tall double door. "Please, God, please," he whispered as he pressed the latch.

It was locked. Henry's forehead fell against its dark wood. How could they lock the church? Even during the Depression, when people were tempted to do all sorts of things to feed their kin, churches had stayed open.

Henry crossed the square to a road he thought led out of town. He paused a moment in the shadows of a slightly grander looking building. Town hall, Henry reckoned.

Suddenly, he recoiled from a dim figure of a soldier. He stared at it in the gloom. It didn't move.

It's only a poster, boy. A poster of a muscled, blond German holding a young boy. The child was eating a slice of bread and smiling. At the soldier's hip two young girls looked up adoringly at him. The caption read: POPULATIONS ABANDONNÉES, FAITES CONFIANCE AU SOLDAT ALLEMAND!

Slowly, painfully, Henry worked out a translation: "Abandoned people, put your trust in the German soldier." He backed away, sickened by the exploitation of children's hunger, and hurried down the street.

Henry came to the last house. What lay beyond it? Henry flattened himself against its cold stone wall and peeped around the edge. He saw nothing but night and trees, and a vast, rolling sea of hilly fields beyond.

He took a deep breath and stepped back onto the road.

Another hour. Still no contact. Henry's throat felt like sandpaper. His legs were numb, his feet throbbing. His wooden shoes had ground a huge blister onto his bad foot. He could feel blood oozing through his sock.

Every sound he heard made his skin crawl: the breeze rattling leaves, the crack of a twig as an animal skittered away, alarmed by his approach. Golden, rosy light was seeping across the earth. Occasionally he heard the tentative morning call of a rooster. What should he do?

Henry came to a rise in the road. He searched the horizon for a place to hide. Far below he saw a farm, four stone buildings clustered together, and several wide, fenced pastures. The buildings were small and low, tucked into protective crooks of the hillside. Smart, thought Henry, to place them where they would be shielded from the winds and snows. Maybe his contact was there. Or maybe the farmer was away and he could hide in the barn. Maybe he could find the well to get a drink of water. Maybe they had stored dried apples or potatoes or something he could eat. Maybe.

Henry walked on cautiously. Anyone looking out a window could surely see him. As he drew nearer he could hear the gentle tinkle of cowbells, the sound of pigs grunting and rooting around, chickens clucking on their roosts.

His stomach grumbled at the thought of food. The *maquis* had only given him a large hunk of crusty bread—

the same dinner they ate—before he began his journey. He carried no water. His throat constricted as he imagined swallowing some sweet spring water.

Henry assessed the buildings. The largest had to be the house. It was covered with climbing roses, ready to bloom. One was the barn. The smallest might be a root cellar. He started to turn for it. Careful, he warned himself, watch out for—

Henry froze. There was an old, stooped man in the paddock by the barn. Henry fought his instinct to bolt. It's an old man, he thought, calming himself. He's seventy if he's a day. I can outrun an old man. I can overpower him if I have to. I have this knife. I can scare him into—

Sweet Jesus. Henry couldn't believe what he had just contemplated. It's just an old man who deserves to go about his business without being bullied for a turnip.

Henry kept moving. He felt the old man's eyes on him. He knew that the man might be a collaborator, might turn him over to the Germans for a few francs, or just for fun. It probably was a good idea to knock him out for a while. But Henry just couldn't do it. There were no telephone wires here. Henry would be long gone before the old man could alert anyone to his whereabouts. Henry hurried on.

Ten minutes later, he came to another slight rise in the road. Henry could see a village maybe twenty minutes farther down the slopes. Was there a way around it? As he searched, he spotted a small figure coming up the road toward him.

Alarmed, Henry slowed. The figure was very small, a child probably. Keep walking, Henry told himself. Don't look scared; don't change your course. Keep moving and nod at him. He's just a kid.

The boy drew nearer and nearer. Just pass him and nod. Don't try to speak. Your French is lousy, remember? Henry's heart pounded wildly, hurting his head.

A few feet from the boy, Henry couldn't help swinging out away from him, like a horse spooked.

"Tonton Jacques!" the child cried.

Startled, Henry backed away as the boy darted toward him.

"Tonton Jacques!" He called again. He caught Henry and hugged him tight. What did it mean? Was this child his contact? A child?

The little boy took Henry's hand. Henry looked down at him, ashamed that his own hand was trembling. The child couldn't be more than eight years old, maybe nine. He had the face of a baby, but his eyes seemed old and sorrowful.

Without another word, the boy turned Henry around and led him back up the road to the farm he'd just passed. When they reached the barn, the boy pulled open the door. The familiar smell of fresh hay and warm, sleepy animals washed over Henry. Just like his barn at home. Henry's eyes blurred with tears. Just like home.

The little boy squeezed Henry's hand. *"Vous serez tranquille ici."*

"Safe?" Henry whispered.

The boy nodded solemnly.

Safe for the day.

Chapter Twelve

The boy took Henry up a wobbly, hand-hewn ladder to the hayloft. The boards were ancient and thin. Bits of straw drifted down through the cracks as they walked. Henry could see the tops of cows and the old man's head through the slats. He heard the sound of milk hitting the bottom of an empty pail, a cow mooing in half-hearted protest over being milked while she ate. They were nice sounds, sounds as familiar to him as breathing.

The boy lay belly down on the straw and hung his head and shoulders way over the edge of the hayloft floor. Henry smiled. How many times had his mother reprimanded him for the exact same move?

"*Grand-père?*" the boy called.

"*Qu'est-ce que tu veux?*" the old man shouted back gruffly.

Henry winced for the boy. The grandfather sounded like Clayton.

Chapter Twelve

"Un peu du lait, s'il vous plaît?"

"Oui," the old man grunted. *"Un petit peu."*

The boy rolled up off the hay. *"Restez ici."* He pointed at the spot where Henry stood. Henry nodded.

The boy slipped down the ladder. Henry fell to the hay. God, he was exhausted. He pulled off his shoe. His sock was caked with dried blood. Slowly he pulled it off to avoid tearing the blister open more than it already was. It was a nasty one, two inches long, very deep, very bloody. He'd have to ask for water to wash it. What was the word for water? *Boisson?* No, that wasn't right. *L'eau.* That was it.

Henry listened to the two talking in whispers below. All he could make out was the grandfather ordering the boy to be more quiet and muttering something about hungry Americans. Then he heard a clink of metal pails and a slosh. Henry's mouth watered. The boy reemerged, carefully carrying a large mug with a rooster painted on it.

"Pour vous," he said proudly.

Henry took the mug. He chugged the thick, frothy liquid. He thought he'd never tasted anything so good. Henry closed his eyes to feel the warm, creamy milk slide down his throat.

He looked at the boy and winked. He'd always loved teasing Patsy's brood of younger brothers. Being an only child, Henry had been hungry for play and never tired of trying to amuse them when he visited Patsy's crowded cottage.

"Mercy buckets," Henry said, purposefully mispronouncing *merci beaucoup*, French for "thank you very

117

much," with absolutely the worst southern drawl he could muster.

The little boy laughed an honest laugh at the country-hick accent. Then he asked, *"Êtes-vous pilote?"*

"Yes, a pilot."

The child repeated *pilot,* rolling the English around in his mouth to get the feel of it. *"Petit ou grand avion?"*

"Grand," Henry answered. "Big planes. Bombers."

Henry saw a shadow cross the child's face. His own flushed. Maybe American bombs had landed off-target and killed someone the boy loved. Or maybe that person had been forced by the Germans to work in a munitions plant the Eighth Air Force had hit. Henry's face got even hotter. It was probably the boy's father. Back on base in England, Henry had read how the Hitler-controlled French government in Vichy was forcing Frenchmen to work in Nazi factories both in France and Germany. The Vichy government called it "compulsory labor," but it seemed little more than slavery.

"Votre père?" Henry asked softly.

The boy nodded and looked away. Henry tried to say something, but no words came. For the first time, he questioned the strategy of dropping bombs on a country they were trying to liberate. It made his stomach hurt.

"La guerre me fait peur."

Henry shook his head. He couldn't understand what the boy was saying. What about the war?

The boy looked hard at Henry, as if he were gauging Henry's soul. Then he held his two index fingers up like guns. *"Tche-tche-tche-tche-tche!"* he shook them as if he were firing machine guns. He stopped and lunged back, pantomiming fear.

"Ahhh," said Henry. The boy meant the war frightened him. *"Moi aussi,"* Henry whispered. "Me, too."

The grandfather's furrowed face bobbed up over the top of the ladder. He ignored Henry. *"Tais-toi,"* he snapped at the boy. He scolded him further and then disappeared back down the ladder.

"Pardon, monsieur," the boy apologized. *"Mon grand-père est très vieux."*

Vieux meant old; Henry knew that word. He guessed the boy wasn't supposed to be talking so much. It also sounded like he had chores to do.

The boy noticed Henry's heel. *"Est-ce que vous souffrez?"* He leaned down, pointed at Henry's heel, grimaced, and said, *"Ouff!"* Before Henry could really answer, the boy had slipped down the ladder.

Warmed by the milk, his hunger cut, Henry fought to stay awake. He could feel his eyelids drift closed. He snapped them open, only to feel them drift shut again. He fell back on the hay. After all those hours of walking and anxiety, the prickly pillow felt wonderful. The smell of sun-dried grass filled his head. The world blurred and Henry slept.

He dreamed he was walking, walking and dragging something behind him. The weight was heavy. It snagged on the rocky road and slowed him down. What was it? He fought to see in the dark, in dream-time slow motion. It was a snarling dog; a huge German shepherd locked onto his heel! The pain was terrible.

Chapter Twelve

He could feel his flesh pulling off the bone.

Henry lurched up in his sleep and grabbed at the pain. He'd shake it off. He'd kill it.

"Monsieur, monsieur, c'est moi! C'est moi." A frightened little voice yanked Henry awake. He had the child by the shoulders.

"Oh, I'm sorry, pal. You okay?" He let go and patted the child gently on the arm. "I'm so sorry."

The boy held a wet cloth in his hand. A bowl of soapy water was beside his knee. He had been washing out Henry's blister. *"D'accord."* He nodded. He was shaken, but all right.

Together they wrapped Henry's heel in clean rags. The boy gave him a new sock.

"Suivez-moi." The child took his hand and led Henry to the back corner of the hayloft, where the golden straw was piled high. He started kicking it away. As the child moved the hay, Henry could see the edges of a small, square door where the wall met the floor.

Henry helped pull it open. There was a deep hole chipped into the barn's fat stone wall, long enough for a man to lie down, barely wide enough for him to roll over. Lord, it's the size of a coffin, Henry thought, hesitating.

The child pointed to a straw mattress lining the burrow. *"Vous pouvez vous reposer ici."*

Henry took a deep breath. He hated small spaces. But he could see what the child was planning. He'd close the door and cover it with hay. That way, if Nazis searched the place, they wouldn't find him. If the boy just tucked him into the hay pile, he'd probably be stabbed with a

Chapter One

pitchfork as the Nazis searched. Okay, he could do this. If he were asleep, the stone box couldn't unnerve him.

He eased himself down onto the makeshift bed. A fist-sized hole punched through the thick wall let air and light seep through. Henry could see the farmhouse through it. There was also a jug of water next to his head.

Henry nodded up at the child, who offered a reassuring smile again. *"Je reviendrai. Je vous le promets. Et je vous apporterai votre dîner."* He closed the door.

Darkness enveloped Henry except for the small shaft of light. It was cool in this hole in the stone wall, which reminded him of the fieldstone cellar at home. Henry pulled the blanket over himself and listened to the child pushing hay over the top of the door.

There was something lumpy under his shoulder. Henry squirmed around until he dislodged it. It flopped around in his hand. Henry pushed it into the beam of light. It was a rag doll, with yarn for hair and buttons for eyes, just like one he remembered Patsy carrying everywhere when they were tiny.

A wistful smile crept onto Henry's face. The boy had obviously left the doll there for comfort. He tucked it under his head as a cushion and fell asleep instantly.

Long shadows were sliding down the farm's steep hills when Henry awoke. He figured it must be late afternoon. He'd slept the day away.

Henry twisted himself around to get a better view of the place through his peephole. Oak and juniper trees forested the rocky slopes that rimmed the horizon just beyond the pastures. There was a large orchard of some kind, maybe apple, maybe pear. A dozen white cows were still out in the pasture, but were meandering back toward the barn for feeding time. Behind the house, a neat rectangular garden laid itself out in a rich brown carpet, awaiting planting. In front of another, low-slung building several huge sows scratched themselves on the fencing. There'd be piglets born soon, Henry reckoned.

It wasn't a large operation, but the farm looked well maintained. How did the old man and little boy keep it up? Henry wondered. He'd offer to help out. He could milk the cows or feed the chickens, at least.

The back door of the house opened and out stepped a woman with a basket of laundry. Henry strained to get a better look at her. She must be the boy's mother. She was small and thin and wore a brightly colored apron. She hung out pants to dry and then waved toward the fields. Henry spotted the boy darting toward her, clutching a handful of white flowers, maybe the edelweiss Henry had seen growing.

As he reached her, the little boy launched himself at his mother. She caught him and whirled him around in a tight hug. Then they disappeared inside. Henry turned away from the hole. His eyes misted over with the memory of Lilly swinging him round and round as he clutched a bunch of goldenrod he'd found in the back pasture for her.

Henry was dying to use the bathroom. How much longer would he have to lie here? He was stiff and cold, too. He pushed against the door to see if he could move it. It wouldn't budge. He peered out through the spy hole again. Beyond the house at some distance was a small shed—an outhouse, no doubt. The sight only made his bladder feel more uncomfortable.

Henry was about to try the door again when he heard a scraping sound. It's gotta be the boy, he thought, but just to be safe he pulled out his knife and held it ready. He tightened with anticipation. The door rattled, then popped open. The boy smiled down at Henry.

"*Bonsoir,*" he said in a singsong voice.

"Hey," Henry greeted him. "*La toilette?*"

Afterward, the boy laid a yellow-and-blue checked cloth, two white plates, and a small cup of wine down on the hayloft floor. On one plate there was a circle of sliced potatoes baked in milk that smelled of nutmeg plus a roasted onion and a small sausage link. The other held a wrinkled apple, dried from the fall harvest, a knot of brown bread, and a thin wedge of blue cheese. Henry was hungry enough to inhale an entire pig, but he forced himself to eat politely.

He knew this was a huge feast. Getting food was tough in France, overrun as it was with Hitler's troops. Madame Gaulloise had provided good but trim meals, food she'd purchased on the black market. She'd shown him her food stamps—the Vichy government allowances for purchases. They weren't enough even for her. Legally, she was permitted to buy only a tiny wedge of cheese per week, about the size of what was on his plate right now for one meal. Her weekly meat ration was nothing more than a scrap, about the size of a good egg.

At least this family had its own farm. Henry knew well that the Depression, though incredibly hard for him and his parents, had been easier on them than it had been on his cousins living in the city of Richmond. On the farm, Henry and his father could hunt rabbit, duck, or even squirrel if they had to. As long as drought or an August hurricane didn't wipe them out, they had their own vegetables to eat in the summer and can for winter. His cousins, on the other hand, had to have cash to buy food at the grocery store. Sometimes they just didn't have any money after Henry's uncle was laid off work. Henry's mother often invited the city cousins to dinner on Sundays and served platters of chicken, corn, and deviled eggs. "This way, I know they get one square meal a week," Lilly had said to Henry. "Always share what you have, honey," she had added. "If you don't, your heart turns to lead."

Henry ate every crumb the boy offered, even the tangy, dry blue cheese. He'd never tasted it before and didn't much like it. It smelled, and the blue stuff had to be mold. But it was food. The only thing he couldn't manage was the wine. It was sickeningly sweet and tasted of walnuts.

Henry smiled at the boy. "That was delicious. *C'est très bon.*"

The boy smiled back. "Del-eesh-oooss," he repeated.

"Do you . . . mmm . . . *tu comprends l'anglais?*" Henry asked.

The boy shook his head, no. Then he pointed at Henry and then back to himself. *"Est-ce que vous pouvez me l'enseigner?"*

"Teach you? I will try," Henry said, speaking slowly. "If you teach me *le français. Oui,* yes?"

"Yess," the boy answered.

"D'accord." Henry shook the boy's hand. "Okay, it's a deal."

"O-K," the boy repeated.

Down below, the cows were shuffling in for their own dinner. The boy threw armloads of hay to them. Henry helped. "This is hay," Henry told him. "Hay." The boy repeated the word, then translated, *"le foin."*

Henry made a silly face and mispronounced it on purpose, *"le fun."*

"Non," the boy giggled. *"Le foin."*

"Oh, oh, *pardonnez-moi."* Henry bowed, made an even sillier face, held his nose, and said, *"fooooooon."*

"Non," the boy squealed with laughter. *"Le foin."*

"Okay, okay, *le foin."* Henry got the uniquely French nasal sound—*fwahn*—almost right.

Henry followed the boy about his chores. They watered the cows, fed the chickens, led the old carthorse to his stall and mucked it out. It pained Henry to see the boy struggle with the huge buckets of slop for the pigs. How many times had he fought to drag buckets that were too heavy for him when he was the boy's age?

"Hurry up, damn it," was what his own father had usually shouted at him. Henry closed his eyes and shook off the memory of Clayton grabbing the buckets away from him and snarling, "What a weakling. I could haul twice that weight at your age."

How old was the boy anyway? That, at least, was a dialogue question Miss Dixon had made them repeat over and over again in freshmen French. Henry had never thought it would be of any use, until this moment. He rattled it off confidently: *"Quel âge as-tu?"*

"Ooooo, magnifique, monsieur!" the boy applauded his pronunciation. *"J'ai huit ans."*

Henry counted up in his head: *un, deux, trois, quatre, cinq, six, sept, huit.* "Eight."

"Haayte," the boy repeated.

"Here, let me carry that for you," Henry told him. The boy gratefully gave up the two buckets. "Why doesn't your grandfather help you?" asked Henry. *"Grand-père?"* He jostled the pails to show what his question meant.

The child shook his head and put his hand to his shoulder. *"Une grave blessure à l'épaule. La Première Guerre mondiale. Son bras n'est plus sain."*

Henry understood enough. The old man's arm and shoulder had been wounded and ruined during World War I, the last time the Germans and French had tried to annihilate each other. Now they were at it again. No wonder the old man seemed so bitter.

There were a few more chores to finish in the growing twilight. Henry was careful to keep to the shadows and not walk far in the open. The child frequently stopped to listen to the air, cocking his head. Each time he did so, Henry's heart pounded.

"What is it?" he finally asked. *"Qu'est-ce que c'est?"*

"La patrouille."

"A patrol passes here?" Henry swept his arm along the sight line of the road.

"Oui. D'habitude à cette heure-ci. Il faut retourner à la grange." The boy pointed toward the barn.

Returning to the barn before a patrol showed up seemed like an excellent idea to Henry. He turned to go. But it was already too late to reach its safety. They heard the sound of a car and motorcycle rushing up and over the hills just beyond the barn.

The boy's mother must have heard it, too. She appeared at the front door and called, *"Pierre?"* Then she spotted Henry. *"Vite! Vite!"* She beckoned them to her.

Henry clutched the boy's hand and sprinted for the house.

At the door the mother grabbed Henry by the collar. *"Stupide!"* she cried. She crammed him behind the thick wooden door, leaving it ajar so that light from her lamps spilled out from the cottage. She threw a soccer ball at the boy. Despite her panic, she spoke to him in a soothing voice: *"Vas jouer là-bas, chéri."* The boy darted to the stone wall and started playing, kicking the ball along the road.

Within moments, the German car and motorcycle pulled up to the farm's gate.

The woman smoothed her black hair, took a deep breath, and stepped out. She called the boy in for bed as if no one else were there, *"Pierre, mon chéri! C'est l'heure du coucher!"*

She pretended to notice the four soldiers for the first

time. *"Bonsoir, messieurs. Voulez-vous acheter des oeufs?"* She walked down to the gate.

Eggs. Henry could translate the final word she spoke. Is she going to try to sell them eggs?

One of the soldiers stepped out of the idling car. He wrote something down on a pad, tore off the paper and handed it to her. A requisition, Henry figured. The jerks don't even pay her.

The mother leaned down to talk to the boy, who ran back into the house. He came back out cradling an armload of large, brown eggs.

She carefully laid the eggs in a basket the soldier held. Then he said something else Henry couldn't hear. The mother vehemently shook her head. The man took a threatening step toward her. The boy took her hand and pulled on it.

What is it? Henry worried. What should he do?

Again, the mother whispered in the ear of her son, who this time ran toward the barn. A few minutes later, he returned, carrying one of their precious hens. As he handed the hen over to a private, the boy let go early enough to ensure that the hen beat the German's face with her large, strong wings. Henry smirked. The boy had spunk, all right.

The patrol commander bowed his head formally at the mother. Then they drove off. Henry felt himself take a real breath of air for the first time in ten minutes.

Hand in hand, as if there were no urgency at all, the boy and his mother walked back to the house. Then she closed the door and glared at Henry. She was trembling all over. She forced herself to speak in a contained voice, but it shook with anger.

"Tu ne dois jamais le mettre en danger!" she said to Henry. She touched the child's head, then her heart, then the child's head again, and added with great emotion, *"Il est tout pour moi! Comprenez-vous?"*

Henry understood her face. Her boy was her life. She couldn't bear it if something were to happen to him. Henry knew if they were caught, he'd most likely be sent to a P.O.W. camp. But the mother, the boy, and the grandfather could all be executed.

Henry nodded at her. He'd never be that careless again.

Chapter Thirteen

Henry had remained with the boy and his family almost a month. He couldn't understand exactly what they told him about the delay. But it seemed that a unit of Germans had camped where he would pass as he continued southwest along the underground's escape route. He'd need to stay put until the French could either find him a new route or until the Germans had moved on.

Except for the hours he spent locked inside the stone wall, Henry enjoyed this time. No bombing missions. No reports of friends killed, disfigured, lost. No need to pretend to be a man enjoying war, happy to be shooting other boys out of the skies.

The farm reminded him of home, and he was growing fond of the boy. They continued to teach one another French and English, laughing over their poor pronunciation. They even played ball in the hayloft. "Bohwl," the boy called it.

Chapter Thirteen

One late afternoon, as the two tossed a ball back and forth, the child's mother silently eased herself up the hayloft ladder. The boy threw the ball at Henry, who let it bounce off his head. "Aaaah," Henry cried. He fell to the ground and pretended to lose consciousness.

The boy hurled himself on Henry. "Up, pilot!" He tugged on Henry's shirt.

"*RRRROOAARR!*" Henry shot up and grabbed the boy playfully. "I've got you!"

The child shrieked with laughter. He squirmed away and grabbed fistfuls of hay to fling at Henry. Henry threw armloads back at him. A flurry of hay filled the air.

"*Chéri,*" the boy's mother called quietly.

Henry and the boy froze. Clouds of hay drifted down around them, covering their heads with spiky fluff.

The mother fought off a laugh and held her hand up to reassure them. "*Ne vous inquiétez pas.*" She motioned for her son to come to her.

"*Oui, maman?*"

She spoke to the boy about his grandfather and of an errand. She paused and glanced at Henry, who had brushed himself free of hay, embarrassed to look so childish in front of her. He understood her to mean that the grandfather was sick. She added, "*Emmene le pilote avec toi.*"

The boy grinned. "*Je peux, vraiment?*"

The mother smiled and stroked his cheek. "*Oui, mon petit.*"

The boy pointed to the hills, to Henry, then to himself. "*Avec moi!*" he told Henry with excitement.

His mother then cautioned him to be serious about the job she was sending them on.

"*D'accord*," the boy answered. To Henry, he said, "*Mon gardien. Pas de bêtises.*"

Henry was to go along somewhere as protection, no playing around. "Where?" he asked. "*Où?*"

The boy pointed to the outside. "*Les pièges.*" He dropped to the ground and crawled like an animal, then pretended to choke.

He must mean traps, thought Henry. His mother wants to give the old man meat. The woman's affectionate smile for her son faded as she looked at Henry. She studied him a long moment before speaking. "*Suivez-moi.*"

Henry followed her down the ladder and to the grain bin. This was the closest Henry had gotten to her except for the night the patrol had passed. The light was fading in the barn as twilight approached. But he could see that her dark eyes were large and pretty, her skin smooth and unlined. She couldn't be more than twenty-six or twenty-seven years old. She was an awfully young widow.

The mother lifted the heavy wooden lid to the grain bin. It was as big and deep as a desk. When she leaned over into it her feet left the ground. Henry fought the urge to grab her, to keep her from dropping in headfirst. She made a racket, shoveling through the heavy grain.

What was she doing? She was grunting and yanking on something. Henry reached over to help. Surfacing in the golden oats was the butt of a gun. Together they dragged it out.

Henry was amazed. This was no farmer's shotgun.

This was a British Sten gun. It was a great black thing as long as Henry's leg. It had a kickstand at one end and a pepper-shaker-like cone at the other. Two triggers unleashed bullets in bursts. The only way the mother could have this kind of automatic gun was if she had picked it up from a weapons drop. Before he had left England, there was talk around the base of the British beginning to parachute supplies to the small guerrilla groups Henry now knew as the *maquis*. It was unbelievably dangerous for her to have such a gun if the Germans ever searched her place. There'd be no pretending then that she knew nothing of the Resistance.

Suddenly it dawned on him. She was probably storing all sorts of weapons. Several times as he lay in his hiding hole he had watched the farmhouse through his peephole. Twice he'd seen men come to the back door. She had given them large bundles. They'd hurried up into the hills. She must be supplying a *maquis* group somewhere with food. She wasn't just a sympathetic mother, taking pity on a lost American boy. She was fighting the war as actively here as he had fought it from the skies. Only her battle seemed scarier, somehow. At least he had a crew with him. She did her part so alone. Secrecy was everything. And if she made a mistake, the price was her son. At least Henry had never had to worry about his actions endangering Ma or Patsy.

The mother handed the powerful weapon to him, clearly as protection if they ran into a German squadron. Henry couldn't help asking why she took such enormous risks. "Why do you do this? *Pourquoi?*"

She stroked the boy's hair. *"Pour que mon fils puisse respirer l'air de la France libre. Il ne sera jamais un esclave des Boches."*

Free French air for her son; no Nazi enslavement.

Henry and his pilot friends had always seen themselves as the saviors of France. He was ashamed of their arrogance. He felt like saluting her as he shouldered the heavy gun. She had already loaded it.

The moon was rising as Henry and the boy climbed over the last fence of the farm. Before them the earth rolled in soft knuckles of green. The meadow was knee deep in grass and wildflowers. Here and there Henry spotted red clover, blue cornflowers, and pink and white orchids. The settling dew strengthened their sweet scent. Henry sucked in the air greedily. The earth was such a beautiful place. He tried to ignore the weight of the gun on his shoulder.

"What are we looking for?" Henry asked the boy.

"Des lapins," he answered.

"Rabbits."

The boy repeated the word and Henry nodded. "You'll be able to be a diplomat when this war is over."

The boy took Henry's hand. Henry realized the only words he had probably caught were "the war." Probably best not to even think about the war being over, if it ever would end. He had no idea how to translate what he meant anyway. Instead Henry said, "You are very smart." He tapped the boy's forehead. *"Tu es très . . . mmm . . ."* — he pronounced the word the French way—*"intelligent."*

The boy smiled.

Rabbit. Henry's mother had made delicious Brunswick stew with rabbit, tomatoes, corn, lima beans, and broth. Henry had loved it. He wondered how the boy's mother would cook it. It would be the first fresh meat he'd had for weeks. The farm's cows were for milk, the chickens for eggs. The sows had just had their babies. The family lived off soups mostly: leek, cabbage, carrot. Henry could tell he was losing weight.

Behind a boulder, jutting up gray and hard among the sea of flowers, the boy checked his first trap. It was just a little rope noose hung on a stake with a carrot stub in front of it. Nothing there.

They walked on. Henry kept checking the horizon. A little ways ahead of them was a narrow road, churned into mud by passing vehicles. German troops no doubt. The French walked, rode their rickety bikes, or used ox-drawn carts.

Without a word of warning, the boy ran to the road. What was he doing? Henry chased after him. The boy came to a three-pronged road sign. When Henry caught up, he could read on it: PONT-EN-ROYANS, LA CHAPELLE-EN-VERCORS, VASSIEUX-EN-VERCORS.

"*Aidez-moi, s'il vous plaît*," the boy said as he tugged on the post. Together they twisted and twisted it so the arrows pointed in the opposite direction. "*Pour tromper les soldats Allemands,*" the boy said, and darted across the road to the other side.

It will confuse more than just Nazis, Henry thought. He made a note never to trust road signs when he started walking for Spain again.

* * *

They checked two more traps. Both were empty of their bait. Some animal had enjoyed a free meal. They moved up through a pine forest now. Their feet moved soundlessly on the carpet of needles. Henry wondered if they'd hear anything coming. The moonlight barely cut through the trees. More than once, Henry stumbled and banged his head on low-hanging branches.

Finally, they found a trapped rabbit. It was long dead, hanged on the rope. *"Merci mon Dieu pour ce repas,"* the boy murmured in prayer, crossing himself as he pulled the fat hare off the line and tucked it into a canvas bag.

They headed back in silence.

As they walked, the hair on the back of Henry's neck began to bristle. A chill rippled through him. He tried to shake off his fears, but instinct shouted at him that something wasn't right. Henry grabbed the boy's shoulder to stop him and put his fingers to his lips. Henry listened and listened and listened to the cool night air. Nothing. Well, maybe he really had gone flak-happy and lost his nerve.

He took two steps forward, but froze when he heard a *SNAP*. There were a few moments of silence, then came another loud *SNAP*. Something was coming toward them—something tall enough to break off branches as it moved.

Henry pushed the boy and himself behind a large tree and into a shallow ditch made by its roots. They flattened themselves to the ground. Henry put his arm over the boy and in his ear breathed: "Shhhhh."

Chapter Thirteen

They didn't dare lift their chins from the dirt, but from there they could see feet passing. One, two, three . . . five, six . . . eight, nine pairs of feet padding quietly along the pine needles. Who were they? Germans? Collaborators? *Maquis?* Better not try to figure out, just hide until they passed. Please God, let them pass, Henry prayed as he slid his fingers down to the trigger of the gun.

The feet disappeared into the forest. Henry waited. Waited for them to be long gone. Waited for his head to stop knocking with his heartbeat. Waited for the frost of terror to leave his hands and feet.

Slowly he drew himself up and motioned for the boy to follow him. They tiptoed back down the path. As they turned a corner through a thick knot of trees, they came face to face with two men.

Henry shoved the child behind him. He pulled the heavy gun up into firing position just as the barrels of two rifles lined up on his head. Henry held fast, his gun aimed at the chest of one of the strangers. It might be two against him, but he'd take one of the men down anyway. Only over his dead body would they get the boy.

The moonlight was patchy and shadowy, but Henry could tell the men were not Germans. They wore regular clothes, and bandoliers of rifle cartridges across their chests. Still, the three guns didn't budge.

Henry felt the boy peep out from behind him. Then take a step. "Don't!" Henry hissed at him.

But the child moved forward. Suddenly he laughed and threw up his arms. *"Tonton Jacques!"*

Henry kept his eyes on his foes. Hadn't the boy called him Uncle Jacques when they first met on the road? Could he truly have an Uncle John?

One gun was lowered. Its carrier embraced the boy. Henry and the other man kept their weapons aimed at one another.

The boy tugged at the sleeve of his uncle. *"Ne vous inquiétez pas, mon oncle."* Then he motioned for Henry to put down his weapon.

"Not until he puts his away," Henry answered.

The uncle waved his hand at his companion. Slowly, the man eased down his gun. Henry did likewise.

The uncle took three quick strides toward Henry. What? Is he going to embrace me? wondered Henry. He'd seen Frenchmen kiss each other's cheeks. Yuck, Henry thought fleetingly.

But instead of a kiss, the uncle whipped back his right arm and punched Henry hard in the stomach. Henry doubled up with pain as he hit the ground and whacked his head against a tree trunk. "Damn!" Henry cried out.

The world spun in front of him, but Henry staggered to his feet. He heard his father's voice, the voice Clayton had used when he had smacked Henry around, supposedly to teach him to box. *Get up, boy, or they'll kick you while you're down.*

Henry forced himself to stand tall, his fists level with his face, poised for a fight. "Come on, you bastard. See what I can do when I'm ready."

The uncle grinned at Henry. *"Pardon, monsieur."* He shrugged. "A test." He explained in bits of English, speaking lines he had obviously been taught and practiced. Apparently, if you hit a man when he didn't expect it, he'd shout out in his native tongue: *"Nazis, allemand. Americains, anglais."* The man shrugged. *"Vous êtes vraiment americain."*

Henry wondered how many other Americans he had slugged. But more importantly how many Germans had he ferreted out that way? So, just because someone spoke English, didn't make him or her safe. He'd have to remember that. He'd also remember that these Frenchmen trusted no one—not even someone who'd lived among them for weeks or who appeared to be protecting a young nephew.

The boy's uncle didn't even say good-bye to Henry. He patted the boy, told him to go straight home, adding, *"La forêt est encombrée ce soir"*—the forest is busy tonight. Then he slid into the darkness of the woods with his companion.

Henry caught his meaning. The *maquis* were on their way to some sort of encounter with Germans or to pick up supplies dropped by parachute from Allied planes. He and the boy didn't want to be in the midst of that.

The boy didn't translate his uncle's statement. He simply tugged urgently on Henry's sleeve and turned for home. He pointed to the rabbit. *"Maman* cook?"—he looked to Henry to see if *cook* was the right word, and Henry nodded—*"demain."*

"Tomorrow," said Henry. "Good." He kept to the boy's small talk and held to the belief that the boy hadn't explained his uncle's statement as a way of protecting Henry from knowing too much. It hurt Henry's feelings to consider that the boy might not completely trust him.

Chapter Fourteen

The next night, the boy's mother invited Henry into the farmhouse for dinner. It was a pretty little stone cottage, wrapped in blossoms. By now the roses had erupted into a froth of pink flowers. Purple hollyhocks taller than Henry lined the walls. Each window had a flower box, overflowing with red geraniums. Blue swallows darted in and out of the eaves.

Inside, ancient, exposed log beams held up the low ceilings. The floors were stone. Delicate, hand-crocheted curtains flanked the windows. They were shuttered for the night but were wide and tall and could open like double doors to the outside. Henry could tell that during the day the house filled with cheery sunlight.

He assessed the lamp-lit kitchen. The dark wooden table amazed him. Eight feet long but only two feet wide, it clearly had been hand-lathed out of one piece of a massive tree many years before. Atop it sat a large handpainted vase stuffed with wildflowers. Everything looked spotless, even the copper pots that brightly reflected the light of the fire.

For the first time, Henry felt ashamed of his appearance. He'd only been able to wash his clothes twice during the past few weeks. His straight, blond hair was now long, dirty, and uncombed. He even had a hint of a patchy golden beard and mustache on his chin and upper lip. He looked sheepishly at the boy's mother. She smiled reassuringly and motioned him over to a ceramic pitcher and bowl where he could wash his hands. He scrubbed his face and neck, too. The soap, though, was little more than lard. It made only a small dent in his grime.

Henry stood awkwardly in a corner and watched the mother cook at the huge open fireplace. A small oven had been built into the side of the hearth, but Henry could tell she did a large portion of her cooking in a black kettle hanging over the fire itself. Must be awfully hot work, he thought. He remembered how thrilled his own mother had been when they finally replaced their wood stove with an electric one. She used to wear herself out feeding the fire of that old thing with shucked corncobs and kindling Henry had picked up around the farm.

Ma. Henry had tried not to think much about home; it always made him go wobbly inside. He'd been so all-fired hot to get out and see the world. All he wanted to see now was that sunny kitchen of white cabinets and sweet smells.

The boy's mother hummed quietly as she stirred the pot. The sound threw Henry all the way back to

Richmond, to the last time he'd been home, on leave right before being shipped across the ocean.

"Boogie Woogie Bugle Boy" had been playing on the radio. Henry had turned it way up, whooping out the bebopping lyrics with the Andrews Sisters: "Come on, Ma, dance with me," he'd said, grabbing his mother and twirling her around.

Lilly followed his moves, sliding her feet and sashaying quickly.

"This is a pretzel, Ma," Henry said as he guided her under his arm and tried to twist them out of the resulting knot. "A gal from the USO taught me."

Lilly kept getting stuck somewhere in the middle of the maneuver. The two laughed and laughed. "That's what you get for trying to dance with an old woman," Lilly had said, pushing him away playfully.

Henry caught her up in a hug and looked down on her head, her own honey-colored hair was just beginning to gray. "You're only forty, Ma. Besides, I'll always love you, even if you can't jitterbug."

Henry's eyes clouded up at the memory and he rubbed them with embarrassment. He caught the boy's mother watching him. "Something's in my eye," he muttered. He nudged the table leg with his shoe and shoved his hands into his pockets.

Smiling again, the boy's mother reached out and squeezed Henry's arm.

"*Que fait-il ici?*" a voice growled. It was the grandfather, staggering through the door supported by the boy.

The mother let go of Henry and answered the old man,

saying something about Henry living with the cows long enough. *"Il peut retourner à la grange après."*

Henry edged toward the door. The grandfather was clearly not happy about his being inside the house. The last thing he wanted to do was cause trouble. But the boy reassured him, *"Maman a dit* okay."

Henry sat down beside the boy. *"Merci beaucoup, Madame.* It smells," Henry paused to close his eyes and sniff appreciatively, "wonderful . . . *merveilleux."*

She smiled, pleased, and set his plate before him. She had cooked the rabbit meat in wine and finished it with cream and its own blood. The plate also held a large fritter of potato and onion.

"La spécialité de Maman," whispered the boy.

The grandfather humpfed and spoke again in sour terms, *"Je te jure, Marie, il va nous apporter de la malchance."*

Henry turned red. He could tell the grandfather had said he was bad luck.

The mother ignored the remark. She took Henry's and the boy's hands to say grace. *"Bon appétit,"* she concluded.

Each bite melted in Henry's mouth. The food was rich and warm and delicious. He savored the taste. He basked in the warmth of the kitchen. He smiled and nodded and attempted conversation. He felt like a human being, not a hunted, hiding thing. He was a guest in a household that, for the most part, seemed to like him. Lord, it felt good.

There was even dessert, a tiny rectangular cake strewn with almonds and a drizzle of honey. Each person had an inch-thick, two-inch-long slice. Henry knew how precious all the ingredients had been. He didn't know how he could ever thank her, for the meal, for his safety, for her kindness this night. He said the first thing that came into his head, "This is heaven, Madame."

She looked at him quizzically. Henry pointed skyward. "Heaven . . . mmm . . . *Dieu maison?* God's home?"

"Aaaah," the boy and his mother murmured. *"Le paradis."* They smiled and nodded. The grandfather scowled.

In that moment of peace came a hurried *knock-knock-knock . . . pause . . . knock-knock.* The mother's smile froze. Her face turned ashen. She put her fingers to her lips, then pointed to Henry, to the boy, and then to the back door. She hurriedly cleared their plates from the table so that it looked as if just she and the old man were there for dinner. She waited until they had exited and pressed themselves to the shadows of the outside wall before she opened the front door.

An urgent male voice sounded through the cottage. *"Les Boches nous ont decouverts! Partez, vite!"* The door slammed shut.

"Nazis," whispered the boy.

His mother reappeared. She knelt to take her son by his shoulders and spoke hurriedly. The boy was to head for the hills with Henry immediately. She would need to get the horse to carry his grandfather. *"Je te verrai à . . ."*

The sound of a distant machine gun stopped her short. The Germans must have found the man who had warned her. *"Mon Dieu."* She grabbed Henry's arm. *"Mon fils, s'il vous plaît. La grange."*

The barn. Henry knew what to do.

Chapter Fourteen

"*Non, non, Maman!*" The child clung to her. "*Je ne veux pas partir!*"

Henry picked him up. The boy struggled to hold on to his mother.

"*Je t'aime, mon chéri,*" his mother covered the boy's face with kisses. "*Vives pour moi.*" Live for me, she told him. She tore herself away and vanished into the house.

Henry raced for the barn, the boy sobbing. He raced as if all the devils of hell were after him.

Henry half carried the boy up the hayloft ladder. He still fought and cried for his mother. "You must be quiet," Henry urged him, "*pour ta maman.* If they find you, they will use you to hurt her. Shhhh, now."

The child quieted.

Henry yanked open the hiding closet and dropped the boy in. He repeated what the boy had first said to him: "I will be back for you. *Je reviendrai. Je te promets.* Trust me. *D'accord?*"

The boy nodded.

"No sound. No matter what you see out that hole. *Tu comprends?*"

Tears streamed down his face, but he nodded.

Henry closed the door. Quietly and quickly, he used his entire body to sweep hay over top it. The pile must be huge and look undisturbed. Within seconds, a golden heaping wall of hay obliterated the child's hiding place.

Henry heard car doors slam, men shouting, one crackling gunshot. Who had fired? Who was dead? Where could he hide?

Henry frantically slid down the ladder. The cows

were wandering into their stalls from the back door. How weird, Henry thought fleetingly, that they'd keep to their routine as their owners' world came to an end. Wait a minute. The cows! Henry had an idea.

He squeezed in with one of the cows, which was blissfully chewing hay from a manger attached to the wall. There was just enough room for Henry to slide up underneath the manger and nearly disappear.

Careful to not spook the cow and give himself away, Henry crawled into place. He packed fistfuls of hay in with him. He prayed that the cow wouldn't eat too fast. Then he flattened himself into the dirt and manure.

The door to the barn rolled open loudly. Flashlight beams darted along the walls. *"Fouillez-la."*

Henry's skin crawled when he heard the French command. French Vichy police were leading the arrest. Or maybe it was the Milice, the French version of Hitler's Gestapo, just as cruel and fanatically anti-Jewish. Maybe someone she knew had turned the boy's mother in—motivated by jealousy, maybe to collect a reward. If the informant had been someone she knew, the Milice might know to look for the boy. There had been no time to find the Sten gun. All Henry had to protect himself and the boy was the knife the guide had given him weeks ago. It would be of little use.

Please, God. Please, don't let them find us. Please. Henry squeezed his eyes shut and silently prayed harder than ever.

He heard the sound of a cautious footfall. Henry's eyes popped open. He could see regulation shiny boots stepping into his stall. This must be a Nazi, a Nazi with a rapid-firing gun and a good reason to kill an American pilot. Henry suppressed the urge to jump up and run. Easy. He locked himself in place. Don't move, don't breathe.

The spit-shiny boots came closer, closer. Henry could have reached out and touched their pristine toes.

"*Verfluchen!*" the soldier cursed. He lifted his foot to look at the sole of his boot. "*Kuh dung!*" He swore again. The boots backed out.

Henry praised God for slimy cow manure.

But his sense of relief was short-lived. He heard men climb up the ladder. The hayloft creaked with their weight. Don't move, boy, Henry tried to throw his thoughts to the child. Don't make a sound. Please, God, don't let him cry out.

Henry heard bayonets stab through the hay, the sound of men kicking it. Had Henry piled it thick enough?

The sounds stopped. Did they find the door? Impulsively, Henry started to squirm out from under. But then he heard a Frenchman shout: "*Rien!*"

Nothing. They'd found nothing! Thank you, God.

There was more tramping, more light beams skittering along the walls and ceilings. Then silence. The men had left.

For a long time Henry could hear banging, shouting, and things being thrown about in the farmhouse. They must be searching the place for a radio or weapons to incriminate the mother, he thought. Then Henry heard car doors slam again, motors starting. Finally all sounds disappeared. He forced himself to count the seconds by one thousands—one one thousand, two one thousand, three one thousand—all the way up to sixty, five times over, before he'd budge. Then he slid out from the manger and kissed the cow's head.

Chapter Fifteen

Henry peeped around the edge of the stall. Moonlight seeped through the open door. All of the guards had left the barn. He tiptoed to the edge of the door. There was one soldier standing by the cottage's front door, waiting to grab whoever approached. Could the guard see into the barn from there? Henry looked back over his shoulder to gauge the German's view. Maybe. He might be able to see Henry as he went up the ladder.

He'd have to pull himself up from the back stall. Henry squatted and ran along the wall to the stall farthest from the door. He couldn't see the soldier from there, so the soldier must not be able to see him.

He climbed up onto the manger. On tiptoe, he could just barely grab the edge of the hayloft. Thank God for all those chin-ups in basic training. His arms shaking, Henry managed to kick, kick, and swing his feet up enough to catch. He pulled himself up to the hayloft floor.

As quietly as possible, Henry burrowed down into the hay to the door of the boy's hiding place. "It's me," he whispered before pulling it open. *"C'est moi."*

The boy was huddled into a tight ball, pressed against the peephole. His shoulders shook. He was crying.

"Ils ont tué mon grand-père. Ils ont emmené ma mère," he choked out the words.

They had shot his grandfather and taken his mother.

Henry picked him up and rocked him. He whispered into the boy's ear.

"There is a man left. A soldier—*soldat*—*à la porte maison. Comprends?"*

The boy nodded. Henry pointed to the back part of the barn. He took the boy's hand and led him to the hayloft's edge. Henry swung down and then caught the boy from below.

Together they slipped out the back door.

The front of the farmhouse faced away from them toward the road. The soldier seemed planted on the stoop. They'd have a chance to make it up the back hill, if they moved very fast. The orchard trees dotted the hillside. They might be able to work their way up tree by tree.

Henry pointed to the trees. "Can you run?"

The boy nodded.

Hand in hand they darted from one tree, to the next, to the next, to the next. Each time they reached a tree trunk and crouched behind it without being seen felt like a miracle. They'd pant for a moment and then go on, zigzagging up the hill, zigzagging between fear and relief, fear and relief.

Chapter Fifteen

When they reached the hill's crest they threw themselves onto the ground and rolled away from the edge onto a wide plateau. They lay there gasping, but out of sight of the soldier at the bottom of the hill.

"Now what?" whispered Henry.

"*Mon oncle.*"

Henry took his hand and pulled the boy to his feet. "Let's go."

They retraced their steps from the previous night. Perhaps the path in the pine forest was one often used by the boy's uncle and they could find him there somehow. Henry looked down at the boy, who clung to his hand. He didn't bother asking the child if he was all right. Henry knew the answer was no.

They passed the boulder, crossed the road, padded silently along the carpet of pine needles in the towering wood. When Henry hesitated, not knowing the way, the child tugged him along. They came to the clump of trees where they had first seen the *maquis* group. "Where to now?"

The boy pointed down a very faint path, where the men had disappeared. If Henry hadn't known to look carefully, he would never have noticed that it existed. There was no choice but to follow it. They squeezed their way through the path for a good fifteen minutes, seeing nothing. Branches raked their faces. Finally, they came to a small clearing. No one was there that night, but Henry could tell from the flattened patches of brush and the circle of cold ashes that someone had camped there fairly recently. There was no trace of where they'd gone.

Of course, there wouldn't be, Henry berated himself. They wouldn't exactly leave a road map to their whereabouts, would they? But what should he do now?

He knelt beside the boy and asked gently, "Is there someone else I can take you to? Aunt? . . . mmm . . . *Tante?* . . . cousin? . . . friend? . . . *ami?*"

The boy sadly shook his head.

Just then Henry heard a *snap* . . . pause . . . *snap.* Someone was coming. Henry jerked them both behind a tree.

A solitary gunman stepped cautiously into the clearing. He was a slight, small man. Henry could tell from his sudden movements that he was very nervous. The gunman circled the clearing's edge. He came nearer and nearer to the tree where Henry and the boy hid. This time Henry wanted the advantage. He pulled out his knife and prepared himself to grab the gunman from behind.

Henry forced himself to wait until the man was just a foot away, his back toward him. Henry sprung, circled the gunman's chest with his arm and held the knife's point against his throat. Henry was unpracticed and awkward doing it, but he held the man tight.

"Who are you looking for?"

The boy translated.

"On vous cherche. C'est Jacques qui m'a envoyé. Je dois emmener le fils de Marie chez le prêtre."

"Pour nous. Us," the boy translated.

Henry let go. The boy's uncle had sent the gunman.

"Où est mon oncle?" the boy asked the gunman.

He told the boy that his uncle was going to attack the

cars taking his mother to the German garrison in Grenoble.

"*Qui la détient maintenant?*" the boy asked haltingly.

"*La Milice.*"

The child dropped his face into his hands. He shuddered. One wrenching sob of grief escaped before he silenced himself.

Henry understood his reaction. If the Milice had the boy's mother, she was in terrible danger. Henry also knew that he, the boy, and this guide needed to hurry. Madame Gaulloise had told Henry that each operative knew to hold out under questioning for at least twenty-four hours. That gave his or her contacts time to burn papers and relocate. After that twenty-four hours, though, they had been taught to give up some tiny bit of old information, enough to get their interrogators off them, at least for a while.

"We'd better go," Henry said.

The gunman led the way through the woods, parallel to the valley road. The boy still clung to Henry's hand. They must be heading south for Vassieux, the village marked by the road sign he and the boy had twisted around the night before. *Isn't heading to a town going into the lion's den?* Henry thought, worrying.

He tried to assess the fighting power of their guide. He certainly hadn't put up much of a struggle against Henry. Maybe Henry should offer to shoulder the gun. He looked hard at the Frenchman's face. *For pity's sake,* Henry thought with disgust, *this guy's just a kid.*

"How old are you?" Henry asked. "*Quel âge as-tu?*"

The gunman swung around on Henry. *"Dix-huit ans,"* he answered hotly.

There's no way he's eighteen, Henry thought. This guy is sixteen at most. He's even wearing shorts that look like they're part of a scouting uniform. Still, Henry admired the teenager's grit. Henry held his hands up. "Okay, okay. *Pardonnez-moi."*

The gunman led on.

They came to the village's outer stone wall. Are we going to try to waltz through the front gate? Henry wondered. They did.

It was another labyrinth of narrow, circling roads. Slowly, the three wound their way into the center of town. Most of the houses' windows had small, wrought-iron balconies that Henry and the French teenager checked for villagers. Nothing there but laundry hung out to dry. There was also a café and a wide scattering of tables in front of it. But it was deserted. Curfew made these villages such ghost towns.

Across the square was a solemn gray church with a rooster weather vane atop its tall tower. That must be where we're heading, thought Henry, but what a risk to walk across the open market. The teenager pulled them back into the shadows. From a sack on his shoulder, he pulled two long black shawls. He threw his around his head and shoulders, hiding the gun. He handed the other shawl to Henry. They were to look like women.

Good thing it's dark, thought Henry.

He tried to feel like a mourner on his way to church to light a candle. Given the circumstances, that would be easy. He took the boy's hand once more and trod as daintily as he could in his clunky wooden-soled shoes. The two-minute walk felt like fifteen.

Once inside the church, Henry gaped. He couldn't help it. He'd never been in a Catholic church, much less one built in the Middle Ages. There were several life-size statues of saints and a huge painting of the Madonna being lifted to heaven by angels. The ceiling vaulted in great tall arches, held up by stone columns. In the flickering candlelight he could make out carved leaves and figures atop the columns. The air had a cool, ancient feel to it, laced with incense.

The little boy let go of Henry's hand to dip his fingers in the font of holy water. He crossed himself and knelt in one of the back pews to pray. Henry slid in beside him.

Only a few minutes passed before they heard footsteps and the swish of long robes. A priest arrived. He had a plump, babyish, pale face. Had it not been for his kindly expression, Henry might have distrusted him instinctively. Clayton had always tried to instill his own prejudices in Henry. "A man who doesn't do any work outdoors isn't worth a spit," Clayton had said repeatedly, dismissing teachers, ministers, county courthouse lawyers—men he didn't understand. Even though he automatically tried to reject anything Clayton had said, Henry still had to fight his influence. He didn't see how this gentle-looking priest could stop a Nazi from dragging off the boy.

Henry listened suspiciously to the way the priest spoke to the boy, who nodded solemnly. The priest seemed adequately concerned about him but it hurt Henry to see the child's smile so gone.

"What did he say?" Henry asked.

The priest himself answered in English. "There is a Cistercian abbey nearby where several children of patriots hide. The Nazis leave the monks alone. It is safe. We have arranged for you to move on. This young man will guide you. *Bonne chance.*"

The priest reached for the boy's hand to lead him away. Henry's head reeled. He felt sick. Now? He'd have to leave the boy right now?

The child backed away from the priest. He ran to Henry and threw his arms around him. Henry hugged the boy hard and blinked back tears. He loved this child. How could he let go? Henry knew that once he did, he would probably never set eyes on him again.

"Maybe I can get him settled in his room before I go?" Henry choked out the words.

The priest started to say no, but instead said grudgingly, "*Cinq minutes.* Five minutes only. This way."

Henry picked the boy up and followed the priest through the back of the church and up a narrow spiral staircase. Up through stone they wound their way. The child's arms and legs were wrapped tight around Henry, his face buried against Henry's neck. They arrived on a floor with three tiny bedrooms. The priest pointed to one and stood outside the door.

Henry took a deep breath and walked into the stark room. There was a small bed with coarse white sheets, a table with a bottle of water on it, and a crucifix.

Chapter Fifteen

"Here we are." Henry set him down on the bed, but the boy wouldn't let go.

"*Pierre,*" he whispered. *"Je veux que vous sachiez mon nom. Pierre."*

"I know, Pierre. I heard your mother call you that. But I didn't want to use your name unless you told me to. I want you to know mine, too. My name is Henry. *Je m'appelle Henri."*

The boy repeated it.

"You have to lie down now, Pierre. Rest." Henry took off the child's shoes and gently laid him down. There was a woolly black blanket at the bottom of the bed. As he pulled it up over the boy, Henry sang a song his own mother had sung to him in hard times, "You Are My Sunshine." It was a song about the joy one person could bring another, and what sadness would come if that sunshine were taken away. The lyrics now were bittersweet to Henry and as he sang his voice became a hoarse whisper.

The boy watched Henry's face, hard, as if memorizing every bit of it.

Henry came to the end of his song. Still he couldn't bear to tear himself away. The boy looked so small and lost in this white bed, this white room. If only Henry had a doll like the one the boy had left for him in the hiding closet, something to comfort the child as he fell asleep. But there was nothing in the room.

Henry reached into his pocket and pulled out the only thing he had that still tied him to home, to his own mother and father—his lucky marble. The marble had symbolized his first triumph over his father, his ability to survive Clayton's hardness. Somehow Henry needed its reassurance less now. The boy, on the other hand, needed all the luck he could get, all the strength, all the love Henry could pass on to him. Henry held it up for the boy to see.

"This is called a cloud," Henry told him. "*Nuage*. See the swirls? It's my favorite marble. *Mon favori*. I want you to have it. That way I'll always be with you. *Henri avec Pierre*."

"*Pour toujours?*" the boy whispered.

"Yes, always," Henry answered, his voice cracking. "Wherever I go, I remain with you."

The priest knocked. "It's time."

Henry nodded. His heart hurt too much to say anything else. He took the boy's hand, squeezed the precious marble into it, and kissed him good-bye.

Chapter Sixteen

Henry stumbled through the night, following the back of his teenage guide. Neither of them spoke. Henry was too upset to ask where they were going. He kept seeing Pierre playing ball, his young mother in her kitchen, the two of them hugging. Would she survive the night? What would the Milice do with her when they finished asking their questions? Would they search for Pierre? Could the priest be trusted?

They were climbing up out of the valley, scrambling along tiny paths scratched into the mountainside. The land tumbled down away from them. The few times he paused to catch his breath and look about, Henry could tell they hadn't gone far, only up, zigzagging back and forth to scale the ridge.

After two hours the ground leveled out a bit where a pine forest grew stubbornly, spread among the boulders. The guide turned off the path into the woods. Here, the moonlight could only sift through the trees in needles of pale illumination. Henry lost his guide in the gloom.

"Hey," he breathed into the night. "Where are you?"

No answer.

Henry waded on, scratching his face on branches.

"*Où êtes-vous?*" he whispered. Had the jerk left him? Or did someone have him by the throat?

Henry heard a twig snap, felt something lunge toward him. "*Regardez!*"

The teenager jerked Henry back. The motion ripped painfully through Henry's shoulder. He shook himself free with irritation. The guide pointed to the ground and swept his hand in a straight line. Henry squinted into the darkness. He could just make out a string running a few inches from his knee. There was a grenade attached to its end—a booby trap.

Taking Henry's arm again, his guide inched them both around the line and down an incline. Within a few moments the world became completely black and dank. Henry could hear water dripping. His feet slipped and he skidded on something slick, making a shrill scraping sound. Instantly there was a racket of thumping wings and high-pitched squeaking. Henry felt a whir of something rush by him.

Only then did the teenager let go. He struck a match. They were in a cave.

"*Nous allons rester ici avant qu'on se met in route,*" the teenager said. He pulled out a lantern from behind a rock and lit it. The light trotted along the stone icicles of the cave's ceiling. Henry trembled in the damp, unnerved. His guide's eyes darted about, checking corners, before he unearthed a jug of water from behind some rocks, drank from it, and then offered it to Henry. This must be a safe house of sorts, thought Henry.

The guide lay down on a sandy spot and motioned Henry to do likewise. Once he was settled, Henry's companion blew out the lantern. Henry thought about the Greek myths he'd read last spring in senior English, in which caves were the entrances to hell. He shut his eyes and forced himself to think of nothing.

The two clambered out of the cave in late afternoon the next day. This time, they walked in a rill carved between the crests of two long mountains. Yellow butterflies speckled with black dots danced before them as they waded through wildflowers.

Henry noted that the youth was extremely anxious, often stopping to listen or to scan the horizon. Once the clang of a church bell reverberated through the crags. Henry couldn't see a village anywhere and realized that sound must bounce back and forth off the rocks for miles.

Henry had difficulty estimating time correctly in France. Twilight fell much later than at home. But right around what he reckoned was 7 P.M. he heard a hum, a motorized whine.

Airplanes!

Henry's heart leapt. He didn't stop to think what kind of planes, who might be flying them. To him, planes still meant freedom, a way home, helpful Americans. Henry darted into the open, searching the clouds for a formation. Maybe if he caught their attention they could radio back to base for help.

"Hey," he shouted, hearing his voice thunder again and again against the cliffs. "Over here!" He waved his hands over his head.

Way in the distance, a small plane was approaching. A small, solitary plane. Confused, Henry just stood, staring.

"*Baisse-toi, baisse-toi!*" The French teenager screamed at Henry. But Henry remained standing, mesmerized by the sound of a plane, the sound of rescue.

The French youth tackled Henry and dragged him, kicking, toward some scraggly bushes that thrust themselves up among the sea of wildflowers and boulders. The bushes engulfed them just in time. Looking up through them, Henry could make out a swastika on the underside of its wings as the plane passed overhead. He hung his head, mortified by his stupidity, overwhelmed with disappointment and the recognition that no American could help him here. It had probably been a reconnaissance plane, searching for *maquis* camps so that a Nazi squadron could come back and finish them off.

The teenager looked at Henry with contempt and spat, "*Je devrais te tuer maintenant.*"

Henry understood why the youth felt like killing him. But the teenager didn't pull out his gun. He just glared. Henry started to raise his fists, readying himself for a fight. But he thought better of it. He owed this guy an apology. He'd been a fool. "Sorry. *Je suis très stupide.*

Chapter Sixteen

Slowly, the youth's face lightened. *"Il est fou cet Americain. Tu dois me rendre une service. D'accord?"*

"A favor? You bet. Anything."

"Quand la guerre sera finie. Tu m'envoies un disque de Louis Armstrong."

Henry started to laugh. "Louis Armstrong? The trumpet player? You want a recording of him?"

"Oui, oui." The teenager turned out to be a serious trumpeter, who had studied in Paris with an orchestra leader. But his enthusiasm turned to sorrow as he spoke. *"Les Boches l'ont déporté. Mes parents m'ont envoyé à la campagne pour me protéger."*

His teacher had been deported to a work camp. His parents had sent him to a children's home in the Vercors countryside when the war started. But Henry didn't focus on how hard it must have been for the teenager to be sent away from home to strangers in the midst of the Nazi occupation. Henry still couldn't believe the boy's request. He didn't know that the French liked American music. And Louis Armstrong? Armstrong was one of his favorites. Henry started singing the song "I Can't Give You Anything But Love," in a low, raspy voice like Armstrong's.

The youth grinned and picked up an imaginary trumpet, humming the blues melody. *"Daaaa-ta-daaa-ta-daaa."* Henry kept the beat, pretending to conduct him as he'd seen big band leaders do. He could hear the trumpet, the trombone answering, and the slow backbeat of the drum set's cymbals. He could see his father singing that very song to Lilly in one of Clayton's rare but adoring displays of affection for her.

Henry and the budding trumpeter finished the song and smiled at each other, forgetting the fears of war. They got up and walked along the hill, continuing their jam with more Armstrong melodies.

At daybreak, they arrived atop the world. Henry gazed in wonder at the vast earth beneath him. He guessed they could see for thirty miles east, back toward where the world climbed into the Alps; thirty miles west, forward to a sloping sea of green pastures and fields of yellow. Any German convoy, any ox cart, for that matter, could be seen long before it became a threat.

"*Col de la Bataille,*" Henry's guide told him, forgetting their code of secrecy.

The *maquis* camp was buried in the woods, back from the peak's vantage point. They walked in without any challenge. Henry realized they'd probably been spotted and okayed long before they entered.

He was amazed by the size of the camp. Twenty or more parachutes were hung through the trees as makeshift tents. On its edge a man was ordering a dozen teenagers to roll under bushes and to dodge behind rocks. Looks like boot camp, Henry thought as he tried to understand their actions. Must be new recruits. Those boys looked even younger than his friend did.

Under one parachute, several men lay on blankets, limbs bandaged, eyes glazed, halfheartedly smoking ciga-rettes. Two young nurses were washing linens and giggling among themselves, like girls in the school play-ground. Near them was stacked a huge stockpile of guns, loaded and ready, boxes of grenades, plus plastics and wires for making explosives. Sitting idle was a large wireless radio, conspicuously marked: MADE IN BRITAIN.

His guide couldn't help but brag, explaining what Henry saw. He talked fast. But Henry did catch that the British and Americans were dropping more and more supplies and that they'd promised some sort of invasion soon. The *maquis* had even been asked to scrape out a real landing strip for large Allied planes.

Henry and his friend arrived at a small hut. *"Le chef,"* the guide said as he knocked. A thin man, maybe thirty-five years old, stepped out. His hair was dark and swept back like Rudolph Valentino's. He wore a turtleneck and blousy riding breeches. In the top of his riding boots was stuffed a Luger pistol he must have stolen off some German soldier. He had a daring, commanding look about him. He reminded Henry of the ace pilots they'd all admired so much back at base. The kind they'd been willing to fly through thunderclouds and a barrage of fighters for. The kind that they all believed could outrun Death and never be hit. But Henry knew better than that now. Dan's death had shown him that even the seemingly invincible could die. He faced the commander warily.

"Bonjour," the French leader greeted him. *"Cigarette?"* he offered as he lit one.

"Non, merci, monsieur."

There was a long silence as the man drew on his cigarette and looked Henry up and down. Henry prepared himself to be slugged again to corroborate his nationality. Instead the leader called his second in command. Henry was surprised to see a dark-skinned man appear. He must be from one of the French colonies in Africa, thought Henry.

"*Emmenez les autres,*" the chief told him.

His aide-de-camp disappeared. Henry waited. What others did he mean? Henry looked to his friend for help, but the teen looked away. Was he afraid of the commander, or just too in awe of him to ruin his surprise? Henry shifted from one foot to the other. He'd only been sent to the principal's once in his life. It had felt a lot like this.

Finally, he heard the *crunch, crunch, crunch* of boots approaching behind him.

"Well, I'll be damned."

Henry knew that voice. Who was it? Maybe Paul had made it out of their plane! Maybe Jimmy! Henry wheeled around with excitement.

It was Billy. Billy White.

Henry's smile froze for just a moment. There were so many people he would have been thrilled to see alive. Mouthy Billy White wasn't exactly his first choice. But Henry shook off his disappointment. It was a familiar face, another flier, another American.

"Hey, Billy," Henry said, stepping forward to shake Billy's hand. "I'm glad to see you in one piece." They shook hands for a long time, a very long time.

Billy was thinner. His left arm was in a sling and there was a thick, new, red scar running from his ear to his collarbone. His dark, wavy hair, before always immaculately combed, fell over his forehead in tangles. His brown eyes looked sunken. "I'm glad to see you, too, Hank. Where've you been all this time?"

Henry was aware of their being watched, closely. It was better to not say where. Hadn't Billy figured that out yet? "I'm not sure, Billy. Around and about. Hiding."

The *maquis* leader grunted. Did that mean approval? Did he understand English?

He addressed Henry in French. *"Vous connaissez cet homme?"*

"Oui, monsieur. Il s'appelle William White." Henry gathered his French for a moment to further identify himself and Billy. The month with Pierre had really helped Henry hone his skills. His accent might still be a dead giveaway that he was American, but at least his vocabulary had improved enough for the French to understand him. He explained that he and Billy had flown B-24s together.

The *maquis* leader looked to his aide, who nodded. *"Et cet homme?"*

Henry hadn't focused on the knot of men standing behind Billy. A young, blond stranger stepped forward. "B-Seventeens, Fifty-Sixth Bomb Group," he said in a clipped manner.

Henry hesitated a moment. Wasn't the 56th a fighter-plane unit? He was almost certain that the 56th was a Thunderbolt squadron that had protected his bomb group many times. He thought some more, but just couldn't remember for sure. The world of English bases seemed so long ago.

"B-Seventeens, you said?"

"That is correct," answered the blond pilot. "Most beautiful birds."

Henry hesitated. The guy's choice of words and pronunciation were odd, forced sounding, almost as if he were unsure of what he was trying to say. But then again on base Henry had heard lots of American accents and ways of speaking that he'd never heard growing up in rural Virginia. The pilot was probably from Boston or some other northern city, with more uppity manners.

Henry shook his head, but explained to the *maquis* chief that his not knowing the pilot didn't mean anything. There were many pilots, many bomb groups in England. There was no way he'd know all of them. He saw the stranger's face tighten.

The leader told Henry that no one had known the pilot or recognized his unit.

"Dog tags?" Henry asked.

"Non."

"Papers?" Henry thought of the counterfeit papers that Madame had provided him.

"Oui, les papiers sont parfaits," the chief said with a wry smile. He turned to Henry's guide and told him to get them something to eat. He added, *"Bientôt nous irons vers les Pyrénées. Il fait beau temps pour traverser les montagnes."* Then he disappeared into his hut. The *maquis* men dispersed, taking the stranger with them.

Henry's friend led them to a kitchen area.

"Damn, Hank. I didn't know they taught French down in the swamps of Virginia," Billy said, but only with a hint of the taunting that used to lace his jabs at Henry. "I

168

Chapter Sixteen

haven't been able to understand anything they've told me. None of these guys speak decent English. What'd the chief just say?"

"They're going to move us in a few days. To the Pyrenees. How long you been here?"

Billy rubbed his forehead. "Two weeks. Maybe three. I'm losing track of time. When I bailed out, I got stuck in a tree. Broke my arm and ripped my neck up so badly, I was sure I was going to bleed to death. I finally cut myself out of the parachute and fell. I whacked my head on something and passed out. When I woke up, I was in a field hospital in the woods, with a group like this. Farther north, I think. Then they moved me here, stuffed under hay in an oxcart. I've been itchy as hell to get going. The entire camp clears out at night. They don't tell me where they're going. Whether or not they're coming back. They jabber something at me, look threatening, and then disappear."

"Didn't they teach you any French at that fancy prep school of yours?" asked Henry. "What was its highfalutin name?"

"Choate."

"Choke?" Henry bantered. He couldn't help it. It was the way he'd always survived conversations with Billy. But he felt bad the instant it came out of his mouth.

To Henry's surprise, Billy laughed. "They taught me Latin because that's what Jefferson and Adams were taught. We were supposed to be great leaders like them. It was in our blood, they told us."

Henry and Billy took a bowl of soup and a slice of

bread and sat down on the ground to eat. The soup was little more than hot water laced with nettles that tasted like spinach.

"To tell you the truth," Billy continued, "I didn't learn a thing that's helped me over here. I'd have done a lot better scrounging around with chickens, like you, so at least I'd know how to find something in the dirt to eat. Look at this slop." Billy held his spoon up to let the thin liquid dribble back into the bowl.

Henry decided to ignore Billy's snobbery. He didn't want the French to think they were two spoiled kids, squabbling. He and Billy needed to stick together now. Besides, Billy didn't even seem to realize he'd insulted Henry again.

Still, he did warn him, "I wouldn't complain about the food, Billy. I think the French often go hungry to feed us. You should have seen the care my family took for me. There were lots of times—" Henry stopped himself. He couldn't trust Billy with Pierre and his mother. He had too big a mouth. Henry looked down into his soup. "They were good people. That's all."

Billy watched Henry eat. Then he said quietly, "You know, Hank, I've given you a hard time. When you're sent away to boarding school at thirteen, you have to pick on the younger guys to prove yourself. Guess I just didn't know how to break the habit. And the stupid thing is, I always hated school."

Henry nodded, accepting the apology. "Why didn't you go home?"

"Couldn't. Wasn't wanted."

Chapter Sixteen

"What do you mean?" Henry couldn't imagine his mother not wanting him.

Billy sighed. "Father was a commodities broker. When the stock market crashed, his partner jumped out of their office window. Dad's business collapsed. He had to quit his clubs, sell the house in Chestnut Hill for a quarter of what he'd paid for it. We moved into Mother's childhood country estate. That's where he drank himself to death. They say he died in a car crash, but I'm sure he drove off that bridge on purpose. Mother has been partying ever since, wearing her flapper dresses because she can't afford to buy anything new. She and my sisters keep up appearances so that at least one of them can marry rich. My grandfather paid my school bills to keep me out of the way. He had some money left because he'd never speculated in the market. And he managed to withdraw a lot of cash before all the banks shut down. But it's borrowed time. I was supposed to graduate and fix all that. Become a doctor or something socially acceptable that still earns a lot of money."

"So why are you here? Why aren't you at college?"

Billy sighed again. "I was flunking out, Hank. Besides, I didn't want to miss the fight, same as you." He paused and stirred his soup. "But I could have done with missing some of the things I've seen now, you know?"

A single gunshot interrupted Henry's answer. He and Billy jumped up, ready to run for cover. But no one else in the camp seemed bothered. Henry looked around for his guide. He spotted him, sitting unperturbed among other French teenagers, eating.

"Qu'est-ce que c'est?" Henry called.

The *maquis* boys all stopped eating to stare at him. His friend called back, *"L'étranger."*

"The stranger?"

"Oui, l'homme que vous n'avez pas reconnu." The youth explained that they'd been suspicious about the blond pilot for a while. He had shown up, out of nowhere, without a Resistance worker escort. English-speaking SS agents sometimes posed as downed airmen to infiltrate the *maquis.* Henry's not recognizing his unit had sealed the chief's decision. *"C'était un espion allemand. Nous n'avons pas de place pour des prisonniers ici."* The *maquis* youths went back to their soup.

A chill swept through Henry. That blond boy was dead on his word. Henry thought he was going to be sick.

Billy tugged on his sleeve. "What's wrong? What did he say? What's happened?"

"They shot that guy, Billy. The guy we didn't know. I can't believe it." Henry swayed with nausea. "They don't trust anybody. The Nazis have gotten into their groups too often, or people they grew up with have turned them in for a few bucks. They decided he was a German spy because of what I said. They can't hold many prisoners, on the run like they are. So they took him out and shot him as a spy. Just like that."

Chapter Seventeen

Around midnight the camp emptied. It began to rain, and Henry and Billy wrapped themselves in some spare parachutes to keep warm. "See what I mean?" Billy said through chattering teeth. "They come, they go. Try to sleep."

Hours later they were awakened by the *maquis* upon their return. The camp swarmed. Wagons pulled by plow horses lumbered in, led by farmers. They were laden with four long gray canisters, tubes about the size and shape of torpedoes.

"*Parachutages,*" Henry's guide explained. It was the first one he had been allowed to help with. He told Henry all about it. Two British planes had completed a drop. All the canisters were recovered.

Often the drops didn't go as well. Canisters got stuck in trees or Nazis patrols followed the sound of plane motors and the *maquis* had to scatter before gathering a thing. Once, by using homing devices hidden in a repair truck to track French radio signals, the Germans had captured one of the *maquis* group's radio operators. The Gestapo had tortured codes out of him. The Nazis then used the codes to signal the British to drop supplies right into their trap. The Germans recovered all the supplies and shot down the plane. This night, however, had been a complete success.

It took six men, heaving and slipping in the rain, to drag each canister off its cart onto the ground. When the *maquis* cracked them open, they yanked out guns, boxes of ammunition, counterfeit francs, and British chocolate and cigarettes. The chocolate and cigarettes caused the most excitement.

Henry helped. Billy stood watching, his bad arm making him worthless for the work. He fidgeted and finally blurted out to the chief's aide-de-camp: "You know, I'm capable of doing something around here. You guys keep me in the dark, ignore me. I'm just as good as old farmboy here."

Henry couldn't believe Billy. Did they really have to compete here?

The man smiled and replied in perfect, upper crust English. "I am certain that we can find something appropriate for your talents, Pilot. Tomorrow."

The next morning the aide-de-camp prodded Billy awake with his boot. He carried two buckets. "You and your friend can collect dinner," he said. He pointed to the ground at a slowly moving shell. The rain had brought out snails.

Chapter Seventeen

"*Escargots*," the Frenchman said. "Fill the buckets."

Henry groaned and got up to take his bucket. He knew this was punishment for Billy's rude outburst. What a jerk. Hadn't being on the run, at the mercy of strangers' pity and courage, taught him anything?

"This is disgusting," Billy complained as he picked up the snails and dropped them into his pail with a little plink.

"I wouldn't gripe if I were you, Billy," Henry warned him. "We're only doing this because of what you said last night. Keep at it and we'll probably have to clean their outhouse."

Most of the snails were to be found on rocks or under bushes. Henry couldn't help but marvel at them, their delicate shells with a whorl of red-brown stripes. He was less impressed with their glistening bodies, which stuck to the rocks. How could you bring yourself to eat these slimy things? he wondered.

He remembered Madame Gaulloise raving about frogs' legs. He'd laughed at the thought of his ma trying to fry up some of the bullfrogs he used to cart home from the creek in his pockets. He straightened up and said, more to himself than to Billy, "What I wouldn't give right now for a plate of Ma's fried chicken."

"So what was it like, farmboy, eating chickens you'd raised?"

Henry thought a moment before answering. "Well, Billy, there's real satisfaction in being able to take care of yourself; to raise everything you need; not having to worry about whether you've got enough money to buy food or if the stores are going to have food to sell. I thought I'd never go back to farming when I finished college. But after all this," his voice trailed off for a moment, "farming looks pretty good."

"Hard work, though, isn't it?"

"Sure. But it's honest work. We have twenty hen-houses. One hundred hens per house. Each house needs two buckets of clean water morning and evening. How good's your math, Billy?"

Billy looked up and made a silly grin, playing the idiot. "Let's see . . . that's eighty buckets a day."

"That's right. Eighty five-gallon buckets to fill and haul, seven days a week. Chickens don't know about Sundays or holidays. So that's five hundred sixty buckets a week; a little over twenty-nine thousand buckets per year. When I figured that out in third grade, I thought I'd about die."

"Didn't your old man help?"

"He had his own chores. While I was hauling water in the morning, he'd be milking the cows, feeding them and the mules, mucking out the stalls. He'd help me collect eggs in the afternoon, after school. If they were laying well, there'd be a thousand eggs a day."

"A thousand eggs! Where did you put them all?"

"We stored them in the basement until the next morning when Dad delivered them to the grocery store just inside Richmond. Planting season was the toughest, though, because we had all that work added on to taking care of the chickens. We tilled about thirty acres and planted watermelons, cantaloupe, strawberries, corn, and green beans. It's sandy soil. Takes lots of turning and manure to plant well."

"Manure?" Billy looked at Henry with disgust. "You put animal poop around vegetables?"

Henry laughed. "It's composted with pine needles so it's not raw manure, Billy. Composted manure is the best fertilizer there is."

"No wonder you farm boys stink."

"We provide food for your fancy, linen-covered tables, White. Somehow I don't see you out hoeing or weeding."

Billy put his hands up. "All right, all right. Don't get in a swivet. Who'd you hire to pick it all?"

"Pshaw, Billy. You really don't know anything. There wasn't money to hire help. Oh, once in a while a hobo would wander up off the Richmond–Norfolk line. Ma would take pity on him and let him work for food. We found out they kept drawing a cat on our barn with chalk to leave word for other hobos that there was a nice lady living there. So one summer we had a whole bunch. But mostly Dad and I did all the work. I hated to pick green beans worst of all. The bushes grow knee-high. There's no way to pick the beans except to bend over and do it by hand. It used to take me about three hours to pick one row out of ten. Felt like I'd been horsewhipped by the time I was done. And the sun gets mighty hot in July in Tidewater Virginia. I was always relieved when school started, 'cause then I wouldn't have to work so hard."

"Funny. I always hated it when school started," said Billy. "I spent my summers lifeguarding at the country club. That was heaven."

Henry imagined so. He'd never even been in a proper swimming pool before boot camp. But he loved swimming, just the same. "You know, Pats and I had this swimming hole down by Four Mile Creek." Henry stopped short. Billy had always ridiculed Patsy. He wasn't up for that. He went silent.

"Go on, Hank," said Billy. "I'd like to hear more. Makes looking for slugs go faster."

"Well," Henry continued cautiously, "it was about a half mile up from where the creek emptied into the James and turned wild with current. The water was real sweet, clear and deep at our hole. Spring beauties popped up all over the creek bank in spring, and by fall there was a soft carpet of moss. There was a big willow hanging over it. Dad had actually hung a tire swing there for me."

Henry stopped searching the ground and just stood, relishing the memory of his childhood's happiest moments. "I'd climb up to the fourth big branch, about fifteen feet up, dragging the tire with me. I'd launch from there. I'd swoop back and forth, back and forth, just above the water. The best part was letting go on the third or fourth swing, before the arc got too low, and dropping into that cool water, *kersplunk*, just like a happy bullfrog. Lord, that was good. Patsy would be right behind me, swinging just as high. When she hit the water we'd have a splashing contest. She had to work about as hard on her farm as I did. Lots of little brothers to help tend to. Those afternoons were such a wonderful break."

"So, did you two ever fool around down there?"

Henry frowned. He had kissed Patsy by the water

hole, last summer, right before graduation. He hadn't planned to. He'd been telling her his plans to join the Air Corps, and she just looked so beautiful, so worried about him and proud at the same time, he'd kissed her, a good long time. It'd been pretty wonderful, too.

That had been the beginning, the beginning of that ache for Patsy. She'd written him that she'd gone down to their swimming hole since he'd left to relive that kiss—*I felt the moonlight creep over me and pretended the touch of the cool light was your hand. I could feel your arms pull me against you, slowly at first, then strong, pressing us into one being, the way I had always hoped to feel your arms embrace me before and pray to feel them again*. . . . The letter was falling apart along its crease because Henry had reread that passage so often. He wasn't about to spoil that kiss by gossiping about it with Billy White.

Henry considered what Billy had told him about his own life. If his mother and sisters had treated him so coldly, no wonder Billy had such a lopsided view of women. Funny how knowing a little about someone made it easier to stomach their flaws. Henry decided to make light of it. "Well, if I had, I wouldn't be telling you about it. How full is your bucket?"

Less than half. Henry's was full.

"My father would have made mud pies outta you, Billy," Henry laughed good-naturedly, still warmed by the thought of Patsy. "Here, give it to me." He took the bucket from him and started filling it with snails. "You know, when I was about ten I passed out from the heat in the field. Must have been a hundred plus that day, and the humidity around the James can make you feel like you're sucking in syrup for air. When I came to I started vomiting. Couldn't finish the day's work. Probably had heatstroke. Dad called me a fool for not drinking water and said if I couldn't pull my own weight around the farm then I couldn't eat. I wasn't allowed dinner that night. Dad said that'd remind me to carry water."

"You're kidding."

"Nope. Ma snuck me some bread and milk later that night. She wouldn't talk to Dad for days."

"Pretty tough old bird, Hank."

"Yeah, he is."

"At least he cared enough to ride you," Billy said quietly. "My father didn't even bother to talk to me at breakfast the morning he drove off that bridge. He sat right across from me, staring into his orange juice, as if I didn't even exist, knowing he was going to kill himself in thirty minutes. I didn't matter to him at all."

They started back to camp and Henry mulled over Billy's comment. He went a ways before adding thoughts that his time spent walking alone, scared, had brought him about Clayton. "Dad's a good farmer. He never gives up. He kept us from going hungry when a lot of families in the county bellied up in the Depression. I'm not sure if the Depression made him so tough, or if he survived the Depression because he was that tough to begin with. But I see how that happens now. I've already thought and done some things since being over here I'm not proud of, but had to do." Henry had also begun to understand how difficult it might be to shed a tough attitude or a wary distrust of people once the bad times were over.

He added more to himself than to Billy, "Sometimes it's almost like Dad's in my head. There've been a couple of moments that mean voice of his has kicked me out of trouble. I just don't want to come out of the war as hard as he is."

His thoughts made him uneasy, and Henry shut off the topic of Clayton with an offhand statement. "Anyway, boot camp was easy after growing up under the hand of Clayton Forester. Let's get these slugs back to camp."

That night they ate escargots. Grilled over the fires, the snails had a nutty flavor that surprised Henry. Billy only nibbled at them, but Henry followed the lead of his teenage guide, sucking the snails out of their shell with a hearty slurp. When they were done, the aide-de-camp approached.

"Time to go," he said, and motioned for Billy and Henry to follow.

At the edge of the camp sat a delivery van. Two more fliers were waiting beside it. They were changing out of British flight gear into plain clothes. They looked shaken and scared. They must have just come down, thought Henry. He smiled and greeted them.

"Wow. Where did you get the van?" Billy asked.

The aide-de-camp turned on him. "You ask too many questions. I told the chief that you were a risk, too curious, that if you ever got caught, you would betray us. But the chief has decided to trust you. Do not disappoint him. Forget you have been here."

Billy slunk into the back of the van, like a dog smacked with newspaper.

Henry shook the aide's hand. "*Merci, monsieur.* Billy's okay, really." Then he took a chance. "*Monsieur,* I know I am not supposed to ask, but my family, the boy and his mother . . . well . . . do you know if she is all right?"

The aide hesitated then answered. "The ambush failed. Two men died in the shooting. She survived the interrogation. She revealed no one. We think she was taken to Ravensbrück."

"Ravensbrück?"

"A German prison camp for women near Berlin. Political prisoners and deported Jews are sent there. It might as well be hell. We cannot get to her."

Henry's heart sank. What were her chances of survival? If the prison life didn't kill her, Allied bombs meant for Berlin might. Henry struggled to respond. "Thank you, *monsieur,* for telling me. No one could ever get anything out of me about them."

The aide's face was grim. "See that they don't. Or I will find you myself. Get in."

As Henry climbed up, he heard feet running toward the van.

"*Au revoir, Louis,*" called his guide.

Grinning, Henry jumped down to say good-bye and promised that when the war was over, he'd send him that record of Louis Armstrong.

The teenage trumpeter smiled and nodded. "*Louis Armstrong, oui.*"

Both of them became serious. "How will I find you?"

Henry asked. He repeated his question in French.

The youth was silent a moment. *"Vivant, je l'espère."*

Henry climbed into the van, joining the three other fliers, and bolted its door shut. The van sputtered into the night.

"What did the kid say?" Billy asked.

"I asked him how I would find him after the war to repay a debt I owe him. And his answer was that he hoped I would find him alive." Henry's voice broke on the final words. He stared out the tiny back window at the retreating mountain.

Ravensbrück. Even the name sounded awful. Did Pierre know his mother's fate? Was he still safe? Maybe the fact she had already been deported kept her son safer somehow. If the Milice no longer needed him to coerce her, surely they wouldn't bother to hunt down a small boy.

Henry hung his head and rubbed his face. Pierre and his mother, Madame, the teenage guide, the old school-teacher—their faces whirled through his head. He'd never known the potential finality of a good-bye before now. Even when he'd held his trembling mother, as he left for England, Henry had been completely convinced that he'd be back, that they'd be eating many a Thanksgiving and Christmas dinner together talking about his adventures. These people—these people who'd risked their lives to save him—he'd never see them again. He felt it in his bones, like an awful ache.

Chapter Eighteen

They bounced through the black night. There was no knowing for sure where they were going in the back of the windowless van. But Henry could tell from the angle of the vehicle that they were heading down the mountains, he assumed to the valley west of camp.

Coal was heaped in the corner of the van's cabin. As the van jolted along, pieces of coal fell off the pile and bounced around like popcorn on a hot griddle.

"What do they need coal for?" Billy asked with irritation one time a lump of it hopped into his lap.

Henry shook his head. Billy'd never figure out how to make things work without directions. If nothing else, Clayton had taught Henry how to think quick, how to improvise. Clayton had been a wizard at jerry-rigging farm machinery. He'd even managed to generate their own supply of electricity with a windmill, pulleys, and a reconfigured truck engine.

Chapter Eighteen

Henry almost pitied Billy. He had obviously known some hard times, but they hadn't strengthened him much. Would Billy have the stoicism to walk over the Pyrenees? Or would he whine and drag his feet? If he and Billy found themselves in a situation that called for a split-second, life-or-death decision, could Billy stay calm and think fast? If the answer to all those questions was no, he'd be a real liability.

Henry had figured out the coal pile immediately. "They're running the van off it," Henry explained aloud. "They can't get gasoline. The Nazis have it all. They've converted the van to coal. Like a steam engine train. That's why it's slow. But it beats walking, right, Billy?"

Billy shrugged.

"Sure does, mate," agreed one of the RAF pilots, clapping Billy on the back to shore him up.

The night turned to dawn and the van lurched into a barn. Not until the barn doors were closed and locked were the pilots allowed to come out of the van.

They were handed milk, cheese, and bread, and told to sleep. Their French driver left.

As he chewed, Henry peeped through a chink in the barn's old walls. The land was flat here. He could see the mountains they'd just left shooting up in the azure sky far away. Before him stretched acres and acres of tightly packed golden sunflowers. They were tall as corn, and their huge yellow faces all turned together toward the sun. Henry had never seen such a beautiful crop.

He wondered what was growing at home. "It's June, right?" Henry asked aloud.

"That's right," replied one of the British officers,

surprised. "The sixteenth. We were shot down just a few days ago. How long you been missing, Yank, that you don't know the date?"

Henry caught Billy's eyes before answering. No need for the Brits to have any information that could jeopardize them somehow. "Too long. I'd hoped to be home by now."

"Then you don't know."

"Know what?"

"The invasion's begun. Allied troops just landed on the beaches of France a week ago. It's not just our air war anymore. We've got boys on the ground now, too."

Henry sat back on his heels. He could hardly believe it. Finally. It's what he and everyone in his combat unit had been fighting for, dying for. Ground troops. With tanks and infantry to worry about, surely the Nazis wouldn't care about a few lost boys wandering around. He'd get home soon.

They bounced through southern France for two more nights, twice exchanging vans and drivers. Henry could make out fields of lavender, hills of vineyards. They passed through a city called Montpellier. Henry began to see flat, white beaches and marshes. Once he spotted what looked like a herd of wild, cream-colored horses, but in the moonlight they looked more like spirits from another world.

At the third day's dawning, they came to an abrupt halt beside a tall, stone wall. The driver kept the motor idling. Another man entered the back of the van. He was

British, a Special Operations agent, parachuted in to work with the French. He quickly briefed them: "We are waiting for two more pilots they're bringing on the night train from Lyon. We are in Narbonne. Usually we would take you through Perpignan to Céret. But our contact there has disappeared. We think the Gestapo got him."

"How is the invasion going?" interrupted one of the RAF pilots.

The British officer answered crisply, "Best not to think about it. They're not much past the beaches yet. You're on your own for a bit longer."

He gave out hand-drawn maps, rough squiggles of compass-point directions through mountain passes.

"We will drive you to Carcassonne. You'll walk from Carcassonne to Quillan. Then from Quillan you will cross the Pyrenees through Andorra to get into Spain. This is our longest but safest ratline. It will take six to eight days to cross. The hardest part is from Quillan to Andorra. Some of that march is snow covered, even now.

"Your guide is new to us. Be careful. He is Basque, more Spanish than French. He was a smuggler during the Spanish Civil War. We think he carried mostly for the Republican side, so he shouldn't have too much love for a Fascist like Hitler. He's also been well paid by His Majesty to guide you. But do keep an eye on him."

The officer distributed small knapsacks containing food and lanterns.

"It is most dangerous at the Spanish frontier. It's crawling with German patrols. No fires. No matter how cold it is. No talking either.

"Mind that you don't get caught. If you are, you will be tortured to reveal everything you can about our French friends. Then you will be shot. Good luck."

With that he closed the doors.

Ten minutes later, two new men hopped into the van. It roared off. They barely spoke English. They were Russians, shot down in Italy. Resistance workers there had gotten them into France. They were husky and strong-looking. They might not speak English worth a lick, thought Henry, but he was glad to have some guys with brawn joining them. He and Billy had always been slight because of their youth, but now they were winnowed down to complete lightweights. Billy's arm was still in a sling. He couldn't tell about the muscle power of the Brits. None of them had weapons. What were they supposed to do if challenged?

It took the day to drive to Carcassonne. At twilight, they got off the van at a farmhouse next to a river. Their driver left them beside a haystack. The Brits and Russians paced, unused to the torment of waiting, waiting, without instructions or any idea of what was coming next.

At least I've gotten more used to that, thought Henry. He recognized that he was again the youngest of the young men. But in this situation, for the first time since being shipped over to England, he had the advantage of experience on them. "Relax," he said. "Save your strength. They'll come. They always do."

Around midnight, a man materialized out of the shadows. He was small, wiry, with a craggy face and few teeth inside his grin. Henry was certain he saw a smile creep over the man's unattractive face as he counted them up and muttered, "Six," in French.

"*Allons-y.*" He motioned for them to follow.

They walked, single file, with Henry repeatedly dragging Billy into the cover of shadows.

Within an hour, the land began to surge upward at a steady incline. Henry could hear the others begin to breathe heavily in the thinning air. They tripped on rocks and stumbled with resounding thuds and curses to the rocky ground.

"Shhhhh," Henry cautioned.

They climbed all night, resting only once. By daybreak they were atop a horizon of billowing peaks. To the south they could see snowcapped mountains jutting brutishly up into the sky, thousands of feet higher than where they now stood, winded and bruised.

Billy whistled. "You've got to be kidding me. They think we can walk over that? Isn't there another way to do this?"

"No, there isn't, Yank," snapped one of the Brits. His pants were torn, his knees bloody from the falls he'd taken in the dark.

"You sure know how to make friends, Billy," Henry said. "Sit down and be quiet."

Squeezed between boulders to shield them from view, they slept through the day.

The next night winds attacked them. Blasting down the slopes, gales scraped their faces and pushed them over. Henry bent forward, virtually crawling up the rocky trail, to brace himself against their force. Only when the group traveled through the sparse pine groves did they get any relief from the roaring winds.

Their guide seemed unperturbed by it all. He often stood on a crag, waiting impatiently for them to scramble up to him. More than once he spat in contempt, watching them struggle.

Their line straggled now. The Russians went first, the Brits following at a considerable distance. Even farther back, Henry waited for Billy. Many times Henry half lifted Billy along. By night's end, he no longer could spot their guide. He kept his eye on the back of the slower RAF pilot.

The third night, melting, muddy snow added to their miseries. The rocks were icy and slick. Once one of the Brits fell and skidded down the ridge, taking Henry and then Billy with him in a tumble of pilots. Billy finally stopped their slide down the mountain by crashing into a boulder.

"Jesus Christ!" Billy cried, clutching his arm. "I can't do this anymore, Hank. I can't. I've got to rest."

Henry stood up and saw the guide making his way down to them.

"He's got to rest," Henry explained. "He's hurt."

The guide shook his head and growled at Henry to move on, to leave Billy if he couldn't hold up: *"S'il ne peut pas tenir le coup, abandonne-le."* He pointed to the crest of rocks above them. *"Marchez maintenant."*

The British pilot picked himself up and said to Henry,

Chapter Eighteen

"Come on, Yank. Leave him. We can't jeopardize five because one gent can't hack the climb."

Henry looked at Billy and lied to encourage him. "The guide says we're almost to the safe house, Billy. It's just a little further. There will be food and a warm bed there. You can do it. I'll help you."

"I can't, Hank. I can't do it. Can't we rest a little while?" Billy's voice cracked.

"*Allez. Vite,*" snarled the guide.

Henry stood his ground. Billy was a complete pain in the neck. They were all tired, weren't they? But Henry couldn't abandon him. He'd never find his own way. He'd eaten all his food. He'd die in the mountains. "I'm staying with him. Go ahead. We'll follow."

The guide stepped toward Henry threateningly. Then he laughed and called them dead men. He turned and climbed away.

The RAF pilot hesitated. "I'll slow him down, if I can, Yank. Try to catch up. Follow our tracks in this mess. See you in Barcelona."

Only the wind kept them company now—wind and the black night and the fear of a Nazi patrol. Henry fought the urge to slap Billy into action. He waited half an hour, then he whispered, "We've got to go, Billy. If we leave now, we may be able to catch up with them."

"A little longer," moaned Billy.

"Look, Billy," Henry tried logic, "their map only shows where the passes are. It doesn't tell where to pick up the next contact. If we lose this guide for good, we may never find the person to take us to the U.S. embassy in Spain."

Billy dropped his head on his knees and said melodramatically, "You go on without me, farm boy. I won't live to tell anyone you deserted me."

Henry saw red. "Get up off your sorry ass, you stupid piece of dirt. I didn't have to wait for you at all. I'm not about to die here after what I've been through and after all that people have sacrificed to save me because some lazy, spoiled Yankee good-for-nothing hasn't got the guts to get up and walk."

Billy's head popped up.

Henry gasped. He sounded just like Clayton. But it was working. He'd gotten Billy's attention all right. Henry went for it: *"Get up now!"*

Half dragging him, Henry forced Billy up the mountain. He hissed stern encouragement, "One step at a time, White. One step at a time. We'll make it. You and me. Then when we get home I'm gonna take you to the farm and whup your butt to make you a real man. Introduce you to my ma and Patsy, women worth knowing. One step at a time, Billy. You and me."

Billy said nothing. He just clung to Henry and climbed.

When they reached the top of the ridge, Henry let go of Billy. He was exhausted from pulling himself and Billy up the rocks. He bent over, hands on his knees, to catch his breath. Both of them were heaving, making great clouds of mist in the frigid air.

As their breathing slowly quieted, Henry could make

out voices down below on the other side of the ridge. The guide and other pilots must have stopped to rest. "Come on, Billy. They're waiting for us. Betcha that old guide has pulled out some food he stored up here. Let's go."

In the moonlight, Billy smiled weakly. "Okay, Hank. I'll follow you."

Henry and Billy hurried down the other side of the ridge more on the seats of their pants than their feet. Henry's relief made him reckless. He followed the sound of voices without really listening to them. He was just a few pine trees from the group when he recognized what he was hearing. There was the French guide's voice. But what answered it was not English. It was German.

Henry froze and dropped to the ground, yanking Billy down beside him. From the ground he squinted into the gloom. There were four German soldiers, guns up and pointed. There were the other pilots—one, two, three, four—hands on their heads.

There was the guide. A fifth Nazi, an officer, was handing him something. Henry gasped. It was a wad of money. The bastard had turned the pilots over for a nice fat reward.

Now the guide was talking. Henry could just barely hear him, "*Et encore deux autres,*" he pointed back toward the ridge, back toward where Henry and Billy hugged the ground.

The officer dispatched two of the soldiers.

"Billy, they're coming for us. Crawl that way, quick." Henry pushed Billy hard.

The two of them shimmied across the ground, fast as lizards, terror finally invigorating Billy. They scooted under one tree then another then another. Henry shot in front to lead them.

Behind him, he heard something catch on a low branch. Must be Billy's sling. Henry turned around to tell him not to struggle, that it would make too much noise. But he was too late.

Panicked, Billy yanked hard. The sling held tight, the branch rustled wildly, then cracked.

The sound led the Nazis right to them.

Bullets exploded in the trees nearby as the German soldiers shot into the grove of pines. Henry put his hands over his head to protect himself against the *whizz* of bullets.

Henry heard shouts, more gunshots, then the sound of men struggling. He looked up and saw the Russians striking the Nazis, grabbing at their guns.

"Come on, Billy! Now's our chance."

Henry and Billy crawled, lunged, threw themselves through the underbrush.

"Hier entlang!" German voices yelled.

Henry could hear feet running after them.

"Hurry, Billy," he urged. "Move!"

There were more shots, too loud, too close, and then Billy screamed and collapsed, writhing. "I'm hit, Hank. Oh, God. Hank, help me!"

Henry grabbed Billy around his chest. He pulled, pulled hard, and dragged Billy through the thicket. Henry could hear the running feet nearing.

"Hier entlang!"

Billy was dead weight, getting heavier each second.

"Leave me, Hank," Billy's voice gurgled. It sounded

like he was choking on something. "Go on, I mean it."

"No," Henry answered, grunting and lurching. "We're both going home."

If he could just make it to that slope over there, they could slide down on their backs and lose themselves in the rocks below. He could hide Billy and try to jump one of the soldiers. He could bash in a Nazi head with a loose stone. The Russians looked to have killed at least one. The Brits had to be fighting as well. They could do this. Just a little farther.

"Hank," Billy reached up and grabbed Henry's collar. "Leave me. I'm dying." Billy's voice was calm.

"No," Henry gritted his teeth. He hadn't saved Dan or Pierre's mother. He would be haunted by them the rest of his life. Come hell or high water or Hitler himself he was determined to take Billy with him.

Concentrating on the ledge ahead of him, Henry lost his footing. He fell on top of Billy. As he pushed himself up he saw that Billy's face was awash in blood that flowed from his mouth. Billy still gripped his collar. Henry could tell that even though his eyes looked up, Billy could no longer see him.

"Hank," Billy's voice was no louder than a breath. "Let go of me. Get home to that pretty girl of . . ." Billy's hand fell away.

He was dead.

With a sob, Henry tried to lift himself up to run, run for his own life. But something cold on his neck stopped him—something cold and sharp.

It was the barrel of a German gun.

Chapter Nineteen

Henry stared at the stiff upright collar of the Gestapo officer standing in front of him. His eyes were so swollen from the beating he'd received from the border patrol that he couldn't lift them to assess the man's face. His voice was cold, though. Cold and frighteningly amused by Henry.

He laughed when Henry had frowned, confused, at the clip of the Gestapo's British accent. "Four years at Cambridge," he informed Henry. "So you see, you cannot hope to play word games with me, American. My English vocabulary is probably better than yours."

The hair on Henry's neck bristled as he listened to the gags and wrenching coughs of the Russian in the next room. What were they doing to that poor guy? Grimly, Henry recognized he'd probably find out firsthand.

Only Henry and this one Russian had been caught alive. Billy, one RAF flier, and the other Russian pilot were left dead and unburied on the Pyrenees. One German soldier and the guide who had betrayed them lay rotting there, too. One among them, a Brit, had managed to escape. He had probably made it to the Spanish frontier within a few hours. They'd actually been very close to Andorra when arrested—a point the Gestapo officer had delighted in taunting Henry with.

Henry was now back deep inside German-occupied France, near Toulouse, in a chateau converted to a prison. He'd been left for a day, in an unlit, subterranean chamber, most likely a root cellar when the mansion had been a home, now fittingly like a tomb. At first Henry had edged his way around the cell, hands to its dirt walls, counting the perimeter. Six feet by five feet.

What would the area be, Mr. Forester? Henry tried to remember the sound of his math teacher's drawl, the big open windows in his elementary school, days when Henry had felt he would live forever.

Before long the terrifying reality of his situation began to seep through Henry, strangling his resolve. He sank to the floor to recite Sunday school prayers, there in the damp blackness. But the words wouldn't come. He closed his eyes and whispered, "Pray for me, Ma. I know God listens to you." His teeth chattered. He wondered how much death could hurt.

By the time his captors dragged him out and up to this stark room for his first interrogation, Henry was already terrified—an effect he realized had been the purpose of leaving him in the dark for so long.

Henry was tied down to a chair. Two guards stood by

the door. There was one table, one chair behind it, and a tin washtub in the corner. The Gestapo officer could tell Henry was unnerved by the sounds coming through the wall. He came to the front of the table, sat against it, and said with chilling sarcasm, "Goodness, what's that? Sounds like a man drowning, doesn't it?" He pointed to the deep washtub. "See that over there? We call that the bathtub. Your head goes in it—over and over and over again—however long it takes for me to get the information I want. How long can you hold your breath? A minute? Two minutes? The Slavic pig next door is not looking very well. It is becoming harder and harder for him to catch his breath."

The Nazi circled Henry as he talked, that cold voice in Henry's left ear, behind his skull, now to his right ear. "I would hate for you to have to go through that. All I need is the name of your French contacts. Their whereabouts. Even a description of their captain. It is no use pretending that you know nothing of what I am talking about. The guide the French assassins hired to take you into Spain— he was one of our agents. So, what will it be, American?"

Henry ground his teeth and reached inside his soul for courage. He thought of the times he felt like Clayton had yelled at him just for fun, how he'd stuck out his jaw and taken it then. Henry struggled to lift his face and open his bruised and bloodied eyes to glare back at the Gestapo officer. "Henry Wiley Forester, second lieutenant American Air Forces, serial number 092—"

The Gestapo officer smiled wickedly. He reached into his pocket and pulled out a thick fistful of American dog tags. He rattled them in Henry's face. "I should have told you—what did you call yourself? Second Lieutenant Henry Wiley Forester?—you won't be needing serial numbers or dog tags. I've collected so many from dead Americans already. Souvenirs of my work." He threw the tags into the corner with a clatter.

"The Geneva Convention will do nothing for you here. You have been with the *maquis*, therefore I am free of restrictions. Your government, your family, will never even know what happened to you. Now, shall we try again? I want the whereabouts of your French contacts."

Henry said nothing.

"Oh, good," sneered the Nazi. "I'd hate for our games to end prematurely."

He snapped his fingers. Two guards dragged Henry and his chair to the tub.

It lasted two days. At first, when they shoved him down into the dirty water, Henry closed his eyes and tried to pretend it was his swimming hole back home. He tried to imagine the sound of Patsy's laugh as they splashed and dove in the clear, sweet coolness. He tried to imagine the smell of summer in Virginia.

Each time they jerked him back up and Henry fought to swallow air, he wondered if the next submerging would kill him, if this breath would be his very last. But he refused to cry out. He barricaded himself with anger. These men weren't human. These men were enjoying this. He hated them as he had hated nothing before. No matter how mean his father had seemed at times, he'd been nothing like this. Nothing.

The last hour of the second day, Henry was sure he was going to die. The guards held him under longer and longer, until Henry began to black out each time. They'd yank him back up into oxygen at the very last moment before his heart was going to explode. But finally, Henry could tell his body was giving out. The guards thrust him under as he coughed and gasped, no time to take a breath and hold it.

Under the water he could hear Patsy calling him. He saw her swimming toward him and motioning for him to follow her somewhere. Henry no longer felt the arms holding him down. He drifted through the water, up toward the sun.

Henry became conscious in a different room, lashed to a different chair. His hair and clothes were still wet. He coughed and coughed and coughed.

The door opened and in strode the Gestapo officer. On a leash he led a huge dog that strained against its line, snapping and snarling. It seemed to have no hair, no tail. Its muzzle was massive, grotesque, lathered with angry slobber. Its ears were cropped into thin points.

In one hand, the Nazi carried a large bone grizzled with raw meat. He sat down opposite Henry and smirked. At that level, Henry could see the Gestapo officer's face. It was fair, sleek and sharp. His eyes were almost color-less, their blue was so light. His mouth was thin and twisted with hatred. Henry could never imagine that face smiling a genuine smile. Could never imagine it as a child's face.

Chapter Nineteen

"This is my Doberman," said the Nazi. He gave the leash a sudden jerk. The dog sat and became motionless. "He has been trained very, very well. He will kill on command. Would you care to see what he can do with a bone?"

He threw the meat shank into Henry's lap. The dog followed it with its eyes. Hungry drool dripped from its mouth. But it remained motionless.

"*Nimm Futter!*" the Gestapo officer ordered quietly, letting go of the leash.

The dog lunged with a snarl at Henry's lap and snapped up the bone. Growling and slobbering, it tore the leg apart at Henry's feet. Henry's heart raced as he listened to its powerful jaws crack the thick bone and rip off the flesh. Within ten minutes the dog had consumed almost all the shank. Speed would have worked on a bone that size for days, thought Henry. He looked back up at the Nazi, his eyes narrowed, waiting.

The Gestapo officer nodded. "Your courage is impressive. But ultimately it is pointless. I will break you."

He stood up and leaned over to whisper in Henry's ear. "At the last moment you American boys always sob for your mamas, just like babies."

He straightened up. "For now, I am going to leave you to think things over. In fact, I think I'll take off those ropes. They look so uncomfortable. But first," he whistled one short blast and commanded, "*Pass auf!*" The Doberman jumped away from its bone and sat down directly in front of Henry.

The Gestapo officer untied Henry, cautioning, "He is

on alert now. He will kill you if you move from that chair. Don't doze off either, because he may interpret any kind of movement as an attempt to get up. And we have seen how much he enjoys ripping things apart."

The Nazi opened the door. "I don't think I'll even bolt this. An escape would be exciting revenge on me, wouldn't it? The guards will probably be asleep at their post later. My, my, it is tempting, isn't it?"

The door slammed shut.

Escape. Was it possible? Had the bastard really left the door unlocked? Or was it just a trick?

Henry assessed the Doberman. How'd that Nazi train this dog to be so vicious? His body didn't look broken from beating. Was he starving him? Or was the dog really the devil hound that it looked, simply born evil?

Still, there hadn't been an animal around the farm— ornery mule, stupid cow, or fusspot rooster—that Henry hadn't been able to tame by talking to it right. He'd give it a go. What did he have to lose?

Escape. Just a few feet away from him, down the hall, and out into air. Was it really possible?

"Hey, boy, nice boy, you want to be friends?" Henry asked in a smooth, low voice.

The dog growled, deep in its throat.

Henry frowned. He shifted his foot, just an inch, to see what the dog would do.

The growl grew louder. The dog curled its jowls back over his teeth, so they all showed, gleaming, sharp, and lethal.

Chapter Nineteen

"Okay, fella, okay. Easy. Easy, now. That's a nice boy, handsome boy," Henry kept crooning at the dog, his voice soft and soothing.

He'd need to wait a few hours anyway. Until the guards were sleepy. Wouldn't do any good to charm the killer dog to walk straight out to watchful Nazi guards. For all he knew that Gestapo sadist was sitting right outside the door.

Henry's body ached. His lungs burned from inhaled water. His head and eyes throbbed with pain. His stomach growled with hunger. But he didn't move, not a flinch. He couldn't, if he wanted to live. Not until he had mesmerized the dog with his voice.

Henry talked to it and talked to it. All the while the Doberman rumbled with a threatening growl.

Finally, when the room had grayed then blackened with nightfall, the dog had stopped snarling. In the dimness, Henry could see the Doberman begin to prick up his ears at his voice. Was it beginning to trust Henry?

The remains of the bone still lay at Henry's feet. He nudged it toward the dog. It snapped and barked at Henry, but it also foamed at the mouth with anticipation of tearing into the fatty grizzle. He is starving, thought Henry. If I can get him to go for the bone, as if I'm rewarding him, maybe he'll let me get up.

"It's okay, boy. Go on, eat it. It's for you," Henry encouraged. The Doberman grew more and more agitated. But it whined more than it snarled.

He's frustrated, thought Henry. He's dying to eat. "Go on, fella. Eat it."

The dog moaned and growled and whined and snarled.

Finally, Henry realized that the dog would only go for the food at a German command. What had the Nazi said? Henry racked his brain. The words had sounded like "name foot." No, that wasn't quite right. *Nim footer.*

Henry took a deep breath and spoke aloud, "*Nim footer.*"

The dog lunged forward. But not to Henry's throat—to his feet. He ripped into the bone, cracking and crunching.

It's now or never, thought Henry. "Good boy. I'm just getting up. You keep on eating." Slowly, slowly, Henry eased himself up and out of the chair.

The Doberman growled, but held his head over the bone, possessive, preoccupied with his food.

Henry inched toward the door, crooning, "Easy, boy, easy. It's all right. Everything is all right."

The dog watched him but didn't move.

Henry's heart began to pound with hope. A little more. Just a little more. His feet reached the end of the room. Slowly, carefully, he lifted his hand to the door. Quietly, Henry warned himself. Don't set off the dog. Don't let the door click loudly.

His fingers curled around the latch. He squeezed. It opened!

Henry could have cried with joy. He pulled the door open just wide enough for his body to slip through. The hall was dark, silent.

Freedom! Henry felt afire with the idea, ready to run,

run all the way across France. He could see his farm. See his ma. Her arms were open.

He tried to quiet his adrenaline. He needed stealth, not speed. He took a cautious step, then another. He reached out to find the wall, to slide along it.

He touched air. Air again. Then something solid— solid but soft—like the material of a uniform.

Henry recoiled.

Lights flashed on like fireworks.

There stood his Gestapo tormenter.

Chapter Twenty

"**D**id you really think I'd allow you to escape?" The Gestapo officer shoved Henry back through the door as he jeered at him.

Henry stumbled and slammed against the wall. He crumbled to the floor and hid his face, hid his tears of frustration.

The officer kicked him. "Get up." He grabbed Henry by the collar and dragged him up the wall. Only when he had Henry by the throat, crushed flat against the ancient plaster, did the Nazi glance over at the dog.

The Doberman cowered by the chair.

When his captor's face turned back to Henry it was so full of rage, it froze Henry's breath. The Nazi ripped his pistol out of its holster and pressed the barrel hard against Henry's forehead.

You're going to die now, Henry told himself, because you ruined the Gestapo's pet killer. At least he won't be able to terrorize another American with that dog. You gentled him. A quiet smile of satisfaction crept across Henry's face. At least he'd accomplished that. He closed his eyes and said in a steady voice: "Go ahead."

Bang!

Henry clutched his head. But there was no blood, only the burning stench of the pistol's explosion. He opened his eyes.

By the chair came a sharp, pained yelping. The dog sprawled on the floor. Underneath him a pool of black-red blood was slowly spreading.

Henry looked back to the Nazi, whose eyes were again controlled blue ice. "Once a thing is no longer of use to me, I rid myself of it." He turned on his heel, and locked the door behind him.

Henry fell to his knees. He gagged and vomited and collapsed face-down beside the mess, convulsed with trembling. He'd never escape. He'd never see home. He'd die, terrorized, broken, a slobbering joke. He heaved sick-ening, retching sobs.

It was a tiny thing that stopped his crying. Something wet and warm touched his fingertips. Startled, Henry tried to focus his eyes along the floor. The dog's blood was oozing across the stones toward him. Pretty soon it would trickle to his face.

Henry looked at the dog. Its eyes were open, staring at Henry. It was still alive.

Henry sat up. The dog whimpered piteously. The Gestapo officer had hit it in the shoulder. It was going to die a slow, awful death, its life seeping out in thimblefuls.

The sight of a dog in such pain knocked Henry into delirium. In the dark, the Doberman became Henry's childhood pet, Skippy—the dog hit by a truck that Clayton had made Henry put down when he was eleven years old.

"Skippy?" Henry whispered. "You hurt bad, fella?" He crawled toward the dog.

Thump, thump, thump. The Doberman's tail wagged weakly at the kind voice.

Gently, Henry picked up the dog and cradled it in his arms.

"Dad!" he cried out. "Dad, help me! He's hurt."

Clayton's voice came out of the blackness. *He's your dog, boy. You gotta stop his misery.*

"I can't, Dad. I can't shoot Skippy. I love him."

What am I going to do with you, boy? Love's got responsibilities. Things you gotta do even if you don't want to. That's the kind of love a real man is capable of.

Is that why his father did the things he did? Is that why he was so harsh with Henry?

"Do you love me, Dad?" Henry sobbed.

Silence.

"Dad? Dad? Do you love me?"

Clayton's voice was distant, fading: *Shoot the dog, boy. Shoot the dog now. . . .*

"Dad?"

The dog whimpered and Henry kept calling until sometime in the night they both fell silent.

✶　✶　✶

Chapter Twenty

A sinister laugh woke Henry the next day. He still clutched the dog's body. It was cold and stiff. Henry was covered in its blood and his own vomit.

"Not a very presentable sight, American," the Gestapo officer mocked him. He pulled up the chair and sat down, inches from Henry. "Certainly not the way you'd like to present yourself to a lady, especially one with elegant taste." As he spoke, he slowly pulled a silk scarf out of his uniform's breast pocket. It was long, rose colored, festooned with flowers.

Henry knew he had seen that scarf somewhere before. But he was muddled from the horrors of the previous night. He pulled the dead dog up against his heart, the way a child hugs a teddy bear.

The Nazi pressed the scarf to his face, breathing in deeply. "Aaaaahhh. It still carries the scent of expensive perfume." He passed it under Henry's nose. "Anything you recognize?"

Slowly, Henry's mind began to clear. The scent was familiar somehow. But it wasn't Ma's. It wasn't Patsy's. It was . . . Henry snapped his eyes to the ground so the Nazi couldn't read them. He knew whose perfume and whose scarf it was. It was Madame Gaulloise's.

The Gestapo officer leaned back in his chair, crossing his legs, seemingly satisfied with Henry's reaction. "This was sent to me by the head of the Gestapo in Lyon, Hauptsturmführer Barbie. He is having some diplomatic trouble because of a prisoner who has Swiss citizenship. He is certain that she has been smuggling Americans, who should have been interned, out of Switzerland into

France. But the Swiss are protesting her arrest. If he can find one American whom she transported across the line, he can hang her. So far, despite all his efforts, she has eluded his questions. You are going to help him with that."

The Nazi leaned over and hissed: "You see, you have betrayed her, without even knowing it. You told me your name, your serial number, thinking as a coward to protect yourself from questioning. You never appeared on any of our P.O.W. lists. So I checked with Swiss authorities. There is a record of you in a Bern hospital, plus the fact you disappeared on route to Adelboden. Now how did that happen, Second Lieutenant Henry Wiley Forester?"

Henry's heart sank. The Army had repeatedly told them to respond with name, rank, and serial number if caught. He had hoped it would save him from interroga-tion. The Nazi was right about that. But he should have known better. Oh, God. What had these monsters done to Madame?

Henry clung to double-talk. "I flew here, sir."

One painful slap knocked the defiant look off Henry's face. "We're driving to Lyon, American," the Nazi snarled. "You will find me gentle compared to Klaus Barbie."

An hour later, Henry had been fed some bread, hosed with cold water, and dressed in black-and-gray-striped prison clothes. His hands were shackled in front of him. He was thrown into the back seat of a plush German staff car, next to the Gestapo officer. A soldier drove.

Chapter Twenty

It would take a long, long day of driving across the rugged plateaus of France's Massif Central to reach Lyon. Strangely, the Gestapo officer described the history of the region and its volcanic origins to Henry as if they were traveling companions. The dialogue unnerved him. What was the sadist after now? Henry refused to look at the passing countryside to which the Nazi pointed.

Instead he focused on the two little red flags with swastikas on the front of the car, flapping in the wind. They were banners of the devil, Henry told himself. No matter how nice this jerk is now, he's evil. Remember that, Forester. The Luftwaffe had been terrifying in their flying accuracy. But Henry bet most of them were just soldiers, doing what they'd been told, fighting to protect their homeland from Allied bombs. This man, though, this man enjoyed causing pain. Henry had to find a way out of the car so that he didn't endanger Madame. He had to.

Once he reached for the door to hurl himself out, but the Nazi only laughed and held on to Henry's chains.

Eventually, Henry realized that the officer's monologue was a way of bragging about new possessions, claiming an appreciation of something to justify stealing it. In all his descriptions of the chateaux, the statues, the churches, there was no mention of the French citizens who had created them.

Only once did the Nazi mention people. He pointed west and said, "Along that road, about two hundred kilometers away, you would come to Limoges. They make excellent porcelain there. I have sent some dishes, very fine, to my wife. They cost me nothing. She was extremely pleased."

He turned to Henry with his familiar sneer. "You would have liked that region, American. Many French terrorists are there. But we have eradicated them—the SS—not regular army, they are such idiots, very squeamish. I believe Oradour-sur-Glane was the name of the village. One of our officers had been killed by the local *maquis* and we suspected the populace of committing other treasons against the Reich. So we rounded up all six hundred inhabitants—men into barns; women and children into a church. We locked them in and torched the buildings. They burned to death. That should stop these French curs from thinking they can resist the Reich."

Henry froze with horror. How could human beings light a fire around six hundred people—children, women, and the elderly included—and then watch them burn alive? He gaped at the Gestapo officer.

The Nazi leered triumphantly. "We will have the world, Lieutenant. Including your precious United States of America. Then we will purge it, as we are purging Europe. It is only a matter of time."

Late in the afternoon, the driver turned and spoke to the officer. He nodded and informed Henry: "About thirty more minutes. Looking forward to seeing your old friend?" He took out Madame's silk scarf, twisted the ends in his fists, and snapped the scarf several times as he continued, "Klaus informed me she was beautiful, very stylish when they picked her up. Of course, she probably doesn't look quite the same these days. I promise to end it quickly for her, Lieutenant Henry Wiley Forester, if you cooperate. If not . . ." He shrugged.

Henry sent a blood prayer, rejecting all of his Sunday school teachings. *Just give me an opening, Lord, so I can get this guy.*

They had descended out of the mountains by now, but the road was still windy and narrow. Fences made of great piles of fieldstones edged the road, blocking the view around curves.

On a wicked twist in the road, Henry's prayer was answered.

The driver swerved to miss a herd of white cows that loitered in the lane, bells tinkling. The sudden lurch threw the Gestapo officer into Henry. They whacked heads and fell into a heap against the door. Henry could feel the Nazi's Luger pistol jammed against his hands.

Grab the gun, boy!

Adrenaline and hatred charged Henry. He grabbed at the Nazi's belt and managed to pull the Luger out. Instantly the Nazi gripped Henry's hands.

It was a life-or-death tug-of-war that Henry would have lost, as beaten down and weak as he was, except for the fact that the car was spinning out of control. The wild swerving and rolling tossed Henry and the Nazi back and forth on top of one another. In all the pitching confusion, Henry somehow managed to hang on to the pistol. The car's spin threw Henry atop the Gestapo agent one last time, pressing the gun against the Nazi's heart as Henry fell on him. The Nazi grabbed at Henry's throat and squeezed hard. Choking, beginning to black out, Henry squeezed the trigger.

BANG!

The Nazi seemed to explode, drenching Henry with his blood.

Henry heard the driver curse, heard him grabbing at something, and struggling to turn around.

Shoot him, boy. Shoot him.

In desperation, Henry fought against the jolting of the car to push himself off the dead Nazi and turn toward the driver. His hands were so bloody the pistol kept slipping. But just as the barrel of the driver's gun came up and aimed at Henry's face, he managed to hold up the Luger. Both guns fired. Henry felt something whizz and scream along his skull.

He clutched his ear.

The driver fell onto the steering wheel.

HHHONNNNNK! The horn blasted as the car careened into a ditch and finally stopped.

Henry slammed his head on the window as he reeled around inside the rolling car. But he remained conscious. Dazed, he dropped the gun and pulled the driver off the horn to stop the telltale noise. Then he fumbled in the officer's pockets, found the keys, and undid his manacles.

Hurry, boy, hurry.

Henry fell out of the car and ran, ran with all he had, ran for twenty minutes.

Finally, he threw himself down in a ravine, beside a small brook. Gasping to catch his breath, Henry reached into the stream to try to wash himself clean of blood. It was everywhere—his hands, his face, his hair, his clothes, his soul. How would he ever be clean of all that blood? He had killed two men—not from the anonymity of the sky—but face to face, with his own hands. Besides that, he'd wanted to kill them, was glad that he killed them so that he could live. He'd had murder in his heart. He couldn't wash that out.

Henry knew that he was changed forever, and not for the better.

Chapter Twenty-one

For two weeks, Henry scuttled into shadows at the sound of humans. He couldn't be seen. His face was battered and swollen. There was a scorch mark along his temple and ear where the driver's bullet had grazed his head. There'd be no mistaking the fact that he was an escaped prisoner, especially if the Nazis had searched for him and alerted residents to his existence.

He'd ditched his prison clothes that first night. He found pants drying on a clothesline. They were too short and soaking wet, but he pulled them on, shivering with the damp. The only top he could find was a woman's red sweater. He knew he must look ridiculous in it, but he wasn't about to chance getting that close to a house again. Dogs had howled and lights had come on inside when he grabbed that sweater. Besides, the sweater was better than the black-and-gray striped shirt that clearly marked him as a wanted man. He buried the prison garb deep in mud under a pig's sty. Then he changed the direction he was walking in case they were found.

Before that moment he'd headed what felt like west. It would be logical for him to push in that direction, to the coast, or south again to the Pyrenees. If the Nazis were bothering to look for him—and surely they were since he'd murdered two of their men—they'd expect him to run that way. So Henry now headed north, following the North Star, the final light in the handle of the Little Dipper constellation. But he had no purpose other than to feed himself and to avoid detection. He had no idea where or how to find the Resistance in this region. He wasn't even sure where he was.

He tried not to think about the two corpses, the men he'd robbed of life. He could dismiss his Gestapo tormentor more easily, but the driver haunted Henry. He was just a driver. Did he have children somewhere who'd now grow up fatherless? A wife who'd become destitute without his paychecks?

Even though it was summer, the nights were cold. Heavy dew settled on everything, including Henry. He tried to keep moving through the night, from farm to farm, looking for something to snatch—dried apples, a bit of milk from a cooperative cow, a jar of honey, grain. He salivated over the fat black hens but knew that he should not light a fire to cook them. He ate the few eggs of theirs he found, slurping them down raw. He counted himself lucky if he found one handful of edible food a day. He refused to acknowledge the fact that he'd become a thief, stealing from people who verged on starvation themselves.

During daylight hours Henry shunned the sunlight, creeping into dark hiding places. He huddled in hollow trees or the four-foot-high ferns that lined the roadside. He tried to sleep, but worry kept him from all rest beyond catnaps. Would the Swiss be able to pressure the Gestapo to release Madame now that he couldn't be used to identify her? Henry tried to imagine her in her elegant suits and scarves, using her wit to befuddle the Gestapo as he had witnessed her outfox other men—not beaten down, filthy, starved. He couldn't stand the idea that this remarkable lady would be destroyed because of him.

And Pierre. What of little Pierre? Had Barbie figured out the link between Madame and Pierre's mother?

Once, Henry spent the day in a rolling landscape of wheat fields, a checkerboard of bounty in shades of new green and harvest yellow that rippled gently with the breezes. He lay down in the thigh-high wheat, relishing the feel of the sun on his bruised face. Yellow-and-black butterflies fluttered above him. Ladybugs and metallic-green beetles crawled about. It reminded him of the hayfields at home, of the hours he and Patsy had hidden in the tall grasses watching ants come and go. It was the one time he slept soundly.

The distant grinding of car gears awakened him. Henry sat up only to hurl himself down again immediately. A German patrol was coming up across the hills toward him. Henry realized that he lay only a few yards away from the road. He ripped off the bright red sweater and squashed it under his chest, wishing he could slither into the cracks in the sun-baked ground. But the wheat, tall and thick, stood like a curtain around him and hid him from view.

The car passed by quickly. Henry caught the sound of young male voices singing. It was choral music of some kind. It reminded Henry of the Vienna Boys' Choir he'd heard on the radio at Christmas. Their voices raised in such gentle songs, they sounded so innocent. Did those boys and the sadistic Gestapo officer really serve the same leader?

Henry pressed himself down until the car's coughing and wrenching faded away. Flattened like that, his eyes completely level with the earth, Henry spotted a huge black beetle with inch-long pinchers waddling toward him. He reached out and grabbed lunch.

"Thanksgiving dinner," Henry whispered to himself. "Pretend it's Ma's turkey with all the trimmings." He broke the beetle in half and popped a piece in his mouth.

The beetle shell crackled as he chewed. Henry retched over the prickly feet still squirming against his tongue. But he swallowed. He could feel it bump and slide down his throat. He closed his eyes and held his breath to manage crunching up the second half.

Henry avoided the small, fairytale castles with golden-brown mortar and cone-shaped roofs that peppered the hills. He figured they would have been taken over by German officers. Mostly, he headed for large, prosperous-looking houses surrounded by high stone walls that protected orchards within. Cherries were ripe now and the graceful trees were low and easy to climb.

One night, in such an orchard, Henry nearly fell as he swung himself up onto the first branch of a small tree—a tree he could have easily scaled as a six-year-old. He was dangerously weak. What little food he found often came back up an hour later or ripped through him—he had dysentery.

He pulled off a cherry and stuck it in his mouth. He chewed it halfheartedly. Its sweetness meant nothing to him. He spat the pit into his hand and examined it in the moonlight. A lump of blackened, hard nothing, thought Henry. You're like this pit now, Forester, skin and bones, no heart, no hope, no mission, no nothing. His hand snapped closed to a fist. He shut his eyes and tried to dismiss the thought: I'm not going make it, Ma, am I?

THWACK.

Something hard and sharp thumped Henry's shoulder.

THWACK.

Another on his chest.

Henry looked around frantically. What was it?

THWACK.

"Voleur! Ne touche pas à mes cerisiers!"

Henry located the voice—a small figure in the shadows of the stone wall. In his current state, Henry assumed everything was scrounging for food like a barn rat. He snarled, "My tree. I'm not sharing."

The figure stepped toward him. It was a clear night and the light of the moon and stars lit it up. The figure was a girl in a nightshirt and sweater. She held another stone in her hand. But she did not throw it. "This is not your tree," she said in heavily accented English. "Get down."

The sound of his own language thrilled Henry. He dropped to the ground in a tumble and staggered to stand up.

"Would you like it if I came to your home and stole your food?" asked the girl. "We have little enough to eat as it is."

Henry froze at the tone of her voice. Her voice had a defensive harshness to it, like older women he'd met and then avoided in English pubs. But this was no woman. She was slight. Her hair floated thick and dark to her waist. She was sixteen, seventeen tops, Henry reckoned. What should he tell her? He instinctively trusted her age, but not her voice. That voice was tinted with suspicion and rage.

She repeated her question. "Would you like it?"

Her words shamed him. Henry hung his head. "I am sorry. I am so hungry."

The girl did not relent. "That sweater is very pretty, handmade. It was probably a woman's favorite. You cannot get scarlet yarn these days. Do you think she misses it?"

Henry felt sick with embarrassment. "I—I—I—" He shook his head. Tears welled up in his eyes.

For several moments they stood in silence. Finally, when Henry thought he could no longer bear the weight of her eyes on him no more, she spoke again, grudgingly, and with a different tone of voice: "*Cerises* will make you ill. Come in the house."

The girl led Henry through a great room with a

cavernous fireplace. Worn tapestries hung on the walls and stag antlers above the doors. They came to a simple kitchen. She lit a candle and set it atop the wooden table, motioning for Henry to sit down.

He caught his breath at the sight of her in the candle's glow. She had a French beauty about her that Henry was coming to appreciate. Black arched eyebrows that had never suffered tweezers accentuated large, almond-shaped eyes. Her nose was prominent, long and straight, giving her a dramatic profile. Her lips were full and sensuous in a way a lot of people back home called trashy, especially when poor farm girls had them. Patsy had lips like that. He had always liked that about her, because she seemed so completely unaware of their exotic prettiness.

The girl looked up at Henry and again he was startled, this time by the color of her eyes. They were a clear, yellow-green, almost amber, like cat's eyes. He'd never seen eyes like that. They turned cold when she caught him looking at her face.

Without speaking, she cracked two brown eggs and cut thin strips off an old ham that was nearly down to the bone to make an omelet. Henry trembled at the sizzle of butter, the smell of frying meat. He tried hard to eat politely when she set it before him, but he inhaled it. Within moments he had finished. Again, he hung his head in embarrassment.

In the great room next door a grandfather clock *tick-tock, tick-tock, tick-tock*ed.

Henry concentrated on the little blue flowers on his empty plate, tugged nervously on the bottom button on his stolen sweater, wishing like mad he could tear it off and magically appear before this girl in full uniform, clean and brave.

"Pilot?" she asked.

"Yes."

"Why are you here? Why do you wear a woman's sweater?"

"I—I," Henry stammered, afraid to tell her the truth. Could he trust her?

He glanced up at her again. She sat ramrod straight, on the alert, with her arms folded tightly across her chest. Her eyes bore into him. His eyes hit his plate again. He shrugged, like a schoolboy caught in misbehavior he couldn't explain for fear of getting playmates in trouble, deep trouble.

The clock ticked loudly and the girl continued to stare at him with a thoughtful, contemptuous look. A look that told Henry she was trying to figure out what in the world to do with him.

He waited and waited, listening to the clock.

Finally it struck the hour—*bong-bong-bong-bong.*

Four A.M.

The clock's chiming saved him. The girl sighed. "I am tired. I must get up in two hours to open *la boulangerie.*" She paused. "Tomorrow I take you to Vézelay, to Basilique-Sainte-Madeleine. The nuns can decide what to do with you. They help ones like you."

She picked up the candle to light her way upstairs. "You may sleep on the bench." She nodded toward the corner.

The girl and the light slid out of the room.

Henry didn't have the energy to walk to the bench. He laid his head on the cool wooden table. Nuns? He'd never met nuns before Switzerland. They seemed kind enough, but cool and intimidating, like this girl. Dan had certainly been full of stories of them—rulers coming down on schoolchildren's knuckles when they'd misbehaved, threats of damnation if they couldn't recite their catechism.

Dan. Henry rubbed his forehead hard back and forth on the table to push out the memory of Dan plummeting to earth. He had traveled such a trail of death and sorrow. Henry knew if all the images—of Dan, of Billy's last breath, of Pierre clinging to his mother, of Madame being tortured, of the men he'd killed—ever caught up with him at the same moment, he'd never be able to take another step. He was running from them as surely as he was running from the Nazis.

Chapter Twenty-two

Whe hen Henry awoke, he found a small loaf of bread beside his head. A note scribbled on the back of an envelope read: *Stay inside.* He turned it over. The envelope was addressed to Claudette Besson, St-Benin d'Azy, Nièvre. Careless of her to leave something with her name on it, thought Henry with surprise. He tore it into little shreds and piled it beside his plate for her to throw away.

Henry ate and dozed again. He was aware of someone moving about upstairs, but he stayed rooted to where the girl had left him for fear of doing something wrong. He also didn't want her to think he was prowling her house to steal something.

The girl didn't return until midafternoon. She carried a half dozen loaves of long French bread under her arm. She also brought a man's undershirt and a jacket. When Henry unfolded it he saw that it was a waist-length khaki jacket of a British pilot's uniform. There were several bullet-size holes across its chest. Henry pushed his finger through one. The jacket's owner must have been shot dead. Henry hesitated to put it on, superstition overwhelming him.

"I could find nothing else," said the girl matter-of-factly. "It is better than a woman's bright red sweater, yes?"

Henry nodded, swallowed hard, and put it on.

They left immediately. Henry reached out and ran his fingertips along the ancient stones of a small tower as they passed through the estate's gates.

Without looking at him, the girl said, "That part of the house was built in one-thousand-ten. My family lived here that long, and stayed when the English occupied Burgundy. The walls are here still, even with men and their wars."

Her bitterness chilled Henry. He tried to charm her, saying, "You speak English very well, *mademoiselle*. How did you learn?"

The girl pursed her lips then answered tersely: "At the convent school. I was a novice before the war."

"A novice?" Henry didn't know what she meant.

"Mon Dieu. Dois-je risquer ma vie pour un tel ignorant?" The girl muttered to herself about having to put up with an ignorant heathen and refused to answer or look at Henry.

Henry told her in French that he did believe in God. He just wasn't Catholic.

The girl stopped abruptly. Henry hoped for praise for

his French. Instead she said, "Then I know you are a fool. If God exists, how could all this happen?"

After that, Henry kept his mouth shut. He knew better than to worry a wasps' nest. He'd learned to keep clear of ornery moods as a child, to avoid trouble with Clayton. He followed a few steps behind this girl. She never once turned back to check and make sure he was still there.

The road they traveled worried Henry. Although the landscape looked serene as the earth swept itself up in gentle hills, he could tell this was a main thoroughfare linking the small villages that nestled in them. Wouldn't German patrols use it? The girl had been so naive about that envelope, was she using any caution? It was still daylight. They'd be easily spotted. Henry hadn't killed two men just to get caught and tortured again.

She carried the loaves of bread. Was she planning to waltz into the next village and make deliveries with him tagging behind in a British flight jacket?

"*Mademoiselle,* I . . ."

Turning around with a menacing look, the girl pointed her finger at him and then held it to her lips.

She kept walking. After a while, she began to whistle. It was a song Henry had learned in grade school: "*Sur le pont d'Avignon* . . ."

Henry stopped in his tracks. This girl was dangerous. Either she was leading him into a trap or she didn't have the foggiest idea how to keep herself out of trouble. He'd seen how hatred and anger made people foolishly brazen. None of these explanations for her behavior reassured Henry. Should he run?

The girl kept walking and whistling. Suddenly she, too, stopped. She cocked her head to listen. Faint, in the distance, came a whistled answer: *"Sur le pont . . ."*

She moved forward again. Henry now dawdled several hundred feet behind the girl. She hadn't looked back for him yet. He followed cautiously, keeping distance between them, unsure what he should do.

The girl turned off the road and waded into a wheat field. Henry crouched down to watch what happened.

Up popped a man. Another. And a third. They were heavily armed with straps of bullets crisscrossing their chests. She embraced one and handed the loaves to his companions.

Maquis. Henry sighed in relief. Why hadn't she told him? Or at least hinted that she knew what she was doing?

He stood up. Henry felt more than saw three guns whip up to take him down.

"Non!" she shouted, then said in quieter voice, *"Il est avec moi."*

The young man she had kissed waved Henry over. Henry hung his head in dismay as the girl explained how she had found him, dirty, sick, stealing fruit from her orchard. Did she have to tell these men how low he had sunk? At least she pitied him enough to leave out the detail of the woman's sweater.

"Qu'est-ce que vous voulez que je fasse avec lui?" Her friend asked gruffly what she expected him to do with Henry.

Henry felt more and more like a mangy alley cat no one wanted.

Chapter Twenty-two

The girl bristled and answered curtly that she didn't expect any favors from him. She was taking the American to the nuns. They could figure it out.

The young *maquisard* laughed and joked that the nuns would see how well he said his prayers before deciding his fate. Then he took her hand and kissed it, telling her to be careful.

One of the leader's companions grabbed his elbow and said, *"Si elle va à Vézelay elle pourrait apporter les trucs de radio à Bernard."*

The girl's friend frowned and shrugged off his subordinate. The companion had wanted the girl to carry radio parts to a man named Bernard. Her friend didn't like the idea at all.

"Elle passera presque sur les lieux du massacre et trop proche des Allemands à Château-Chinon. Non." He turned to the girl and told her again to go hide with the nuns.

Henry gladly turned to leave, relieved to be away from men who knew his shame, relieved to be avoiding a town the *maquisard* said had a German garrison in it. But the girl didn't budge. She wanted to take on the mission.

She spoke in a tumble of words, telling him she'd carried parts before tucked in her umbrella and bicycle basket.

"Pas cette fois-ci, mon enfant," the young man answered. *"C'est trop dangereux à ce moment."*

The girl turned red. Her boyfriend had called her a child. Lord, Henry could only imagine what Patsy would do to him, if he ever called her that.

The girl swung back to slap the *maquisard*. He grabbed her hand and grinned. She only proved his point, he said. She acted like a child.

He let go of her arm and marched himself and his team away down the hill, over the next, and then they were gone.

The girl stood seething, breathing hard until they disappeared. She whirled on her heel and ran, skirt and hair flying. Henry started after her.

"Wait!" he cried. In his sad shape, he'd never keep up. She didn't.

Henry struggled after her, calling again, just when he knew he was going to faint or vomit.

Finally, she halted. Her fists clenched by her side, she stormed back to Henry. He was bent over, breathing like a horse about to die.

"*Vite.* Do you understand? I have to be rid of you so that I can fight *les Boches*. I want to kill as many as I can."

Henry straightened up, panting between words, "No, you don't. It won't make you feel as good as you think it will."

"And how would you know, thief?"

"Look, I'm not proud of what I've done to survive. But I've seen a lot of things you haven't."

The girl narrowed her eyes and slid up close to him. "I saw my mother killed because she would not let a convoy of drunk Germans into our home. They shot her dead, then they ran into the house. One of them finished the meal she was eating just before. When they left they took everything—the pigs, the cows, the silver. Everything except my hens and my fruit trees. Last month, in Dun-les-Places, the Nazis said we shot at them from the church tower. They hanged the priest from that tower. Then a Gestapo informant pointed out people who helped the *maquis*. The collaborator grew up with those people, ate supper with them, worshiped God with them. The Nazis shot them all—thirty people—in front of the church. My eighty-year-old uncle was one of them. I went to Dun-les-Places to find my aunt and bring her home to live with me. Their blood is still on the church walls.

"I have seen all this. Last month, I am seventeen. I will kill every Nazi I find and every collaborator. And I will smile when I do it."

An awful silence hung between them. Henry couldn't take his eyes off those furious yellow-green ones. He was horrified by what she reported, by what she planned. He wanted to run far away from her fury and at the same time he wanted to hold and comfort her. His confusion kept him immobilized, wordless, arms by his side.

Then they heard gunshots.

The girl's eyes darted to the horizon behind Henry. *"Mon Dieu. André."*

She brushed by Henry and ran, ran again with skirt and hair flying. This time Henry managed to keep pace.

They came to the top of a hill and could see a jeep fly-ing up the road, pursued by two brown-and-black camou-flaged trucks and four German motorcycles. A heap of men clung to the open back of the jeep, some firing back toward the Nazis. Their aim was terrible because of the wild jolt-ing of the jeep. The Germans were closing in fast.

Just then three small figures rose up out of the grasses. *"André!"* the girl screamed.

BOOM!

The first German truck exploded into flames and careened off the road. André's group must have thrown grenades into it. The second truck screeched to a stop. A dozen soldiers jumped out and opened fire into the wheat field. The *maquis* jeep turned left, roared into the field across the road, looped back and tried to mow down the Germans caught in the crossfire between them and André in the wheat field.

The girl began to run.

This is suicide, Henry warned himself. But he ran after her, watching the skirmish unfold before him.

German soldiers screamed, fell, and writhed on the ground.

Frenchmen screamed, fell off the moving jeep, and slammed down dead on the roadway.

A dozen yards from the fighting, Henry caught up to the girl. He tackled her to the ground. "Crawl," he whispered.

They shimmied through the grasses to the first of André's companions. He was dead. *"Non, non, non,"* cried the girl. She thrashed on.

Henry paused over the dead *maquisard*. No beard on his face. Another teenager robbed of the chance to live his life.

Henry picked up the boy's gun. As he yanked it up, the dead boy's hand fell limply from the trigger to his belt. It bumped against a grenade.

Henry's heart hammered against his chest. A grenade.

Chapter Twenty-two

He'd never used one. Pull the pin and throw, right? That's all there was to it. Henry glanced back up to the fight. The French were definitely outnumbered. The jeep doggedly kept circling the German truck and the soldiers huddled beside it, but one after another the *maquis* fighters were being gunned down. Soon the jeep would be empty of French fighters. A grenade that found the right mark might save them.

Henry no longer needed his father's voice to prod him in life-or-death circumstances. He picked up the grenade. It was heavy, cold, scaly. It felt like a thing of death. Henry pulled the pin, stood up, and hurled it.

BOOM!

The explosion knocked Henry back and over. His head hit the ground hard and the world went black.

Chapter Twenty-three

Henry surfaced to consciousness to the sound of sobbing and gunshots. He sat up, woozy, but on the alert. A *maquisard* was shooting at a pair of German soldiers running away through the fields. He missed his mark and turned, cursing himself.

When the fighter noticed Henry, he strode toward him, gun in hand.

"No!" shouted Henry, scrambling backward like a crab.

The Frenchman halted, shoved the pistol into his belt, and put his hands up reassuringly. He pointed to Henry, to the smoldering truck, and back to Henry. With a bow, he said, *"Merci."*

Henry nodded and replied, *"Je vous en prie."* He rubbed the back of his aching head and watched the four *maquisards* who had survived loading the jeep with their dead and wounded.

Where was the girl? He could hear her heartbroken crying somewhere in the wheat. André must have died. Henry ground his teeth. If only he'd run faster, thrown the grenade faster, maybe the young man would still be alive. He forced himself to get up to find her.

The girl was deep in the golden wheat. She clutched André's body, rocking the two of them back and forth, her face pressed to his, cheek to cheek. In whispers she asked him to wake up; to look at her. *"Tu dois te reveiller maintenant. S'il te plaît, André."* She gently picked up his hand and kissed it. *"S'il te plaît, mon amour. Réveille-toi maintenant."*

Embarrassed, Henry looked away from the intimacy of the embrace. They had obviously held each other like that in happy, twilight moments, moments they had promised each other their futures.

Henry stood and waited.

The *maquis* leader quietly joined him. After a few moments, he told the girl that they must take André's body.

The girl ignored him.

"Nous ne pouvons pas rester ici." The man grew more insistent. They could not remain on the open road. The two soldiers who escaped would report their position soon enough. They had to move on immediately. He would bury André for her with his comrades.

The girl still ignored him.

The man motioned for his fighters to separate her from her love's corpse.

Wild with grief, the frail, seventeen-year-old girl

turned on them with a viciousness that startled the muscled men to a halt. *"Non! Ne me touchez pas!"* She picked
up André's gun and turned it on them, threatening to kill
them if they dared touch his body. *"Si vous le touchez, je
vous tue!"*

Henry could tell the *maquis* were losing patience.
Soon they would tackle her, perhaps hurt her without
meaning to. Maybe she would shoot one of them. Maybe
they would shoot her. He took a step forward.

She swung the gun on him. "Get back, thief," she
snarled. "Thief!" Her hand shook uncontrollably. "Are you
after his sweater, too? And him, not even cold yet." She
sobbed hysterically. But the gun remained aimed, wob-
bling dangerously.

Henry flushed hot. He had been degraded by Clayton's
name-calling a thousand times. But not like this. This hit
an awful truth. It had occurred to him to take one of the
dead German's shirts or a pair of new, soft boots. He had
become a scavenger, as loathsome as turkey buzzards picking at roadkill back home.

He took a deep breath. Maybe if he could help her, he
might redeem himself.

"Claudette, give me the gun. Let them take André.
They will give him a hero's burial. I will take you with
them so that you can see it. And then I will make sure you
get home safe, to your aunt. I owe you that. I promise. *Tu
comprends?"*

In the corner of his eye, Henry could see the *maquis*
closing in behind her as she concentrated on him, on gun-
ning him down.

Chapter Twenty-three

She shook her head vehemently. "Thief," she shrieked. She squeezed the trigger.

Henry gasped, expecting to explode inside.

Click.

Click.

Click, click, click.

The gun was empty.

The men grabbed the girl.

Henry sat in the back of the jeep crammed between two injured men and a pile of dead bodies. He forced himself to stare at the wheat rushing past him, not the mangled corpses. Claudette sat with her back against his. She trembled with silent sobs.

They were heading toward a chain of dark mountains, rippling low on the horizon, reminding Henry of the Virginia Blue Ridge near Charlottesville. He thought of home and of his mother, Lilly. She'd know what to do for Claudette, thought Henry. His mother had been able to comfort everyone. Henry stole a glance at the girl. No, he had no idea how to soothe someone this cut open by grief and so many tragedies.

The man riding in the passenger seat, the one who seemed to be the group's leader, turned to ask Henry about himself.

Henry answered that he was an American pilot. The man nodded and then spoke quickly to the driver. The driver shrugged. *"Oui. On peut le garder. Sait-il peut-être réparer la voiture?"*

Claudette was asked to translate. She snapped out of

her sorrow to refuse angrily. She told the Frenchman she was tired of speaking to a thief.

Henry spoke for himself. He had caught enough of the front seat conversation to understand that this *maquis* group did not run an escape line and that the driver had said something about a car that needed repair. Henry told the leader he didn't want to be any more trouble. But if the group had a car engine that needed fixing, he might be able to do that in exchange for dinner. His father was an ace mechanic. He knew a few things.

The Frenchman grunted and nodded. They rode the rest of the way in silence, climbing the black mountain range along narrow dirt roads. Henry clung to the jeep's edge as it jolted through the dense, forested hills. More than once he had to catch a corpse as it began to slide off the back. The wounded men groaned.

Finally, when the moon was high, the jeep plunged down a narrow path. Henry had to duck to avoid being cracked in the skull by the branches that twined themselves into a tangled thicket overhead. To him it looked like a matted, eerie dead-end, but then brakes screeched and the jeep skidded into a camp.

Like the camp in the Vercors, this one teamed with an odd assortment of boys, men, and even women carrying mostly German guns. Some wore bits and pieces of Nazi uniforms, the luckier ones replacing their wooden clogs with German field boots. Despite their hodgepodge of clothing the camp was tidy and regimented. Wooden walkways made of tree branches lashed together kept the fighters out of the dank mud. They crisscrossed the camp connecting the tents made from parachutes. A dozen bicy-cles ringed a large beech tree in the center of camp.

Henry was led to a table built in the same fashion as the walkways and given a thick potato soup to eat. He practically drooled at the savory smell. Claudette sat across from him and ate nothing. It took all the will-power Henry had not to grab her bowl.

A tall lanky man wearing a tweed coat and tie sat down next to Henry, and handed him a cup with a few spoonfuls of golden liquid in it. *"Salut,"* said the man, clinking his glass against Henry's.

Henry gulped it as the Frenchman did. The liquid burned all the way down his throat to the pit of his stom-ach. He coughed. The man smiled in a friendly way.

"A good cognac, yes? My last bottle. I was a lawyer before the war and could afford such things. Now," he sighed and gestured to the forest. "We must live as Robin Hood, yes? They tell me you saved the jeep. I thank you. The British dropped it just a few days ago. It would have been a shame to have lost it so quickly."

"The British dropped a jeep?" asked Henry in surprise.

The man nodded. "And many other things. The jeep took four parachutes. It was beautiful coming down."

He assessed Henry carefully before continuing. "You look as though you have been in our country a while. I am sorry I cannot move you now. You must stay with us. We are busy fighting. The leader of the Free French army, Charles de Gaulle, finally broadcast the order for the *maquis* to rise up against the Nazis as an army. We are to disrupt the German troops as much as possible. We are to distract them with small ambushes as they retreat from the coast. We must break their telephone and telegraph lines to prevent them from communicating orders about counterinvasion tactics. This should slow their regrouping and keep them disorganized. The men you saved had just set a detonator on the railroad tracks to break the supply line to the German garrison in Autun. I am grateful to you for the men who lived. They are my best explosives men."

Henry was amazed at the *maquisard*'s candor. Perhaps because he was openly fighting the Nazis, the man didn't feel the need for secrecy. But Henry knew the openness reflected a do-or-die attitude. There was no middle ground. Even though he felt he was acting as part of De Gaulle's Free French army, the *maquisard* would not be treated as a soldier if caught. The Nazis would shoot him instantly as a terrorist.

The man stood up and extended his hand. "My name is Martin."

Henry stood up. "Mine is Henry, *Henri*." They shook hands. Henry's grasp lingered for a moment. Hesitantly he asked, "*Monsieur*, there was a lady, a very kind lady, who helped me. She is being held in Lyon. The Gestapo was transporting me there to testify against her when I escaped. Is there anything I can do to help her?"

Martin's face turned grim. "No, nothing. Her best hope is that the Allies retake France quickly."

Then he addressed Claudette and told her his sorrow about André. He had been a good boy. *"Je regrette beaucoup André, chérie. C'était un bon garçon."*

Claudette rose to go with Martin and bury her love. Henry followed. Atop a grassy hill, bathed in moonlight, a handful of people stood around five shallow graves. Henry could count at least ten other newly dug and filled trenches nearby.

The bodies with which Henry had ridden in the jeep were wrapped in parachutes. One by one they were gently lowered and covered with earth. Claudette sobbed as dirt hit André's body.

As the group turned to leave a sudden clap of thunder echoed through the mountains. Henry glanced up, but saw a clear canopy of stars, no clouds. He looked to the horizon. A fiery plume shot up in the valley below them.

Martin smiled. A passing train had ignited his *maquis'* booby trap. Whatever had been in the train was no more.

The next morning, Henry looked for Claudette. He knew he was asking for more abuse from her, but he couldn't help it. There was something about her—something about her looks, something about her spirit—that ate at him. It went beyond his desire to prove himself respectable to a person who'd caught him at his lowest. That was a matter of trying to reclaim some smidgen of self-respect. This was something more.

He found her, predictably, in a hot argument. Martin had instructed one of his *maquisards* to escort her home. He wanted her to go back to work at the bakery so that she could continue to supply them with bread. She didn't want to. She wanted to stay and fight.

Henry watched at a safe distance as Claudette

clenched her fists and shouted up at the still well-dressed Martin. Even though he towered over her in height, he seemed to recoil from the fury of the petite teenager.

What a spitfire, thought Henry. A slow smile spread on his face. The scene reminded him of the time Patsy had kicked that brat Jackson who had been picking on Henry in the schoolyard. That's what it was! Henry suddenly recognized what it was about Claudette that lured him, bothered him. She had spunk like Patsy's, but it was spunk turned unforgiving and vengeful. He could imagine what he loved about Patsy twisting the same dark way if she had to endure what this French girl had.

Martin was losing patience. He grabbed Claudette by the arm and pulled her to his waiting subordinate. The man took her the same way and starting dragging her out of the camp. Claudette sat down in the mud, kicking and screaming like a toddler having a tantrum. When the *maquisard* tried to continue dragging her along the ground, she tripped him up, so that they both sprawled and thrashed in the mud. The men observing laughed loudly. The *maquisard* jumped to his feet, humiliated, and shouted angrily at Claudette. He raised his hand as if to strike her.

Without knowing exactly why he did it, Henry stepped forward. "*Monsieur Martin?* Your men told me that one of your cars needed fixing. Maybe she can help me. See how small her hands are? My Dad always needed me when our truck broke down 'cause he couldn't get his big hands all the way down in the gears to fix them. I bet I can use her hands."

Chapter Twenty-three

Everyone froze. Lord, what have I done now, thought Henry. But he walked over to Claudette and pulled her to her feet. "Yep, look at her fingers, long and thin. I bet she can be a real help, *Monsieur.*"

Martin laughed. "You do not know what you are getting yourself into, Henri. But I lost my mechanic two weeks ago, killed in town. If you can fix the car it would be very helpful. And if you want Claudette's company, you are welcome to her. I don't think my man would be able to drag her all the way back to St-Benin anyway. Come," he gestured to the people surrounding them. "We have work to do. Claudette, show Henri the cars." He held up his finger. "Be good."

In frosty silence, Claudette led Henry out of camp, up a narrow road that ran through more knotted woods. Coppery beech trees grew up in many forks, more like massive, woody bushes. It would be nearly impossible to run quickly through them to hide from German troops, Henry noted.

After about ten minutes of uphill walking, Henry saw cars tucked into screens of briars along the roadway. There were a small Peugeot and a Citroën plus two stolen Nazi Mercedes. It was the larger Mercedes that didn't run. Henry could see why the *maquis* wanted that one fixed. Not only could they slip in and out of places masquerading as Germans in that car, they could probably stuff eight gunmen in it, easy.

Henry lifted the hood with a great *creak*. He could see smears of oil and rust all over the motor. Something wasn't right. He searched the makeshift garage for tools and could only find a wrench. Not much good that would do him. He'd need more than that to take the engine apart and get it back together. No, he'd have to try to spot and fix whatever was wrong by reaching past the gears and wheels and belts and wires. Henry peered between the carburetor and battery and saw a wire from the distributor dangling uselessly. Could it really be that simple a problem? If there wasn't anything else wrong with the engine, reconnecting that cable should get the motor to fire.

Henry straightened up. What do you know? he thought. Claudette really could help. It would be difficult for him to wriggle his hand in there to reconnect the electrical wire. But she could easily.

They had it repaired and running within the hour.

As they worked, one of Martin's assistants watched. When Claudette switched the car key at Henry's cue and the engine turned over, sputtered, and then hummed, the Frenchman stuck out his lower lip and nodded approvingly.

He led them back to a shed on the edge of camp. Laid out on a table were bundles of plastic explosives, timing devices, and fuses—the cache from a British parachute drop. The *maquisard* pointed to the instructions attached to the fuse packages. The instructions were written in English. The foreign words were useless to him. He wanted Henry and Claudette to read them and build the bombs, setting some to explode two hours after setting, some six, some eight.

Henry nodded and sat down gingerly to read the

instructions. One false pinch with the pliers or a clumsy flinch could set off the plastic, killing him and the girl instantly. He took a deep breath and looked up at Claudette to ask if she was okay with this.

He'd never seen her so happy.

Chapter Twenty-four

Ｊuly slipped into August in a haze of midnight para-chute drops and the nerve-racking business of making bombs. Claudette stayed in camp, helping Henry twist fuse lines and time pencils into the detonators of hand grenades or bundles of plastic explosives.

As he worked, Henry listened to the men argue politics. Some were admirers of de Gaulle. Others hated him for fleeing to England. Some still trusted Marshall Pétain, the World War I hero who headed the pro-Nazi Vichy government. They claimed the old fox was simply waiting for the right time to turn on the Nazis. But most detested him as a traitor. When members of another *maquis* group came into camp looking to borrow a wireless radio, Martin's men almost turned them away empty-handed because they were Communists. Henry's hosts accused them of being loyal to the cause only after Hitler attacked Communist Russia and because they wanted to overturn the French establishment.

The only thing that anyone agreed on was wanting the Nazis out.

At night the camp emptied. The fighting was getting fiercer, deadlier. The *maquis* blew up railroad lines to stop trainloads of gasoline and munitions running from Paris to Nevers to Autun. They knocked down telegraph wires passing orders and information from German garrisons in Avallon to troops in Dijon. Occasionally they attacked Nazi truck convoys, always losing some men. Henry helped dig at least two dozen more graves.

Henry was not allowed to go on these missions. But he was often sent down into the villages with Claudette to collect cheese, bacon, and loaves of bread with counterfeit food stamps the British dropped for them. These visits terrified him. Claudette continued to march through the streets, as if daring German soldiers to confront her. Henry constantly had to throw himself into the thick hedgerows lining the roads as bicycle patrols passed, three to four young German soldiers pedaling swiftly, rifles across their backs.

Claudette laughed at him as he crawled back out, brushing prickles from his face and arms. But she was softening slightly. Henry figured what must be her instinctive kindness was winning out over her angry resolve—just as it had on the night she first found and fed him. About a week after they began their bomb making together she approached Henry with a long, thick sweater and clean pants.

"These were André's," she told him. "I looked in his tent. He would want someone to use them."

Henry gratefully shed the bullet-torn British flight jacket. He turned to thank her but Claudette had already walked away.

Martin was rarely in camp. He seemed to commute among several *maquis* groups hiding in the low, junglelike mountains to coordinate their operations. The travel couldn't be easy. Henry had learned that the range was called the Morvan, meaning "black mountain." The name suited. Wind had been the constant in the Vercors. Here in the Morvan, heavy, cold rain drenched the rocky hills constantly, leaving the thick forests always dripping, the paths slick with mud.

One afternoon, however, Martin was in camp for a meeting. After the men finished talking, Henry approached him. Since he seemed to be a commander of sorts for the *maquis* movement, Henry hoped to hear some word of the Vercors group that had sheltered him. Pierre was always in Henry's mind. Unlike poor Madame, Pierre should still be free and safe. And what about his friend, the trumpet player?

"Monsieur Martin?"

"Oui, Henri? I have wished to speak with you. I hear you tame Claudette. That is a service to us all."

"She's all right, *monsieur*. You just have to watch your step, that's all. My dad is the same way." Henry sat down at the table. "I really hoped to ask you a question, *monsieur*."

"Oui? I will answer if I can, Henri. I cannot tell you

much, though. I see that you are trustworthy, but I do not tell my own men everything I know. If it is about the woman in Lyon, I truly know nothing. The Gestapo has that city by the throat. We have lost touch with every-one there."

"It is about Vassieux, a village near . . ." What had the teenager called that pass in the mountains? Henry searched his mind. It was hard to remember exactly where he had been in all those dark nights, so afraid and hurrying. "Col de la Bataille, I think that's it, *monsieur*. I came through there and was taken care of by a family. They got caught. The grandfather was killed. The mother was taken to Grenoble and maybe deported. There was a son. A young boy. I took him to people his mother asked me to. To a priest. He said something about an abbey. I don't know where. I . . . I . . . ." Henry didn't really know how to phrase his question. "Please, *monsieur*. If you know of him or that area, I need to know. I need to know he is safe."

Martin sat back in his seat and sighed. "I do not know about the boy, Henri. There are many families in our movement. If you took him to people his mother re-quested, he has probably been hidden safely away. But Vassieux was hit last month, Henri, some say abandoned by the Allies. The British and Americans asked the *maquis* to build a landing strip in the Vercors. The Allies want-ed to bring in troops to attack the Nazis as they retreat from Normandy back into Germany. The *maquis* built it. Then on Bastille Day, the Allies dropped arms and rations in broad daylight. More than a thousand parachutes. It led the Nazis right to Vassieux. They bombed the village, completely destroying it. Then a week later the Nazis used the landing strip the *maquis* had built for the Allies to bring in their own SS troops. They hunted down all the *maquis* in the region and massacred everyone they found, even the wounded in a field hospital, even children. The British and the Americans never came. Vassieux is no more."

Henry jumped up from the table. He had to go back. He had to find Pierre. He couldn't just leave him lost, unknown. If Americans were on the move, Henry might be able to get Pierre to the Americans. His ma would adopt Pierre, for sure. Maybe even Henry could adopt him. He'd be an adult legally in a few years. He sure felt like one already, an old one, one wiser than a lot of the fools back home.

Martin stood and held Henry by the arm. Henry's thoughts must have been all over his face. "You cannot help him, Henri. If you go to look for the child you would probably lead the SS right to him. If he was in an abbey, he was out of town at the time of the attack. The monks would know where to hide him. The only good thing about the Nazis is that most still respect the church."

"But, Monsieur Martin, I have to know if he's all right. Maybe you could get a message to one of your people there to check on him. Pierre is eight, brown hair. His smile is a little shy, a little sad." Henry tried to think of other features that would identify him. "He has a marble I gave him, a cloud. It's for good luck."

Martin held up his hand to stop Henry. "I cannot take the time for one boy. And if I ask about him, it links him to the *maquis*. It is safest for him to disappear into oblivion, Henri. The best thing you can do for him is pray and never seek him out."

Never? Never know Pierre's fate? How could Henry bear that? Stricken, he pulled himself loose and walked away from Martin into the woods.

Too angry to pay attention to his feet, Henry stumbled over tree roots and stones. He pushed his way off the path through brambles toward the sound of rushing water. He fell to his knees by a tiny waterfall and pool and clasped his hands. He hadn't prayed, really prayed, in months. He hadn't known how to find the right words in such chaos, in such misery, in such violence. And his thoughts hadn't exactly been what his church called Christian:

Please, God, protect me even though everyone else around me might die.

Please, Jesus, help me kill my enemy before he kills me.

Please, God, give me the cunning to blow up a train just as it passes, never mind who's in it.

What kind of prayers were those?

Speechless, Henry stared into the water, his hands still palm to palm.

There came a rustling behind him. Self-protection was second nature now. Henry reached down for a stone to murder whoever threatened him. But it was Claudette.

Sashaying up to him, she taunted: "Do you really think God can help you now? He has turned his back on us. If He exists."

"Go away, Claudette." Henry threw the rock into the water and sat down, clasping his knees with his arms.

"I listened to you and Martin. Now you know a little of my pain." Ignoring his request, she plopped down beside him. "I prayed, too, when all this started. God never answered. The devil has taken the world and laughs at us."

She picked up a rock and skipped it across the water, one, two, three, four times. Henry looked at her in surprise. Patsy had been the only girl he'd known who'd been able to get a rock to hop that many times. Homesickness overwhelmed him. He'd give anything to get away from all this horror and stomach-wrenching sorrow, to get back to that swimming hole, stripped clean. He buried his head in his knees and fought back tears. Even so, his shoulders heaved.

A few moments went by and then tentatively, lightly, Claudette's hand brushed back his hair. "Shhhh. I am sorry, Henri."

It was the first time she had used his name. Henry reached out for her and wrapped himself around the small body. He could no longer fight crying and sobbed against her hair. She held him and cried quietly herself. Then she kissed his cheek, his neck. The kisses were sweet, warm. Henry pulled away to look at her face, to understand her tenderness. Her eyes were closed. He closed his own and found solace in her lips.

France disappeared.

"Patsy," he breathed, without realizing he spoke aloud. "God, Pats, I've missed you."

Claudette held her lips to his ear and whispered gently, "I am not Patsy. You are not André. Let us pretend we are."

They walked back to the camp later, silent, holding hands but separate in their thoughts. If he ever got back, Henry promised himself, he was going to tell Patsy he loved her. He couldn't believe it had taken all this to recognize it.

He looked at Claudette and smiled at her. She was gorgeous, especially when her face was peaceful, clear of hatred. But it was awash in sadness. Henry didn't say anything to her, respecting her grief.

They found the camp in an uproar. After questioning one of the *maquis*, Claudette beamed and told Henry, "The Allies have reached Paris! The people are rebelling. Soon we will liberate it. *Vive la France!*" She joined the cry of the men. "*Vive la France!*"

Many of the *maquis* embraced. Some danced a little jig, slapping each other on the back. But their jubilation was terse. Within a few minutes, the men were pulling on straps of bullets and loading their guns. Others ran to the cars with boxes of grenades.

"What's going on?" Henry asked.

Claudette didn't know. She went to ask. Henry ran after Martin, who was striding through camp.

"*Monsieur! Monsieur Martin!*"

"I am in a hurry, Henri." Martin kept walking, buttoning up his coat. "What is it?"

"Where is everyone going? Are German troops near?"

"Henri, I don't have time for questions. Speed is imperative." He put his hand on Henry's shoulder to stop the next question. "You cannot go with us. You must stay here. But be on watch. The Nazis attacked the *maquis* in

Vernay and are strafing the roads near Montsauche and Ouroux. Those villages are only a few kilometers away."

Martin motioned his assistants to follow. He darted up the hill to the awaiting cars.

Henry bit his lip. He was sick of feeling so useless. He turned round and round searching the rushing crowd for Claudette. She was shouting and shaking her fist at one of the men.

Within moments the camp emptied except for the wounded and the village women who were tending to them. Claudette ran to Henry with tears of frustration on her face. "It is Pétain. He is in Saulieu. They go to intercept him as the coward flees south. They won't take me with them!"

Pétain and his Vichy-government cronies! If they could catch the head of the Hitler-controlled French government, maybe the *maquis* could force the Gestapo or the Milice to release some Resistance prisoners. Like Madame Gaulloise! Like Pierre's mother! "How far is Saulieu?" asked Henry.

Claudette stopped crying. "Ten kilometers. We could use the bicycles." She laid her hand on his chest. "Will you help me, Henri?"

Henry looked down at the pretty face. It was no longer quiet. Her eyes blazed with a ferocity that had once unnerved him horribly. But after today's news of the slaughter of the Vercors people, Henry was in for a little revenge himself. He nodded grimly. "You betcha."

Chapter Twenty-five

The month he'd spent eating the Morvan's simple but regular food had strengthened Henry. They flew down the mountains on their bicycles, Claudette's skirts flapping loudly. Saulieu lay low at the edge of the Morvan, where the knotty woods gave way to the fertile fields of Burgundy. They could spot the cathedral of Saulieu long before coming to the town. The sun was rising slowly, washing the countryside pink. There was very little to hide them. But Henry refused to acknowledge the lunacy of what they were doing.

They left their bicycles propped against a stone wall encircling an ancient graveyard. He held Claudette's hand to slow her down and keep her against the wall as long as possible. She was trembling with excitement.

The town was already stirring. People hurried by them, carrying baskets of flowers, fruit, milk bottles, and loaves of bread. In the market square, a farmer led his

255

horse to drink from the splashing fountain. A scroungy-looking dog chased a gray cat. A young girl swept the front stoop of her house. It seemed an ordinary morning. No high officials. No sense of impending conflict. Claudette left Henry to gossip with a shopkeeper. Maybe she'd learn what was happening.

Nervous, Henry sat down on a stone wall wrapping the edge of a closed café. A Nazi propaganda newspaper blew down the street toward him. He picked it up and buried himself behind it.

When he glanced over the edge of the paper he could see Claudette inside the bakery and an old woman sticking her head in and out of a glass case. He guessed she was responding to Claudette's questions about the contents. He'd seen Claudette do this a dozen times now, playacting at being a customer, all the time wheedling information out of people without their ever knowing it. This time, though, he wished she'd hurry it up.

A good ten minutes passed. Then, up a road came the whirring sound of several bicycles, pedaled at breakneck speed. Henry forced his head even farther down behind the newspaper and hunched over.

Whoosh . . . whoosh . . . whoosh . . . whoosh.

Four German soldiers whisked past Henry and careened through the market, sharply turning on a street and disappearing into the labyrinth of village alleys.

Moments later, up the same road, rushed the whine and grind of a car being shifted into high speeds on tight curves. A jeep flashed into the courtyard. Four men clung to the back of it, a long machine gun stuck out the back.

Maquis. Henry recognized the hodgepodge of uniforms and German and British guns. But he didn't recognize the band of men. The jeep circled the square, its driver trying to decide which spoke to take. But before Henry could signal the direction the bicycle patrol had fled, the jeep *vroomed* down the larger roadway on which he and Claudette had entered town.

C'mon Claudette, Henry fumed. Something's up. He was going to motion to her, when he heard more car sounds roaring toward the marketplace. This time two black Nazi sedans hurtled into the square and disappeared up another street.

Damn, that's enough of this, cursed Henry. He ran across the square, into the bakery, and grabbed Claudette. "We're leaving now," he said, forgetting to speak French.

The elderly shopkeeper gasped.

Oh, God, thought Henry, don't make me have to do something to this old lady to keep her quiet. But the woman hurriedly shoved more bread loaves into Claudette's arms. *"Bonne chance, mes amis."*

As Henry and Claudette opened the door to leave, the *maquis* jeep reappeared in the square then raced up the road the Nazi staff cars had just taken. Henry dragged Claudette across the square into the crook of an arched garden gate.

Panting, they peeped around its edge. They would be completely exposed trying to escape along the road on which they had entered town. "Do you know another way out?" he whispered.

Claudette shook her head.

"Do you know what's going on?"

"They missed Pétain. He made it out before dawn with six hundred Milice guarding him."

"Six hundred! Was there a fight with Martin?"

"I don't think so," Claudette said with irritation. "I think they completely missed him. The fools."

"But what's all the hubbub about?" asked Henry.

"What means hub-bub?"

"Why the staff car, the bicycle patrol, and *maquis* jeep? Who's chasing whom?"

Before Claudette could answer they heard the sharp crack of rifles and the loud chattering of the machine gun.

Dropping the bread, Claudette pushed away from Henry and ran back through the square. Henry dashed after her. They weren't armed. They didn't know where they were heading. They just ran on like hound dogs crazed by a fresh scent.

The fight was over before they got anywhere near it. The *maquis* jeep rushed past them yet again, the Frenchmen triumphantly shaking their rifles and cheering. Claudette and Henry had to press themselves up against the buildings for the vehicle to pass. In the back of the jeep was a bloodied Vichy officer.

Claudette was ecstatic. She ran after the car, shouting back at Henry, "Come!"

At the edge of town, they came across a crowd of people, shouting, jeering, shoving. Eagerly, Claudette pushed her way through them. Henry followed gingerly. There was something terrifying about the seething anger of the mob. Henry could feel it rippling toward a tidal wave of violence.

When Henry squeezed his way through to the center of the throng, he saw a teenage girl. Accused of collaborating with the Nazis, her hair had been shaved off, her dress torn open. Bald, half-naked, vulnerable, she quaked before the people who spat at her and called her vulgar names. A pregnant woman held a long horsewhip and stood before the girl. She was asking who in the crowd would be first, the first to whip her captive.

Disgust choked Henry. This was crazy. This was a witchhunt. There'd be no telling what these people might do. Henry needed to get Claudette out quick.

He reached her just as she shouted, *"Cochon!"* Before he could stop her, she jumped into the circle. She pulled a knife out of the belt of a man standing nearby.

"Kill her," Claudette shrieked in French. "I will kill her for you. She has betrayed all of us."

"Oui, oui! Tuez-la, tuez-la!" the crowd began to chant.

Henry recoiled. He couldn't believe Claudette's bloodthirsty rage—that the murderous person holding the knife was the same girl who had comforted and kissed him so tenderly just hours before. He couldn't let her do this. She'd never be able to live with herself later if she slit this teenager's throat. Claudette would be as dead inside as if she had been killed.

Henry tackled her from behind and held her fast. "Don't do this, Claudette. Don't."

Claudette screamed and kicked and cursed him. The

crowd shouted at him. But Henry held fast. "Look at her, Claudette. Look at her. She's just a kid. Maybe she fell in love with a young soldier stationed in town, some home-sick boy who before the war probably would have been embraced by the whole town as a great match. Maybe she fell for him because he was strong and brave and could treat her to some decent meals on his soldier's pay. Maybe he loved her enough to write her poetry. Love probably made her stupid. She's going to have to live with what she's done. She'll be shunned here the rest of her life. That's punishment enough."

Claudette still struggled. "Let me go. Coward! Coward!"

"Think of André, Claudette. Don't dishonor him with this. He died for France's freedom, not for this. And if you kill her, you're as bad as the Nazis. The one thing I've learned from all this hate and death is that when the war is over, it has to be over. If it's not, we'll just have an-other bloodbath in a few years. Don't do this, Claudette. You're better than the Nazis. I know you are."

The crowd went silent, waiting.

Claudette's hand trembled. The knife dropped to the ground. Claudette went limp and covered her face.

Henry carried her out of the crowd and laid her down on the grass.

"I hate you," she mumbled. But she held onto his sweater and buried her face in it and cried. Henry heard her whisper a prayer asking forgiveness from God.

He was only able to cradle her for a moment before someone cried out, *"Les soldats!"*

Chapter Twenty-five

Henry looked up and saw a German truck barreling down the crowd from the village. Another one approached up the country road. The trucks screeched to a halt. Soldiers jumped out the back, guns up and ready.

Henry pulled Claudette to her feet. They scrambled through some bushes and ran—ran with all they had—ran to the cemetery where they'd left their bicycles. Maybe they could pedal to safety.

The bikes were gone. Henry could hear tramping feet doing double time up the graveled road. There was nothing to do but hide behind the gravestones and pray they passed.

He and Claudette huddled together behind a huge stone topped with an angel. It was missing a wing. Henry looked at Claudette. Terror was all over her face. She looked so young. He couldn't let the Nazis get her. He couldn't.

The gate squeaked open. Henry chanced a look. Two young soldiers were threading their way through the tombstones. They'd find him and Claudette for sure.

Henry looked again. The soldiers looked scared. New recruits, Henry reckoned. Still, there were two of them with two guns. They'd make a racket even if he did manage to jump them. Then the rest of the troops would be on them within seconds.

There was nothing else to do but for Henry to draw them away from Claudette, just like he'd seen mother quails do when someone approached their nest. He cupped Claudette's face in his hands. He didn't know if he'd ever see her again. He kissed her gently. "Stay here," he whispered. "When they run after me, run for the hills."

Henry crawled from grave to grave. When he neared the gate, he stood up in plain view.

"Halt!"

Henry bolted. He ran back toward town. He looked over his shoulder to make sure both soldiers were chasing him. They were.

He glanced back again. In the distance he saw Claudette creep out of the cemetery and disappear up the hill. The soldiers chasing him saw nothing.

So long, Claudette, Henry thought. Be good now.

He gritted his teeth and ran on.

A shot rang out behind him.

Another one twanged into the ground beside him.

"God, give me wings," Henry prayed. He imagined the fields back home where he'd run pell-mell into the March winds, arms out, waiting to be lifted off the face of the earth, up, up, into the blue.

Another shot. But it was way behind him now.

He'd done it. He'd outflown them. Now all he had to do was get out of town and find someplace to hide.

Henry darted around a corner.

He came face-to-face with a German squadron.

Two months later, Henry just knew his life was over. He'd never get home, never hold Patsy, never see his mother and father. He had watched for every opportunity to escape from the Germans who held him and there had been none, absolutely none. They'd transpored him north-east from towns to fields to villages to mountains in their wild, disorganized retreat. American fighters had strafed them. *Maquis* groups had ambushed them. Many of the German soldiers in the convoy had died along the road. And all the while Henry remained shackled to the back of a camouflaged truck.

These Germans were regular army. They had treated him pretty well. He'd eaten once a day. They didn't bother to ask who had helped him. All they focused on was retreating. Worn-out, afraid, ill-supplied, dogged by their enemy, they had scurried eastward, back to Germany.

But now they were meeting up with other German columns and massing. Clearly Hitler was preparing some sort of counterattack to the Allied invasion. The last road sign Henry had seen had been for Metz. He remembered from his flying days that Metz was pretty close to the German border, not far south from Luxembourg.

Henry could sense the growing desperation of his jailers. They were heading for a do-or-die fight. Waiting, watching, hoping for some kind of miracle, Henry had written dozens of letters home in his mind:

Dear Ma,

Try not to be too sad when they tell you I'm gone. I got to skim along winds just under heaven. I also got to see the very best of people—even as I witnessed the very worst in them. Remember how you told me that people would amaze me? So many people risked everything to help me. There was a young French mother who took me in who remind- ed me a lot of you. She was kind and pretty and brave and a real good cook. She loved her son fiercely, with all her being. Just like you. Look for me in the clouds, Ma, because I hope to fly there now in peace. I'll be watching you.

Dear Pats,

   I wish I had told you I loved you before getting shipped over. I guess I didn't recognize it until I was here without you. Your pretty face followed me everywhere. Your beautiful letters kept me going. Many times when I was afraid I thought of you and the joy we shared as children and could have shared as adults. I wish I had a whole life to spend with you. Go swim in our creek for me once in awhile. I'll be waiting there in spirit to hold you in my arms. My body may not have been able to walk home but I know my soul will fly there. I do love you.

Dear Dad,

   You and I have never had a real good talk. But I learned a lot about you over here. This war has taught me that people sometimes do the wrong things for the right reasons. I think you treated me harsh to prepare me for this. Well, I've got to admit it helped. Love's got responsibilities, like you always said, things you've got to do even when you don't really want to. I understand that now. I put up a good fight but, you know, Dad, they play for keeps in a war.

It was an old regimental sergeant who came to get him. Henry had seen him before. He had brought Henry meals many times. The man clearly had no affection for his Nazi commanders. He never did that to-the-sky salute and he always seemed to fume after they left him. But he followed orders, loyal to his homeland. Given the man's age, Henry figured he had served in the First World War, too.

When the old German came to get Henry, he carried a shovel. He wouldn't look Henry in the eye. Henry's stomach lurched. The sergeant's orders must be to take the American out and shoot him, after making Henry dig his own grave.

In the field, Henry scratched out a trench very, very slowly, trying to buy himself some time, time to think, time to live. Maybe he could whack the old man with the shovel and run. He could hear the distant rumble and grind of tanks, the shouting of men. Somewhere, toward the west, mortar shells were exploding. If he ran straight into a battle would they really bother chasing him?

Henry looked up to the sky. Locked in the truck, he hadn't really seen the daylight sky for weeks. It was a clear, crystalline blue, stretching up forever, with a bright day-moon shining. The autumn air was crisp, invigorating. What a day for flying, thought Henry. Up in the sky he'd be away from all this killing and pain. There'd be no dead-end alleys, no bullets to stop him. Would the air lift him up into silent, soaring glory if he wished it hard enough?

Henry closed his eyes and tried to smell a breeze. If he made himself light, shed the war and his fear, maybe he could just slide up into the heavens like a kite, the way he had pretended to do a million times over as a kid. He opened his eyes and focused on the translucent day-moon, the boundless blue that reached toward it. Without really realizing what he was doing, the words of his favorite poem came out of his mouth like a prayer: "'Oh, I have slipped the surly bonds of earth, And danced the skies on laughter-silvered wings; Sunward I've climbed. . . .'"

As he recited, the words vaulted Henry's soul into the clouds, to freedom. For a few moments, he hovered, strong, unafraid, on the winds. But when his words stopped, his flight did, too. Henry remembered his own grave lay at his feet. His eyes fell from the sky to the dirt. Slowly, sadly, Henry turned to face his executioner.

The sergeant's resolute expression had turned to a troubled, conflicted one. He sighed heavily and shook his head. Reaching into his breast pocket, he pulled out a thin sheet of paper folded many times. He handed it to Henry.

It was orange and carried American and British seals. The top half was written in German. The bottom half translated: *The German soldier who carries this safe conduct is using it as a sign of his genuine wish to give himself up. He is to be disarmed, to be well looked after, to receive food and medical attention as required, and to be removed from the danger zone as soon as possible. Signed, Dwight D. Eisenhower, Supreme Commander, Allied Expeditionary Force.*

Henry looked up in surprise. The German's weather-beaten face seemed softened by a mix of compassion and remorse and plain old weariness. Allied planes must have dropped the leaflet. Hope flared in Henry. Were the Americans really that close? Was the Nazi defeat really that inevitable? Clearly the old German thought so. Maybe he even hoped so.

The sergeant kicked dirt into the empty grave to fill it. He undid Henry's shackles and pointed his thumb west. *"Auf, geh heim."*

Henry wasn't sure he understood. Was it a trick? Could someone in this hellish war still have that much mercy? Henry backed away tentatively. He looked to the sergeant for approval. "Home?"

The old German nodded and repeated, *"Auf. Geh heim."* He lifted his rifle and fired it once into the air to make the officers back at camp think he'd shot Henry. The sound reverberated in the chill air. Then he turned and walked away, very slowly, to his own unit.

Henry was alone, free, just a few miles from American troops. All he had to do was skinny through enemy lines, avoiding detection and the bombs of his own countrymen, then walk up to tanks rolling into battle and give himself up without getting shot.

Somehow, on that clear, cold morning—when his enemy had chosen to spare Henry's life rather than kill him—the journey seemed completely possible.

Chapter Twenty-six

Thanksgiving Day, 1944.

Lilly Forester's kitchen smelled of a harvest feast. Inside her stove a wild turkey sizzled, stuffed with apples, onions, and corn-bread crumbs. Succotash—corn and lima beans in a thick creamy sauce—bubbled on top. The biscuit batter she had mixed early that morning was slowly rising. In a few hours it would be light and fluffy enough to roll and cut and cook.

Right now she was making pumpkin bread. Covering her whitewashed table were blue bowls full of ingredients: thick molasses, cinnamon, ground cloves, nutmeg, raisins, creamy butter, cracked walnuts, and brown speckled eggs.

Lilly measured out two cups of sugar ever so carefully. Rationing being what it was she couldn't afford to lose one precious granule. Because of the war, people were allowed to buy only a pound of sugar—two cups worth—every two weeks. She'd needed to plan way ahead to have the two cups for the bread, three cups for the apple pie, plus a little left over for the relatives to have a dash of sugar in their coffee after dinner.

Clayton had called her a silly, sentimental fool for making Thanksgiving dinner to begin with. He was in no mood to entertain what he called his deadbeat cousins. "What do we have to be thankful for this year?" he'd snapped. The farm's output was way down because Clayton was having to work it alone without Henry. Then he added, "You know the boy is dead, Lilly."

Lilly had reached for wood to knock the instant Clayton said it. "Don't you be burying him before he's gone, Clayton Forester," she'd said, fighting her irritation with him. Clayton had gotten even harder since the telegram had come informing them Henry was missing in action. Lilly tried to tolerate her husband's surliness because she knew it was his way of grieving.

But she had to believe Henry was alive somewhere. She couldn't go on otherwise. She'd heard tell that some of the French people were helping pilots get out. And weren't Patton's tanks crossing France quickly now? She fought off the idea of her son caught between two great armies, dodging bullets from both sides.

Lilly sat down at the table, remembering other, happier Thanksgivings—when Clayton had actually stopped picking on Henry to talk about how lucky they'd been that season. When Henry had danced around her begging for a taste of dessert before the dinner even started. And her favorite memory—when Henry had been all of three years old. After lisping through the blessing he had added, "Please God, when I grow up I want to be a bird."

She glanced at the photo of Henry, so tall and proud in his uniform, hanging on the wall. What kind of thanks could she offer this Thanksgiving? "If I am to have no more time with my son, Lord, thank you for the blessing of having him at all." It was a halfhearted prayer at best.

"Henry, honey, where are you?"

Tap, tap, tap.

"Mrs. Forester, you home?" called a voice.

Lilly wiped her eyes with her apron before opening the back porch door to a blast of frosty air and Patsy's smiling, cold-red face.

"Hey, honey, you look about frozen," said Lilly. "Come on in."

Patsy stood shivering and stamping her feet. "Mmmammma sssent me to bbbuy a half dozen eggs," she said through chattering teeth. "Sssshe doesn't have enough for the ccccake."

"Hush now, we have time for that. Come warm yourself a minute," said Lilly. "Mr. Forester's out collecting this afternoon's eggs. He'll be back in a few minutes and then you can have really fresh ones."

Patsy crept close to the stove to warm herself.

"How are those little ones at your place? Are they getting excited about Thanksgiving?" asked Lilly. Their church had placed a hundred London children with parish families to protect them from Hitler's bombings. Patsy's family had taken two little boys into their already enormous brood. Lilly had wanted to shelter a child—he or she could have used Henry's room—but Clayton had refused.

"They're fine," said Patsy. "They don't really understand the holiday. But I've told them it's a time of celebrating everything, all the bounty, this country has given us. A time that the pilgrims and Indians were friends even though they were so different. A time for family to be together. I think the ten-year-old, Wesley, feels kinda bad about being here, like it's charity. Talking about Thanksgiving seems to make it worse for him. He wants so bad to be fighting the Nazis himself. So I've got him doing salvage. He's peeled off enough tinfoil from old cigarette packages and gum wrappers he's found at the dump to make a lump the size of a baseball. One of my teachers told me he could get fifty cents for that ball over at the Richmond Engineering Company. They use the tin in bombs."

Patsy was finally warm enough to take off her worn overcoat.

When she did, Lilly laughed. "What in the world do you have on, child?"

Patsy blushed. She looked down at the jeans she wore, rolled up to her knees, her father's shirt with its tails hanging out. "It's what the girls working the munitions factories wear. And see," she pointed to a black ring on her left hand. "Any girl who knows someone fighting in the war is wearing one."

Patsy held her hands up like that for a moment before dropping them awkwardly to her side.

Lilly knew what Patsy wanted to ask. "I haven't heard anything, honey. As soon as I do, I'll come tell you. Or better yet, Henry will tell you himself."

Patsy nodded. Embarrassed, she looked away. Her eyes fell on Lilly's china cabinet, on a tiny wooden airplane tucked beside a delft blue teapot. "Did Henry make that?"

"Yes. That boy was always crazy for flying." Lilly put her arm around Patsy's thin shoulders. "In grade school, he knew everything there was to know about clouds—cumulus, nimbus—oh, I can't recall all the types he told me about. But he knew all about them, just like he was part of them. You know, we must try to not grieve too much if we've lost him. Henry got his chance to fly, to climb up into the clouds." Lilly's voiced cracked and she added softly, "But you have to promise to keep coming to visit me so I don't get too lonely. Okay, honey?"

The sound of Henry's dog, Speed, barking outside interrupted Patsy's answer. Car wheels grated along the driveway's gravel.

"Goodness, who could be coming here now?" mused Lilly. "It's too early for the relatives. No one else would waste the gasoline to drive over here. They'd telephone." Then she froze, fear stopping her heart. Sometimes the Army delivered death notices in person. "Oh no." She reached for Patsy with a shaking hand. "You don't suppose?"

Patsy couldn't answer.

Slowly, Lilly removed her apron and smoothed her skirt. "Don't cry," she muttered, half to herself. "It would embarrass Henry." She forced herself to put her hand on the old iron doorknob and twist it open.

When the taxicab had turned up his farm's half-mile-long driveway, Henry had wanted to leap out the door and run all the way himself. How could the driver be so slow? Didn't he know how badly Henry wanted to see his folks? He'd been waiting, about to explode with impatience, for a month since American troops found him, running toward them on an open road.

That moment had been perhaps one of the most dangerous of his time in France. He had waved and shouted to the foot soldiers clustered around the fast-moving tanks. "Hey! Am I glad to see y'all."

Ten men had surrounded him with pointed guns. Shriveled down to a hundred pounds, covered in grime, wearing German boots and filthy civilian clothes he certainly hadn't looked like the American pilot he claimed to be. Pulling out the safe conduct paper the old German sergeant had given him hadn't helped matters at all.

The infantry had passed him back down the lines under guard. Eventually someone believed Henry. But then it had taken two weeks to make it back to the coast and across the channel to England. Another week to get on a transport plane filled with wounded men heading first to Iceland and then to New York.

In New York City, the Army had insisted on interviewing him again about the *maquis* and the German troops he'd seen. Then he'd been run through more medical tests. Finally, the Army issued him back pay and a uniform. Only then could Henry get permission to catch a train to Virginia.

"Want me to wire your parents, son?" a colonel had asked.

"No sir, I want to surprise them."

Now Henry leaned forward from the taxi's back seat to peer out the front window. Poison ivy vines, turned crimson by the frost, climbed up the dark green cedar trees lining the drive. The fields lay golden and shorn, asleep for the cold season. And there, finally, he could see the white Victorian farmhouse between two enormous oak trees that had been the goal that kept him alive. Home. It was the most beautiful sight he'd ever seen.

Cccccccrrruuuunnnch.

The taxi skidded to a halt, the driver having to veer to avoid Speed, who was charging the car and barking like mad.

"How much do I owe you, sir?" Henry asked, reaching into his pocket.

"Nothing, Lieutenant. I'm proud to have brought you home. It gives me hope that my two boys will be home by Christmas."

Henry adjusted his uniform's tie and hat. Then, trembling all over, he eased himself out the door.

Speed danced around him, moaning, hopping, and blocking his way to the house.

"Hey, boy, easy. Easy, now. I'm glad to see you, too, fella."

Dipping his head, whining and wagging, the dog

refused to budge from Henry's side. Henry knelt down to pet him. "Good boy, Speed. Everything's okay now."

Henry heard the screen door creak open. He looked up and was thrilled to see his mother standing in it. But she didn't run to him. She kept the door in front of her as if to protect herself from something. "Can I help you, sir?" she called in an uncertain voice.

Henry straightened up, Speed still jumping all over him. Lilly kept standing there, her hand to her heart. Henry realized she wasn't sure who he was. Had he really changed that much? "Get down, boy," he said gently to Speed, trying to clear his path to his mother.

"Strange," Lilly murmured. "I haven't seen Speed act that way since. . . . Oh, my Lord." She flung open the door. "Henry! Henry!"

She flew down the stairs. Henry rushed to embrace her. She seemed so tiny to him now. They held each other a long, long time. Biscuits, apples, sugar, she still carried that wondrous scent of warm things baking in the kitchen. "I'm so glad to see you, Ma," he whispered into her hair.

Lilly looked up at him, her eyes shining.

"Hey, Henry."

It wasn't until then that Henry realized Patsy stood patiently by the front door steps, giving Lilly her time. Henry caught his breath. She was even more beautiful than he remembered. Still holding his Ma's hand, he strode over to Patsy and caught her in a tight embrace with his other arm. He kissed her once and gave her a smile that promised more later.

"What's going on here, Lilly?"

The three of them turned together. Clayton was strug-gling up the hill with two big wire baskets crammed full with eggs. About a hundred per basket, remembered Henry. Mighty heavy.

"Go on, honey," Lilly said in a low, emotion-choked voice. She let go of Henry's hand and stepped back, pulling Patsy with her. "Go on to your father."

Henry stood in a kind of awkward attention. He'd composed a dozen different speeches for this moment and he couldn't think of one word of them.

Clayton stopped short, confused by all the commo-tion. "Lilly, is that . . . ?" But before she could answer him, Clayton knew.

Eggs flew as Clayton threw up his hands and ran to his son. He caught Henry in his arms.

For a moment, Henry wasn't sure what to do. Clayton had never hugged him. But it only took a moment. Henry reached up, patted his father's shoulder, then held on to him tightly.

When Clayton finally stepped back, he kept his hands on his son's shoulders. They stood eye to eye, Henry now as tall and straight as his Dad. Clayton's eyes brimmed with tears. "Where did you come from, son?"

Henry thought of the confusion, the contradictions, of all he'd seen—the beautiful mountains and sunflowers, the ancient villages, the destruction, the death, the hatred, the courage, and the kindness. He saw the faces of the people who'd helped him and whom he'd lost.

He shook his head. "I'm not really sure, Dad. But I'm home now."

Afterword

May you think sometimes of the reasons you are free.
—*Pierre Meunier, general secretary of
the National Council of the Resistance*

This novel was inspired by the stories my father told me of his and his friends' experiences with the French Resistance during World War II. Like Henry, my father was a B-24 pilot who spent several harrowing months behind the lines. As resourceful as he was, it is doubtful that he would have survived without the amazing willingness of some French people to protect a stranger, their quick-witted courage and self-sacrifice. He met many individuals like Pierre and his mother, Claudette, and the Resistance fighters. He did, in fact, surprise his parents by arriving unannounced at their farm after months of being missing in action. Eggs did fly.

But this is fiction. It is not the story of just one young

idealistic farm boy who grew up at war. Although my father's resilient and kind spirit permeates the character, Henry's odyssey is culled from the experiences of thousands of American aircrew who had to bail out or land crippled airplanes on enemy territory.

During the conflict with Germany over Europe, 51,000 men in the American Air Forces went missing; many were captured and interned. It is less clear exactly how many airmen—young, often badly hurt, certainly terrified, and all alone—managed to evade capture or escape prison and then make their way through Nazi-controlled land to Allied front lines. Many died in the attempt, perhaps lost in mountain ranges, perhaps executed without any record of who they were. However, MI9, the British escape service that helped Resistance movements establish underground escape lines, calculated that more than 4,000 British and American servicemen were brought out of Belgium, the Netherlands, and France along these escape routes before the Normandy landings in June 1944. Allied forces liberated another 600 servicemen after D-Day. (Several thousand men also made it to Allied front lines in Italy and Russia.)

Each successful escape, however, carried a high price. MI9 estimated that for each Allied serviceman who made it to safety, one Resistance worker died.

This novel, then, is also the story of the French children, women, and men, who risked everything to help American boys. The schoolteacher, Madame Gaulloise, Pierre and his mother, the teenage guide, Claudette, and Martin are fictional, but represent ordinary people who did extraordinary things to save lives and to resist Hitler's oppression.

Children as young as Pierre did serve as guides and couriers. Teenage boys, particularly scouts, filled the ranks of the armed fighting groups known as the *maquis* (pronounced ma-KEE). These youngsters had to fight like grown-ups because so many of France's adult men had been shipped off to work in German factories under compulsory-labor laws. The *maquis* leaders who organized them were typically not trained soldiers. In the Morvan region, for instance, one chief had been a dance-band leader, another a lawyer, yet another a veterinarian. War and necessity taught them how to fight back.

Women, young and old, operated radios, broke secret codes, and forged identity papers. They baked bread for the *maquis* guerrilla groups, stored their guns, and hid escaping servicemen in their closets, attics, barns, and even outhouses. They carried messages and the parts of radio transmitters, guns, and explosives. Since women and girls were expected to be out daily doing grocery shopping and other household errands, females like Claudette had a better chance of transporting clandestine items hidden in umbrellas, handbags, and bicycle baskets.

Europe still adhered to a rigid class system in the 1940s. This attitude allowed well-dressed, well-spoken women such as Madame Gaulloise to slide through checkpoints and other dangerous situations by intimidating regular German foot soldiers with their wit, fashionable clothes, and aristocratic elegance. Teenage girls, on the other hand, had to improvise in other ways. A girl guide —like the one who helped Henry in the Swiss train station—might playact a tearful, passionate good-bye with an airman she'd just met to embarrass a passing German soldier into looking the other way and forgetting to check their identification papers. One twenty-year-old agent, code-named "Michou," who often used that ploy, is credited with helping one hundred fifty American and British airmen to escape.

Even nuns braved arrest to shelter airmen. If German troops searched their cloisters, the sisters might choose to lead them straight to a clinic where airmen had been told to feign madness, an illness that many Germans of that day feared.

The Resistance movement began in simple, nonviolent ways. In May 1940, Hitler's forces rolled through Western Europe in a *Blitzkrieg* or "lightning war". They overran Denmark in one day, Holland in four and Belgium within three weeks. The French army held on six weeks, but eventually was overpowered by German tank squadrons, known as Panzer divisions. On June 14 German forces marched into Paris. Brave French citizens immediately began defying the Nazis who occupied their homeland. They gave incorrect directions or pretended not to understand German soldiers who asked for their help. During the night they would scrawl *Vive la France* (Long live France) on prominent buildings to keep up French morale. Anti-Nazi newspapers sprung up and were passed out by schoolchildren. Railway operators adopted a noncooperative, "go-slow" attitude. And as the

Nazis began to deport Jews, many French hid and helped to evacuate their Jewish neighbors.

The price for defiance was high. On Bastille Day 1941, for instance, many Parisians publicly celebrated their independence day despite Hitler's ban of the holiday. One man was gunned down simply for singing the French national anthem. Hitler also held more than one million French soldiers hostage. For each German killed by Resistance workers—whom the Nazis labeled "terrorists"—several French prisoners were taken out and shot.

Hitler's pervasive racism extended to the French, whom he dismissed as "the monkeys of Europe." Following their leader's twisted thinking, some Nazis— primarily his elite Gestapo and the SS—could be horrifyingly cruel in their treatment of captured Resistance workers. Ironically, their ruthlessness was matched by a French unit of "shock troops" called the Milice, which had been formed by the French puppet government in Vichy. These French police were just as fanatically anti-Jewish and pro-Hitler.

The first organized groups of French fighters came into being to smuggle out British soldiers trapped at Dunkirk during the *Blitzkrieg*. They led them into neutral countries: Spain, Switzerland, and Sweden. They continued operating escape lines for the Allied aircrew who seemed to fall out of the sky like rain. Workers would watch the skies for parachutes and race on bicycles to try to reach downed crewmen before Nazi troops did. After the Allies' invasion of Normandy, however, most escape routes disintegrated in the fray. Many airmen had to remain with the *maquis* groups then, helping to unload supplies parachuted down by the Allies, repairing trucks, cars, and radios, or building explosives.

The Resistance was also critically important to the Allies in providing information about Nazi troop movements, encampments and fortifications, and advancing bomb technology. Resistance spies discovered, for instance, two secret German weapons that had devastating capabilities—the V1 buzz bombs and V2 sonic rockets. Both unmanned rockets could be launched from ramps in German-occupied France to hit Britain. Anti-aircraft guns could not down the rockets once they were in the air. The only way to destroy them was to bomb the launch sites. French agents provided the Allies with the location of V1 and V2 launch sites. One man discovered 100 launch sites before he was killed by a German patrol.

On the eve of D-Day, Britain's BBC and the Free French radio broadcast two seemingly nonsense messages: "It is hot in Suez" and "The dice are on the table." But Resistance workers knew what they meant. The Allied invasion was on. The Resistance cut telephone and telegraph wires, and blew up bridges and railroad tracks to prevent German troops deep inside France from coming to the aid of those stationed on the Normandy beaches.

Already in the French countryside, the *maquis* had been harassing German troops throughout the war. The guerilla bands hit German convoys and patrols, then darted back into the cover of mountain ranges such as the Morvan and the Vercors. *Maquis* is a word in the dialect of Corsica for the dense forests and undergrowth on the hills of that French Mediterranean island. *Maquis* groups were fiercely independent of one another, each identifying with one particular strong leader. Before the war, France had been divided by its politics—there were Communists, Socialists, and Fascists. Such division was replicated among the *maquis* groups. But they united in their resolve to oust the Nazis, especially as the war dragged on and more and more outrages were committed against French civilians.

The barbaric massacres at Oradour-sur-Glane, Dun-les-Places, and Vassieux-en-Vercors did occur. Horrifying Gestapo interrogations did as well. So, too, however, did French executions of captured Germans suspected of spying. The *maquis* and their supporters could retaliate with brutality against citizens believed to have collaborated with the Nazis. In "popular trials," some suspected collaborators were shot without a chance to legally defend themselves. Women thought to have had romantic relationships with German soldiers were shaved in front of large, jeering crowds. It is one of the great marvels of humankind that during such madness, there were individuals—on both sides—brave and compassionate enough to act with kindness, generosity, mercy, and conscience.

There is a small, very moving museum to the Morvan's *maquis* in St-Brisson, a pastoral village located a few miles from Dun-les-Places. Lining its walls are photographs of *maquisards* and villagers who helped them. Most haunting are the clear-eyed, hopeful faces of several teenage agents who simply disappeared, never to be found.

There are also heartbreaking letters. Perhaps forseeing

that he would die in his fight against Hitler, twenty-three-year-old Paul Sarrette prepared his will and wrote: "I'm going to fight, not for a word, not for glory or for a flag, but for you—men, women, and children—so that you may live without knowing the horrors of a war."

Let us, then, think sometimes of the great humanity and courage of young Europeans such as Paul Sarrette and American aircrew like Henry who volunteered to fight terrible battles for our freedom. In such a cruel time, they could still dream of a better world and of better people.